AN INNOCENT CHILD

ROBERTA KAGAN

MARGOT'S SECRET

ISBN (eBook): 978-1-957207-55-1
ISBN (Paperback): 978-1-957207-56-8
ISBN (Hardcover): 978-1-957207-57-5
ISBN (Large Print): 978-1-957207-58-2

Title Production by The Book Whisperer

DISCLAIMER

This is a work of fiction. Names, characters, businesses, places, events, and incidents are either the products of the author's imagination or used in a fictitious manner. Any resemblance to actual persons, living or dead, or actual events is purely coincidental.

PREFACE

In the year of 1939, in a small village called Pomssen just southeast of Leipzig, Germany, a boy was born. His small body was deformed, and he was completely blind at birth. When they looked at the son, his parents were appalled, so they sent a petition to the Führer asking that their child be euthanized. The Führer, believing that the child was damaged and therefore of no use to anyone, got in contact with his personal physician, a doctor by the name of Karl Brandt, who then proceeded to end the life of this tiny boy whom the Führer referred to as nothing but a useless eater.

PROLOGUE

1939

A small secret gathering of men dressed impeccably in their pressed black SS uniforms sat around the table in the quaint two-story house at Tiergartenstrasse 4 in Berlin. This quiet, unassuming location was designated to serve as the headquarters for Hitler's newly approved program they were about to put into place.

A pretty young woman walked into the room. She did not meet the eyes of the men who were seated there. This was a top-secret meeting; the less she knew about it, the better off she would be. So, she placed a tray of pastries in the center of the table. Then she returned to the kitchen area and retrieved a second tray that contained a pot of coffee, a bowl of sparkling real sugar, and a small pitcher of fresh milk. After she placed the second tray on the table, the woman quietly left the room and closed the door.

A tall, dark-haired man with sunken, deep-set black eyes that matched his black SS uniform stood up. He walked over to the door and then locked it. The other men in the room watched him as he turned around and surveyed each of them. Then he walked back to his chair at the head of the table, and in a soft but warning voice, he said, "As you have already been told, this program is of the utmost secrecy. Each of you has been hand-selected because of the racial purity of your bloodline and your true devotion to our cause. The program I am about to share with you is not for the faint of heart and may even seem abhorrent to some of you at first." Then he smiled. He was trying to send a message with that friendly and warm smile. But the true nature of the man shined through, and his smile was terrifying because it never reached his eyes.

"I'm sure that each of you must realize how important it is that our Aryan race is not mottled or destroyed by lesser races. So, if we are to survive and rule the world as intended, we must not concern ourselves with the individual. Instead, we must do what is best for our Fatherland." He coughed a little. "I realize that what I am about to share with you may sound, well, like murder. However, it is not. It is a mercy killing that must be done, and you must always remember to think of it that way. We are doing a service to our country and to the future of our children. And for those who must be sacrificed in the name of progress, always remember we are doing them a favor. No one wants to spend their lives as a useless eater, so this is, in fact, to be considered a good death. We shall refer to this cleansing program as T4."

CHAPTER 1

Adelaide Schroder cursed under her breath as she opened the door to her husband Alex's room. It was a difficult task to carry his breakfast tray and open the door at the same time. Although he knew what time she would bring his breakfast, he made no attempt to open the door and help her. Still, she never missed a day; she had been doing this for him since he'd returned from the war, his face disfigured from when he was burned by mustard gas. Alex almost never left his room and preferred staying in the dark. Once, he had been a handsome, rakishly charming, and desirable man whom women sought after. And he adored their attention so much that he had never been one to be faithful. However, much had changed about his return. Now, he was no longer handsome, and instead of being charming, he was bitter and angry. The years since the war had ended were empty years for Alex. He no longer cared for his wife or their three daughters, who had grown into beautiful young women. And he knew Adelaide, his wife, whom he had rejected, had become lovers with his brother, Leo. Leo was once his best friend and saved his life in that fateful

3

battle when he'd been disfigured. To an outsider, it would have appeared to be an odd situation. The three of them, Adelaide, Alex, and Leo, all live together in the same house. But it was natural to them. Before the war, Leo had met and fallen in love with Adelaide; before his brother Alex had ever noticed her, Leo hoped to marry her. They had all been very young. Alex was twenty-five, Leo was thirty, and Adelaide was only twenty-two.

Adelaide had been working at the bakery when Leo first saw her. They flirted each week when Leo bought bread. One day, Leo finally mustered up the courage to ask Adelaide to have dinner with him. On his way to the bakery, he saw Alex walking home. Alex had insisted on accompanying Leo to the bakery. And that was the first time Adelaide saw Alex. He was painfully handsome, and she was instantly smitten by his sculptured face and tall, slender body. Leo was hurt. But because he was crazy about her and wanted her to be happy, he pulled back and didn't pursue her. Instead, he acted like a good brother and blessed the marriage between her and Alex.

Adelaide looked around the dark room where Alex spent his days. His unwashed body's musty, unclean odor made her want to gag. But then she noticed a picture on his dresser. It was a photograph of the three of them, Alex, Adelaide, and Leo. It was from before the war. She stared at it for a moment. It was not there before. *When had he put that picture there? And why?* As she stood staring at the smiling faces in the photo, she was transported back to when they were first married. Then, Alex was infatuated with Adelaide, but it didn't take long for him to become bored. After she gave birth to their twin daughters, he grew restless, and once he lost interest, he became a terrible husband. He went out at night, and everyone in town knew he was running around with other women. He spent time and money at the brothels, refused to work, and drank too much. But worst of all, he paid little attention to his young wife and their two infant girls. If it had not been for Leo, Adelaide and her daughters would have starved. But Leo was the man who took the responsibility of supporting the family seriously, not to mention that he was still in love with Adelaide. So, he got a second job and shouldered all the expenses for his parents and Alex's family. Leo asked for nothing but friendship from Adelaide in return. This was not unusual for Leo. He'd taken care of Alex all their lives. Even when Alex made a mess of things by arguing with older boys at school and causing them to threaten to beat him, Leo always came to his brother's aid. Leo didn't like to fight, but he was a power-house of a man. He was not handsome like his brother but had a pleasant face and a strong, muscular body. Leo didn't mind providing for Adelaide. In fact, he took pleasure in it. But then, one night, a young woman came to the door looking for Alex, who was out carousing as usual. The young woman was desperate. She didn't know which door in the apartment building belonged to Alex. All she had was an address. So, she began screaming in the hallway of their building. Leo lived with his parents in an apartment in the same building as Alex and Adelaide. When he heard a female voice calling for Alex in the hallway, he left his apartment and went to speak to her. She was very young and trembled with fear when he saw her standing at the bottom of the stairs. He ran up to her, told her he was Alex's brother, and asked her what she wanted. She told him that her sister was a prostitute and was currently in trouble. She said that her sister was dying in childbirth and that the child belonged to Alex. Leo was not surprised. In fact, he didn't doubt the girl at all. He knew that Alex always left loose ends wherever he went. So, Leo agreed to follow the young woman to the brothel. When they arrived, her sister died after giving birth to a little girl. Leo was ashamed to admit it but had been to that brothel before. After all, he was a single man, and he had needs. But he didn't want to hurt a woman by getting involved with her, knowing his heart was not free. It belonged to Adelaide. So, occasionally, he accompa-nied his brother to visit the prostitutes. Leo knew the woman who had given birth. He'd seen her at the brothel. Her name was Mia. She wore a Star of David on a chain around her neck, and everyone at the brothel knew she was Jewish. Leo tried to give the baby to the girl's sister. But she refused to take the child. "I can't raise a baby by myself," she said, and then she told Leo that she was sure the madam would send the child off to an orphanage in the morning. Leo looked at the baby. Her tiny red face was scrunched, and her little hands were balled up in fists. The baby looked ready to fight. And something about the child touched Leo's heart. Perhaps it was that she was so small and helpless, but she was not giving up. He knew she might fight without someone caring for the child, but she would not last until morning. Leo could have left; he could have walked away. This was another mess that Alex had left behind. And Leo knew it was not his problem or responsibility. But Leo could not turn his back on this child. He was a man of honor whose heart was often too big for his own good. So, he wrapped the infant in a blanket and lifted her out of the bed, where she lay beside her dead mother. Then he carried her out of the bedroom, through the noisy, smokey brothel, and then to his home. When he arrived, Adelaide was awake and waiting for him. Leo didn't want to cause his brother trouble, so he told Adelaide the child was his. He explained that the mother was dead. When she saw the helpless baby, she fell in love with her. And since she was still nursing her twins, she told Leo she would feed and nurture the child and raise his little girl as her own. Leo hated to lie to Adelaide, but he was grateful because he knew the child needed a mother. In his opinion, there was no better mother than Adelaide. Leo and Adelaide stood in the kitchen that night and named the little girl Margot. Several years later, Adelaide discovered the truth that the child was Alex's biological daughter and her mother was a Jewish prostitute, but it didn't matter. She already loved Margot just as if she were her own child. Margot was a spirited child who was both warm and independent. Adelaide smiled when she thought of Margot. Then she looked down at the food tray in her hands and remembered why she was in Alex's room.

"Alex, I've brought you your breakfast," Adelaide said, as she did every morning.

The room was dark and cold. It was the middle of winter, and it was so hard to heat the house in the winter. "Alex," she repeated gently. "I brought your breakfast." He didn't answer. He hardly ever spoke to her. Never thanked her for bringing his meals. Never asked her how she was. Adelaide sighed. She put the tray down on the dresser and pulled open the drapes. The sun burst through the window, filling the room with light. Usually, he cursed her when she did this each morning. But today, he was silent.

Adelaide turned to pick up the tray, and as she did, she glanced at Alex. The tray dropped from her hands and went crashing to the floor. The glass dish that held the bread and glass coffee cup shattered. Adelaide let out a scream. Leo ran into the room. "Addie, what is it?"

Then his eyes fell on Alex. "Lord in heaven." He said as he sunk down to sit on the bed beside his brother. Then Leo said to Alex, even though he knew Alex could not hear him. "Why did you do this?" But both he and Adelaide already knew the answer. Alex had no life. He had been a prisoner of his own misery for over ten years. Blood as red as dark cherries covered the white sheet.

"He was always so depressed. I guess he just couldn't go on anymore." Adelaide said. Tears ran down her cheeks.

"I know," Leo answered.

CHAPTER 2

Alex's burial was on a Monday. He had lived in the same house his entire life, but no neighbors or friends were present. The only friends that were at the funeral were Heidi and Artur Kraus. But they were not Alex's friends. They were Adelaide and Leo's friends and the father of Max, Margot's husband. Alex had no friends because he had lived as a recluse since the great war. His scarred face made him feel more comfortable locked in a dark room alone than going out. Only Alex's immediate family was in attendance.

Leo stood on one side of Adelaide, with Margot on his other side. Margot held the hand of her four-year-old son, Erik, who stood quietly by her side. Margot's husband, Max, was a good-looking young man. He held his son's other hand. Mattie, Margot's unmarried sister, was on Adelaide's other side. Next to her was Trudy and her newlywed husband, Rudolf, looking very proud in his crisp new Nazi uniform.

Adelaide's parents were not present at the funeral. They had never truly cared for Adelaide, especially after she stood up to them and told them how terribly they had treated her when she was a child. She told them she could not trust them to watch her children while she was working at a job during the Great War. But that seemed to be lifetimes ago, and it didn't matter anymore. Whatever they'd done to Adelaide was in the past. She had found happiness in Leo's arms, and she no longer let the pain of what her parents had done to her control her life. They were old and growing feebler each day. Adelaide's parents seemed to have given up on living after receiving a letter from a man in Russia claiming to be a friend of her brother, Felix, who was their only son. Adelaide's mother said this letter told them that Felix had been imprisoned. It explained that the man writing the letter had made a pact with Felix that if one of them survived and the other did not, the survivor would write to the family of their dead friend and tell them what had happened. So, this was how her parents learned Felix had been tortured and finally died somewhere in the frozen land of Siberia. This horrifying news of the death of their only son broke both of them. And Adelaide knew why. It was because, from the day Felix was born, they had loved him far more than they'd ever loved Adelaide.

Heidi and Artur, Max's parents, were Adelaide and Leo's best friends. They stood quietly in the back of the cemetery. Artur wore a dark suit and Heidi a navy blue dress. Although they hardly knew Alex, they had met him only a handful of times. They came to pay their respects and stood quietly, hand in hand. Their faces were solemn.

The sky was an incredible shade of ice blue, and the day was so bright from the sun's reflection on the newly fallen snow that it hurt Adelaide's eyes. She felt a single tear drop freeze as it ran down her cheek and wished she could say it was because she was grieving for losing her husband. But she wasn't. It had been a long time since she'd loved Alex. It had been a long time since she had even cared about him. And as far as her daughters were concerned, they didn't recognize him as their father. They'd grown up thinking of Leo as their father. In fact, Adelaide had never told them that Alex was their biological father. Or even the fact that Alex and Adelaide were still married. They had never divorced because of the social stigma it would have caused. But Leo and Adelaide had been living as man and wife since Leo and Alex returned from the great war.

The girls were still toddlers, so Leo was the only father they had ever known. To the three young women who had grown up with Adelaide and Leo as parents, Alex was nothing more than their scary uncle who only came out of his bedroom once in a while. When they saw Alex, he was always in a foul mood. And they found his scarred face difficult to look at. It was hard for the teenage girls to believe that Alex had once been handsome. Leo said women had fallen at Alex's feet when he was young. But of course, that was before he'd been destroyed by the mustard gas.

Alex would never have returned home if Leo had not been beside his brother on that fateful day. He'd come so close to death that he had looked directly into her eyes. But Leo was there, and although he could have let his brother die and come home to claim Adelaide for himself, he didn't. Leo put his own life in danger while rescuing his brother. Adelaide told her daughters how Leo had been a hero in the great war. She told them their uncle Alex was alive only because of Leo's heroic gesture. This was all the three Schroder girls really knew of Uncle Alex. They were young when their mother tried to explain what had happened and caught up in the drama of their own lives, so they never found out anything more.

CHAPTER 3

After the funeral services, everyone returned to Adelaide and Leo's apartment. Leo was devastated. Everyone was standing around sipping coffee or beer and talking. But Leo couldn't join them. He had lost his only brother, best friend, and worst enemy, the only person he'd ever felt completely attached to. So, Leo went to his room to be alone. His relationship with his brother had always been full of contradictions and was difficult to understand. But it was deeper than any canyon. And only Adelaide understood it. Because she did, she knew the best thing to do was to leave Leo alone to grieve in his own way.

Everyone except Leo was gathered in the living room of the small apartment. Mattie immediately got up to help. She quickly spread her mother's best tablecloth over the dining room table. Then Margot, Trudy, and Mattie helped their mother bring plates for cake and additional cups for tea and coffee. Adelaide put a pot of water on the stove and set it to boil. While the women in the Schroder family were busy, Max watched over his son, Erik, who slept quietly in his pram. At four years old, Erik was probably too old for a pram, but Erik was a small child. He'd always been a sickly boy and had never grown as he should have. He was born with an arm longer than the other and short little legs. But he was a sweet boy filled with affection, and his parents adored him. Trudy's husband, Rudolf, was standing alone because Trudy was also helping her mother in the kitchen. So, he walked over to say hello to Max. "How have you been?" Rudolf asked in a cheerful voice.

"Good, but busy." Max smiled.

"Of course. Me too."

"How are you, Rudy? I haven't seen you since you and Trudy got married."

"I'm doing fine. Enjoying the life of a newlywed," Rudy said, smiling. He was not really handsome, but he had a way about him that gave one the impression that they were in the presence of an important man. He never slouched. His smiles were quick, and it was hard to read what he was feeling in his eyes.

"Yes, those early days of marriage are fun," Max agreed. "So, have people stopped teasing the two of you about the fact that your names rhyme?"

Rudy laughed, "No, actually. Everyone who hears our names finds them to be adorable. Trudy loves it when people say, 'Rudy and Trudy.' Everyone we meet says it over and over. Trudy says her girlfriends tease her, too. Ahhh, the pain of having rhyming names." He winked at Max.

Max smiled.

Mattie walked over to the two men and said, "There's cake and coffee on the table."

Rudy patted Mattie on the back, then said, "I'm going to introduce Mattie to some nice single fellows."

"So, you say," Mattie teased. "You've been promising me this since you and Trudy got married. But so far, you haven't introduced me to anyone."

"Ahh, you're absolutely right. It's my fault. I've been very busy. But that is no excuse. I will make sure that I take care of it by the end of next week," Rudy said.

Trudy had made a point of telling everyone that her husband, although he'd been young at the time, had been a hero and had been awarded medals in the Great War. Because Leo had also served, he was impressed by this. Whenever there was a family gathering, he and Rudy would be busy chatting about their time in the service. But not today. Today, Leo wanted no part of anyone else. He needed to be alone.

"Oh, I hope you will introduce me to some nice men. I am quite excited to meet them. All I ever seem to meet are married men or ones who don't want to get married." Mattie said.

"We're going to have to change that," Rudy said, winking at her. "All you need is one good man. And I'll see what I can do to find him." Then, he turned his attention back to Max. "So, tell me about you and Margot? Have you two looked into purchasing a home yet? I'm sure that you would love to have a home with a backyard where Erik could play."

"Of course we would, but unfortunately, it's too expensive for us, I'm afraid," Max admitted. "We looked into it, and it's just not affordable right now."

"Yes, things are expensive, that's true. However, I have a solution. Perhaps you might want to consider joining the party. From your age, I assume you were too young to serve in the war. But I'm sure you served your time in the Labor service."

"I did."

"That's good. That will be a plus when you join." He smiled. "As far as I'm concerned, I was already in a good position when our Führer came to power. It just so happens that I became involved with the party right after the war. I like to think that my involvement with the youth groups was instrumental in helping to mold our precious Aryan youth."

"Oh? I didn't know you had been a party member for that long."

"Yes, you see, I helped to form youth groups for the party right after the war ended. The youth needed direction. So many people, young and old, were hurt and disillusioned by Germany's loss of the war."

"So, you truly believe in all of this?" Max asked.

"All of what? Exactly what do you mean?" Rudy asked. His tone was slightly caustic.

"Well, do you actually believe in the party's principles?"

"Of course I do. And so should you. I believe that you and I and other pure Germans are the race created to rule the world. You and I are Aryan men. We and other Aryan men like us are born of pure blood. Our wives, Margot and Trudy, and also Mattie. And all pure Aryan women are a wonderful addition to our cause. And don't forget that they, too, have a big responsibility to our fatherland. Their responsibility is to produce as many pure Aryan children as possible. Children like your little boy, Erik, who will someday take their rightful place as rulers of the world. This is the New Reich, and I promise you, it will last for at least a thousand years. It is a wonderful time to be alive and to be a German. The world is opening its arms to receive its rightful leaders. And we are here to take our rightful place in history."

"That was some speech, Rudy. I'm impressed. You almost sounded like Hitler himself," Max said with just a touch of sarcasm. "So, what about all of this nonsense that Hitler has been spewing about the Jews being the cause of Germany losing the Great War? You can't actually believe that. Do you?" Max asked.

"Yes, I do. And it's not nonsense, I'm afraid. The Jews are one hundred percent responsible for it. Just look at all the rich Jew bankers. They are thieves and liars, and they just can't be trusted. Every pure Aryan returned from the war poor and broke. But they didn't. Instead, they prospered. They got richer and richer. You see, my friend, the Jews are a dangerous bunch. You might not have ever known any, but I do. And I can tell you from experience that everything our Führer says about them is true. They are crafty and underhanded, and if they aren't controlled, they will bring our fatherland down even before we even have a chance to rise."

Max looked directly at this brother-in-law. He wanted to punch him. But he knew his wife, Margot, would be furious. After all, this was a funeral and no place for an argument or, even worse, a fist-fight. So Max held his tongue and just nodded.

"Anyway, I wanted to say that I have a lot of friends who are rather high at the party. And consequently, I have a bit of influence." Rudy said confidently. "I might be able to help you get a good posi-tion, even though you never served in the war and aren't a party member. But if you would like, I'll try to get you a job where you would earn enough to afford to purchase a home."

"I don't know," Max said, shaking his head.

"I would accept Rudy's generous offer if I were you, Max. I think it's really nice having a brother-in-law with so much influence in the government," Mattie said, smiling at Rudolf, who was tall and sturdily built. He would have been handsome had his face not been pockmarked from a battle with measles as a child. His light brown hair was combed perfectly, but upon closer observance, it was apparent that it was thinning.

"She flatters me," Rudolf said, putting his arm around Mattie's shoulder. Then he removed his arm and turned his attention back to Max. "But, seriously, you really should consider joining. The work will be much easier than carpentry. And if you join, things will be better for your son when he's old enough to take his place at our party."

"Thank you so much, Rudy. I do appreciate your offer, and although I can't give you an answer right now, I will think about it."

Across the room, while they were setting the table, Margot spoke with Adelaide about her father, Leo. They discussed with her how close Leo and Alex were. "They were always inseparable," Adelaide said. "And Leo always put himself in harm's way for his brother. Once, when they were young men, Alex got into trouble with a girl. This was before I met them. The girl's father came to the house to challenge Alex. Now, Alex was no fighter. He was not a physical man. But Leo would not allow this man to beat on his brother. So, he fought for him. He really loved him. And now, he's going to be heartbroken living without him."

Margot was crying. She could imagine Leo fighting for Alex. She had always known that there was a special bond between them. And since she loved Leo, the only father she had ever known, so much, it was painful to think of him hurting. She didn't want Max to see that she had been crying because she knew it would upset him. So she went to the bathroom to wash the tears from her face before Max saw them. Margot didn't particularly like her Uncle Alex, and she knew her Uncle Alex was not the most well-liked man in town. In fact, she couldn't say she would even miss him. But she was crying for her father. She had never seen Leo cry before, yet today, he cried at the gravesite.

While Margot was in the bathroom, Erik awoke crying softly. His face was flushed, and when Max picked him up, his body felt hot. Rocking Erik gently, Max waited for Margot to return. He looked down at the little boy with concern.

"I hope you're not sick, little fellow," he whispered to Erik.

Erik didn't answer. He just nuzzled into his father.

Then Max noticed Trudy, who was standing across the room. Trudy's eyes caught Max's eyes, and she smiled at him. Then she walked over to where he stood. Everyone else in Alex's immediate family was dressed in black, but Trudy wore a hunter-green wool dress that fit her tightly, hugging the curve of her hips. She sauntered slowly over to Max, letting her hips sway gently. When she reached him, she said coquettishly, "Let me see my handsome nephew. He's getting so big. I'm surprised he will still allow you to cradle him like a baby."

Max smiled a little and said, "He doesn't always. But I think he might be a little under the weather. It could be that he was out in the cold for several hours during the funeral today. I'm a bit worried about him. I hope he hasn't gotten sick."

"I hope so too," Trudy said, trying to sound concerned. "Let me take a look at him. I haven't seen him in a couple of months." Erik was wrapped in his blanket, but he was still shivering. Trudy moved the blanket back away from the child's face. "Well, he is certainly a very good-looking boy, just like his father." She winked at Max.

"Except for his blond hair, which he got from me, I think he looks more like Margot," Max said.

"I don't think so. I think he's the spitting image of you, Max. He's just so handsome." She smiled up at Max. "I'd love to hold him. Would you sit on my lap for a while?" she asked Erik.

Erik nodded.

"I guess he is willing," Max said as he handed the child to Trudy, who sat down, and Erik climbed onto her lap. Erik sat quietly for a few minutes, then grew restless and began looking around the room franticly. "I want Mutti," he said. Not seeing his mother anywhere, he began to cry.

"Shhh, don't cry," Trudy said. But Erik must have sensed the insincerity in her voice because he cried even harder. Just then, Margot returned from the bathroom. "It seems your son doesn't like me very much," Trudy snapped.

Margot took Erik from her sister's lap and sat him on hers. "He's too young not to like you, Trudy," she said. "He just doesn't know you well."

"Well, I can't come by as often as I did before I got married. I mean, my husband and I have so many parties and things we are required to attend."

"Of course," Margot said. "And I wouldn't have it any other way." Then Margot turned to look at Max and said, "Erik feels very warm. I think he might have a fever."

Max stared at Margot with concern in his eyes.

Erik began coughing. "Oh my," Trudy said, her face showing that she was repulsed.

"It could just be the smell of your strong perfume," Margot said sarcastically. But then Erik let out a terrible whooping sound. He sounded as if he was choking. "Max, something is not right. What's wrong with him?"

"I don't know," Max admitted.

Erik was choking in a fit of unstoppable coughing. His face was red, and his eyes and nose were watering.

"I think he's having trouble breathing," Margot said.

"We should take him to a doctor," Max said.

"But no doctor is open at this time of evening."

"Then let's get him home, and we can try to give him steam."

"Yes, let's go." Margot was holding Erik close to her chest. She walked over to her mother, still carrying her son. "We have to leave; I think Erik is sick."

"Oh no," Adelaide said. "What can I do to help?"

"Nothing. We are going to try to get him to a doctor."

"Yes, of course, you must," Adelaide said.

Erik stood straight like a soldier as Margot dressed her son in his warm coat and hat.

Max went to the bedroom to tell Leo that they were leaving. The door was closed, and he didn't want to open it, so he knocked and spoke loud enough for Leo to hear him through the door. "Leo, it's Max. Margot and I are going to have to get home. Erik has started coughing, and I am going to try to have the doctor come out to our apartment."

"Okay," Leo said, but he didn't open the door.

"Of course, you must go home and take care of your son." Adelaide walked over, took her grandchild from her daughter's arms, and held him close for a moment. "You should do your best to get a doctor right away."

"We will, Mother," Margot said.

Trudy sat beside her husband, drinking a beer. She wore a wicked smile that disappeared as soon as Max looked her way. "I hope Erik feels better," she called out.

CHAPTER 4

On the walk home, it snowed, and the temperature dropped considerably. Margot took off her scarf and covered Erik's face with it.

"His face is so red. I'm afraid he has a fever."

"I know," Max agreed. "And would you just look at this weather? It looks like we are going to have a storm. What doctor is going to come to our apartment in this? I'll do my best. I'll go to the doctor's house and plead with him. But chances are we're going to have to wait until morning."

"Not necessarily. I can always ask Ben for help. He'll come to our apartment."

Ben and Margot had been friends in school. Unbeknownst to Max, Ben and Margot had once declared their love for each other, and this love had not disappeared. However, it changed, and that was because of the laws in Germany forbidding marriage between Jews and Gentiles. Since Ben dared not try to marry Margot, he became Margot and Max's best friend after Margot married Max. Since Ben was a young boy, he had wanted to go to medical school, but because he was Jewish, this dream had been thwarted when laws were put into place under the Nazi regime that forbid Jews from attending the University. However, Ben refused to let these stop him. There were too many people in need of medical care. He was so driven to save lives that he went to the local doctor in the Jewish sector and offered to apprentice under him. It was there that he learned the art of medicine. Although he had no license, Ben was as good a doctor, and as time passed, he might even have gotten to be a better doctor than the one he had been studying under.

"I'll leave you and Erik at home and go to Ben's house. I'll leave right now," Max said.

Margot nodded. "Hurry, please. I'm worried."

"Boil some water and hold him over the steam until I get back," Max said.

"I will," Margot agreed.

CHAPTER 5

Ben was still single, and so he was still living with his parents, who knew nothing of his friendship with Margot and Max. So, when Ben's mother answered Max's knock on the door, she was surprised and unnerved to see someone standing there who was clearly not from their Jewish neighborhood. Max was blonde and tall, and for a moment, Ben's mother was afraid he might be from the German police. Plenty of their friends and neighbors had been arrested and taken to the police station for questioning for no reason at all.

"Yes, can I help you?" she said. Max was still standing outside with the snow falling all around him, covering his coat and hair.

"My name is Max Kraus. I need to see Ben. I am a friend of his. Please tell him I'm here," Max said. But the woman just stood looking at Max. "I have the right house, don't I? This is Ben's home, right?"

Ben's mother was trembling. *My son. What could this goy, this non-Jew, want with my son? I can't let the Nazis get him.* "Ben doesn't live here anymore. He moved, and I don't know where he's gone," she said bravely.

"Please, please, may I come in for a minute? I have to know where to find him."

She still did not allow Max to come inside.

He doesn't sound like a Nazi. They never ask politely, and they never beg. Who is this man, and what does he want from my son?

Just then, Ben came out of his room. He was dressed for bed in a thick flannel robe, but when he saw Max, he said, "Max, what are you doing here? Come in. You must be freezing." Ben walked over and pulled Max into the house. "Take off your coat. It's soaked from the snow."

Max shook the snow from his hair and wiped the icicles from his eyelashes. "I hate to bother you so late in the evening, but Erik is sick," Max said. "Margot sent me here to see if you would come and help. She's very worried. Frankly, so am I. He's so tiny for his age, and he's coughing so hard."

Ben nodded. "Of course, I'll come. Give me a minute to put on some clothes."

"You know this man?" Ben's mother asked. A look of surprise on her face.

"Yes, mama, I know him. He's the husband of a very good friend of mine."

"Goyim?"

"That's not a nice word, mother. But in answer to your question, no, they're not Jewish," Ben said. He was a little embarrassed that Max had heard her use that derogatory term for non-Jews.

His mother looked at him in disbelief. *All this time, he had goyish friends that I never knew about?*

Ben hurried to his room, and within minutes, he returned, buttoning his fly and throwing on his coat. His hair was uncombed, and he looked disheveled. But he quickly set his black bag down on the table so he could slip on his coat. Then he wrapped a wool scarf around his neck and put on his hat. "Let's go," he said without looking back to see his mother's anxious expression.

CHAPTER 6

R udy owned his own home before he and Trudy were married. He was the only child of a wealthy lawyer and a socialite mother, who had both been killed in an auto accident. At twenty-one, he had inherited the house. When he was in his late thirties, he met Trudy. She seemed like the perfect wife to help him to further his career. If he were to advance in the Nazi party, he needed a wife, a wife who was fertile and would give him lots of Aryan sons he could be proud of. When he met her parents, he liked them immediately and decided she came from good German stock. Her father was a war hero. At the time, he thought her uncle was a war hero, too. Only later did he learn Alex had gone insane from his war injuries. Even so, that didn't matter. That fact was hidden. What did matter was that he and Trudy were the perfect couple on the outside. He knew Trudy had fallen in love with what he had offered her. It was not a romantic partnership. And he knew it. But he knew how to woo and win her. So, he set out to do just that. When they were together, his manners were pleasant. He was always well-spoken, and he carried himself with dignity. But he knew he was far from handsome. The sex was mediocre as far as he was concerned, but he realized, even on his wedding night, that he would always need to have other women to keep from being bored.

After seeing his wife interact with Max the evening of their wedding, Rudy was certain she was destined to be miserable because it was not him but Max that she truly loved.

"Max and Margot's baby is growing so fast," Rudy said. "He's a cute little fellow, don't you think so?"

"Yes," she said tersely. She did not really care much about Erik.

"Wouldn't it be nice to have our own child?" Rudolf said. He was ten years older than his wife. He had been married before, but it only lasted a little over a year because she had died in childbirth. "I'm not getting any younger, you know, and I would love to have a son as soon as possible."

"I know. You tell me all the time." Trudy was annoyed with him. But he didn't seem to notice.

Rudy said he was tired and had to be at work early in the morning. So, they left Adelaide and Leo's house soon after Margot and Max left. When they arrived home, Rudy didn't wait for his wife to prepare for bed. He helped her to remove her coat, still standing in the doorway. He took her into his arms and undressed her.

He doesn't even know that he's getting on my nerves. I wish he'd just let me get in the house before he started this. He can be so dense sometimes.

"Have I told you today that you are very beautiful?" Rudy said.

"No, not today." She answered, realizing that he would have his way and if she tried to pull away from him, he would get angry. So, she closed her eyes tightly and secretly wished he were Max.

"Well, you are. Very beautiful," he said, his voice husky with passion.

Trudy managed to smile. He unbuttoned her dress, and it fell to the floor, which was wet from the snow on their coats. Trudy grabbed the dress and looked at it to see if it had gotten wet. It hadn't. "I want to hang this up. It's my best dress," she said, pushing him away gently.

"I'll buy you another one," he said. He picked her up and

carried her to the bedroom. She laid the dress on the dresser on her way. Then he laid her on the bed and kissed her breasts. Trudy shut her eyes tightly, and as she always did when Rudy made love to her, she pictured Max.

CHAPTER 7

When Max and Ben arrived at Max's apartment, Erik was burning up with a fever. "Poor little fellow," Ben said compassionately as he rubbed Erik's back. "You two go into the living room," he told Margot and Max. "Try to relax. I'll take care of him from here."

Erik knew Ben, and he was comfortable with him.

"Is he going to be all right?" Margot asked. She was almost in tears.

"I think so," Ben said. "Let me take care of him."

Ben spent the night at Margot and Max's apartment. Margot and Max fell asleep in their street clothes, sitting on the living room sofa, waiting for Ben to tell them what to do next. But Ben did not sleep at all. He was awake all night with Erik.

A little after four a.m., Margot went into the kitchen, where she found Ben still awake. But Erik was wrapped up in a blanket and asleep on the kitchen table. "Do you have any idea of what's wrong with him? It seems like he has a very bad cold. Last week, his nose was running, and he was coughing a little. I thought nothing of it. I thought it was just the weather," Margot said. She was frantic. "But today, we went to my uncle's funeral and had to stand outside for a few hours. When we got back to my parents' house, Erik fell asleep. But when he woke up, he was coughing hard, making a terrible sound. It seemed like he was choking on mucus. It was horrible. I'm afraid he got sick from being outside. You know how cold it's been."

He nodded. "Yes, I know," Ben breathed.

"Oh, Ben, he was making this horrible sound. It scared me. It was a cough, but a strange and horrible cough like I had never heard before."

"I know. I know what that cough sounds like. I'm pretty sure he has pertussis."

"What is that?"

"It's commonly called whooping cough because of the sound of the cough that you heard."

"Is it fatal?"

"It can be. But don't worry. I am going to stay here with him until he gets well."

"You can sleep in our room. I'm sure Max won't mind."

"Thank you. We'll see tomorrow. But for now, I am going to stay here in the kitchen with Erik and keep a watch on him. Don't you worry, Margot. I'll do whatever I can for him. But, unfortunately, tomorrow morning, you must let your parents and everyone else you saw at the funeral know that they have been exposed to whooping cough. You and Max must stay in the house because this is a very contagious disease, and we don't want to spread it."

"I never even thought about that."

"Yes, we have all been exposed. So, we must stay here until we are sure we don't have it."

"How long would that be?"

"About ten days."

"I can't. I need to go to the market to buy food," Margot said.

"You don't have any here in the house?"

"No, not enough for ten days."

"Then I suppose you must go." Ben tried to smile.

CHAPTER 8

The next ten days were an emotional rollercoaster for Margot. Sometimes, she would go into the bedroom where Erik and Ben now slept and find Erik sleeping comfortably. She was encouraged to believe that all would be well on those occasions. But then there were nights when Erik's coughing fits were so intense that Margot covered her ears and wept, terrified that he would crack his ribs. When fits of vomiting followed a coughing fit, she was afraid that he would never recover. And then, once he'd vomited until his stomach was empty, exhausted by the effort, he would fall into a deep sleep. She kissed his brow, wet from sweat, and then wiped it gently with a damp cloth. Ben held her hand and looked into her eyes to let her know he would be beside her no matter what happened. Erik slept deeply for almost four hours, and then he was awakened when another coughing fit came over him.

As Ben had instructed, Margot finally telephoned her parents. She spoke to her mother and told her that Erik had whooping cough and that they had been exposed. She asked Adelaide to please get in touch with Mattie, Trudy, and Heidi and let them know that they, too, had been exposed. Margot's and Max's lives hung in the balance as little Erik's condition worsened. Ben was exhausted from not sleeping and sick with worry. He had been informed several months earlier that groups of doctors and scientists had been working on a vaccine for whooping cough, and he wished he had access to more information about it, but he didn't. And as he sat watching the child suffer, he felt helpless. Especially since it was Margot's little boy, he would have done anything to save the child. He left for about a couple of hours one day. He spoke to the doctor he worked for to see if there was more information about the sulfa treatments for whooping cough. But he knew these medicines were not without danger. Many patients he'd read about who had been treated with various sulfa treatments died. After a long discussion with his employer about administering sulfa to Erik, they both decided it was too risky. Erik was very young, and whooping cough was treacherous, even for a healthy child. But for a sickly child like Erik, it was doubly terrifying. Ben telephoned his parents and told them he would be under quarantine with a child who had whooping cough for at least the next two weeks.

Erik slept in the bed, and Ben slept on the floor beside him. But he hardly slept. And twice Margot found him dozing off while sitting up in the easy chair, holding a sleeping Erik in his arms. Her heart still swelled with love for Ben. But now, that love was more than a young girl's fascination with a young boy. Now that they were both adults, Margot's love for Ben was different. It was fueled by admiration. Admiration for Ben's devotion to saving lives and his tremendous understanding and kindness.

On the third day of Erik's illness, Erik woke up out of a deep sleep and let out a shrill scream. Margot was sitting on the bed beside Erik, and Ben was sitting on the chair. They looked at each other, and for a moment, they were both frozen by the high-pitched sound that came from the lips of the child. Then Erik grabbed his ear and pulled at it, screaming repeatedly. Margot was shaking. "It's his ear," she said. "His ear must be hurting."

The sound brought Max running into the room. He looked at Margot and then at Ben. Then he picked Erik up and held him close. "What's wrong with him, Ben? He sounds like he's in terrible pain," Max said.

"Yes. He is in pain," Ben said sadly. "And it's breaking my heart because I don't know what to do for him. You see, this disease can cause inner ear infections. And they are very painful," Ben said. Margot saw Ben's hands shaking as he removed an instrument from his black medical bag and gently placed it into Erik's ear. Erik tried to pull away. But Margot stood up and rubbed his back while Ben looked. Then Ben nodded. "Damn it," Ben said, almost in tears, "this poor child." Then he took Erik from Max and rocked Erik in his arms, trying to calm him. But Erik continued to scream. Because Erik was so young, Ben had been trying not to give him an NRI treatment. He had the recourses available for the NRI radiation treatment to reduce the swollen tissues that surrounded the Eustachian tubes. And it didn't require anesthesia or hospitalization. But it could be painful and often ineffective. As he held the screaming toddler, Ben couldn't bear to see the child suffer anymore, so he finally gave in and administered the drug. A little while later, the pain subsided. Erik stopped screaming and fell asleep. His small body was sweaty, and he was exhausted from the ordeal. Margot took a rag and wet it, then without a word, she sponged the sweat off Erik.

Ben was glad to see that Erik was resting comfortably and that at least his pain had subsided. However, he had been reluctant to give Erik this medication because he knew that the primary side effect of NRI was that it caused a severe loss of appetite. And Erik was already so small and thin for his age. *I hope I made the right decision.* He thought. Then, when Erik awakened, it was just as Ben had feared; Erik refused to eat. It was a struggle to get him to drink even a little water.

Max insisted on going into town to purchase vegetables for Margot to make soup. "I think he will eat it because it's hot," Max said. "And maybe the cold water hurts his ear. Or maybe his throat is sore from coughing." He reasoned. Before Erik got sick, he loved hot soup. So, Margot hoped Erik would eat a little if she made the soup. But he didn't.

Then, the following day, while Erik was asleep, Ben asked

Margot and Max to watch Erik for a few minutes. "I just have to take a quick shower. It's been a few days, and I need to clean up."

"Go ahead. You haven't had a nice hot shower or a good night's sleep in a long time," Margot said. She was worried about Ben. "I don't want you to get sick, too."

"I'm all right. I'll be back in just a minute."

And although Ben wasn't gone long, and everything should have been fine, it wasn't.

While Ben was showering, Erik awakened and shook uncontrollably. His arms and legs were jerking wildly, and his eyes rolled around. He clenched and unclenched his small fists. Margot let out a scream. Ben must have heard her because he returned soaking wet and wearing only his pants. Shirtless, he took the child into his arms. "He's having a seizure," he said. "Dear God, what am I going to do? All I can do is ask you to please help this little boy."

Max's hands were shaking. "What can I do? How can I help?" Max asked.

"Nothing you can do. All any of us can do is wait. Hope and pray," Ben said.

That night, in the middle of the night, when everyone but Ben and Erik were asleep, Erik had a second seizure. As his eyes rolled and he trembled with muscle spasms, Ben held him in his arms and cried.

CHAPTER 9

The following afternoon, Mattie called to find out how Erik was and also to tell Margot that Trudy had contracted whooping cough. "She went to a doctor, someone Rudy knows from his association with the party. He gave her medicine, and she says she's doing all right," Mattie said. "We've all been praying for Erik. Have you taken him to a doctor?"

"My friend, Ben, has been looking after him," Margot said.

"Ben, you mean Ben, the Jewish fellow you knew from school?" Mattie asked.

"Yes."

"What does Max say about Ben treating your son? I mean, he is a Jew and all. And you went to a dance with him as well."

"All of that nonsense about Jews doesn't matter to us. And I'm not sure why you would ask what Max would say about this? Max is a reasonable man. He's glad that Ben has come to help us. Besides that, Ben and I went to the dance a long time ago. Now that Max and I are married, Max and Ben are friends."

"Oh, Margot. I can't understand how you can justify having a friendship with a Jew, especially with the way things are in

Germany right now. They hate us. So how can you trust this one with your child's safety?"

"You are so wrong, Mattie. Ben would never hurt Erik. I would trust Ben with my life."

"I think you're making a huge mistake. If you ask me, you should take Erik to a Christian doctor. It can't hurt to get a second opinion. Besides, you know the laws; German citizens aren't supposed to have anything to do with Jews. So, you are actually breaking the law by allowing Ben to treat your son."

"I can't stress enough how much I hate those laws. Jews are German citizens, too. And Ben is a good friend."

"The Jews are not German citizens anymore, Margot. They aren't. And because they're not, it's best that you stay away from them. The last thing you need is trouble with the law. You'll have to ask Rudy for help if you get into trouble."

"I don't need help. And I really wish you didn't feel like this, Mattie. If you only knew Ben, you would love him. He's a wonderful man."

"I believe you. I know you are smart. You were always the smartest of us girls. But it's not about being smart. It's about taking risks. And all I am saying is that with the way the country is lean-ing, I think your friendship with a Jew is really unwise. If you don't care about yourself or Max, at least won't you consider your sister, Trudy. She is married to Rudolf Schulze, and he is a high-ranking official in the Nazi party. It just doesn't look good for Trudy or her husband that you are friendly with a Jew."

"Please don't tell Trudy anything that I tell you. She and I are very different. I know her husband is a Nazi, and because he is rich, she believes everything he tells her. But I don't. I believe what I know is true, not what Hitler tells me. Anyway, let's face it, Mattie, Trudy never really liked me. And I can't trust her or her Nazi husband," Margot said.

"Don't be silly. Of course, she likes you. You're her sister. She would never do anything to hurt you. Besides, her bad feelings towards you were because of jealousy. When we were young, she had a serious crush on Max, and she was miserable because he was in love with you. But now she's married, and she's happy. And that childhood crush she had on Max has long since been forgotten."

"If you say so," Margot said. "Anyway, did the doctor tell her for sure that what she has is whooping cough?"

"Yes, for sure. But he said she'll be all right. I guess the doctor said not to worry because she doesn't have a bad case."

"Is everyone else all right? Mutti, Vater, you?" Margot asked, concerned.

"Yes, actually. No one else caught it."

"That's good news. I'm glad everyone is all right. But I am so worried about my son. I wish he would get better."

"Don't be so darn stubborn. Just listen to what I am telling you and take him to a Christian doctor. It can't hurt."

"All right. I guess you're right. I don't know what else to do. And Ben seems to be out of options, too, right now. So, I will."

Ben was not opposed when Margot told him that her sister said she should get a second opinion. "Of course. I think it's a good idea. You should take him. I would never want to stop you. Perhaps this other doctor can do better than I. He will have access to medicines I can't get my hands on."

"Your feelings are hurt?" she asked.

"No, I swear to you. They're not. I want what's best for you and what's best for Erik. I know a little about medicine, but not enough. They wouldn't let me go to medical school. So, I've done the best I can with the resources available to me. I would never want you to put Erik at risk to satisfy my ego. Your child's health is very important. In fact, I would go with you to see the doctor if I could, but you know I can't."

"I know," she whispered.

That afternoon, Margot dressed Erik warmly, and then she carried him to the bus stop, where she caught the bus and took him to the doctor's office.

When the doctor examined Erik, he said, "His throat is red, but not dark red. And there are still some signs of infection in his ear. But from the way he looks, I'd say I think he is recovering."

"I hope so, doctor," she sighed. "He has been coughing less."

Then, the doctor shined a light into Erik's eyes. He pulled the lid down and looked inside the eye. Erik cried.

"Did he have a seizure?" the doctor asked. "Do you know what that is?"

Margot nodded. "I know what it is. And yes. He did."

The doctor grunted. "I hope I'm wrong. But I think he has some brain damage from the seizure. But the good news is that he's going to live. I just don't know if that's going to be the blessing you've been hoping for."

Margot was shaking. "Brain damage? What does that mean?"

"We don't know yet. We'll have to wait and see as he gets older. Bring him back to see me again in a year or so, and we'll probably know more then."

Margot thanked the doctor. She quickly dressed Erik in his coat and hat, paid the bill, and left the office.

Margot shook as she boarded the bus. She sat holding her son in her lap. Erik was quiet, and she thought he'd fallen asleep from the motion of the vehicle. But when she looked at him more closely, he stared blankly ahead. The bus arrived at her stop, and Margot, still carrying Erik, got off and walked home. When she arrived, Ben was waiting. He helped Margot change Erik into comfortable clothing and put him in bed for a nap. Then Ben and Margot went into the kitchen, where he put a pot of water on the stove for tea. Margot plopped down in the chair. She was emotionally and physically drained.

They sat across from each other in silence for a few minutes. Ben took Margot's hand and squeezed it gently. Then, the teapot whistled.

"What did the doctor say?" Ben asked as he poured her a cup of tea.

Margot told Ben everything the doctor said. She told him how worried she was about the possibility of brain damage.

Ben hung his head and nodded. "Yes, I knew that already. But even if it is true, and he does have brain damage, he's your son, and at least he's alive."

Margot wept. Ben stood up and walked over to her to put his arm around her shoulder.

Ben and the doctor were right that Erik was recovering. After two long and terrible weeks, by some miracle, Erik had survived. He began to eat again and to drink water. The fits of coughing grew shorter and less often. Ben was ready to go home. He was tired. He needed a day or two of rest and then wanted to return to work. So, he told Margot that he would be leaving. She and Max told him they were so grateful for his help. But even as he was walking home, Ben thought about Erik. He worried about Margot and Max because he knew raising a child with brain damage would be difficult. His heart broke for Margot because he still loved her, and although he would never want to hurt Max, the feeling did not go away. So, he kept them hidden and did whatever he could to help her little family. Ben had to accept that he was only human and had done all he could. Erik was in God's hands. Only time would tell how badly Erik would be affected by the seizures.

CHAPTER 10

JUNE 1938

O n a beautiful cloudless day in early spring, after Max left for work and while Erik was still asleep, Margot baked a batch of cookies. She wrapped them in a clean, freshly pressed kitchen towel. Then she waited until Erik awakened. When he did, she gave him his breakfast, then dressed him and got dressed herself. "Where are we going, Mama?" he asked.

"We're going to see Ben. I want to bring him some cookies to thank him for his help when you were sick."

"I like Ben, mama."

"I know you do," she said, smiling. Now give me your hand, and we'll walk to the bus stop.

Erik gave his mother his hand, and they walked together. She glanced at the top of her little boy's head and said a silent prayer of thanks to God that Erik had survived.

While they waited at the bus stop, Erik told Margot how excited he was to see Ben. She smiled, and when the bus arrived, she helped him to board. They took the bus to the Jewish sector of town. Margot knew exactly where Ben's house was located. She had been there many times before when they were in school. She and Ben had been lab partners in science class and often studied together after school. It was easier to find the peace and quiet to work on science projects at Ben's house because he was an only child. At Margot's home, there was plenty of love from her parents, but her sisters were always doing something, so it was difficult to find a quiet space. She felt comfortable as she walked through the streets of the Jewish sector of town. As she turned the corner and headed towards Ben's house, she noticed a middle-aged woman standing in the middle of the street, hunched over. It appeared that she was frantically picking things up off the ground. As she got closer, Margot could see that the woman must have come from the market because it seemed she had spilled a bag of potatoes and was trying to chase them as they rolled away. Margot whispered to Erik, "Let's try to walk a little faster. I want to help that lady."

"Why?"

"Because she's old, and I think she needs help."

"All right, Mama." He was satisfied with that answer.

They sped up there until they reached the woman. "Let me help you," Margot said.

"I slipped somehow, and I almost fell. I didn't fall, but I dropped all of my potatoes," the woman complained.

Margot put the cookies down on the walk and told Erik to stand still and not move. "I'll be right back. You can watch me, but don't come into the street, all right?"

"Yes, Mama."

"And you be a very good boy and keep an eye on those cookies for Ben. Can you do that for me?"

"Yes, Mama."

Her heart swelled with love. Then she went into the street, and while watching for traffic, she began to help the woman gather up her potatoes. When they had gathered all of them, Margot put them into the burlap sack the woman carried. "*Oy*, such a help you were to me today," the old woman said. "You're such a *gute mädel*, such a good girl. Your mama should be proud."

"Thank you. That's very sweet of you to say." Margot was used to the strange way some Jewish people spoke. Margot knew the lady was sincere, so she smiled and added, "I was glad to help."

"*Nu?* So, I don't recall having ever seen you around here before. Have I? *Oy*, who knows. I'm getting so old. What's your name?"

"I'm Margot Kraus. I've been here before. But you might not have seen me."

"Margot Kraus," the woman repeated as if she were making a mental note of Margot's name. "Ehh, I don't remember. Anyway, I'm Frau Feiner. I live across the street right over there." She pointed. Then she looked at Erik and said, "Such a sweet little boy you have. Do you and your husband live somewhere around here?"

"No, we don't, I'm afraid. I'm here because I'm visiting my friend, Ben Weisman. Do you know him?"

"Of course, I know him. How could I not know him? I've been living here for a hundred years. Well, maybe not for a hundred. But sometimes it seems like it." She smiled. Then she said, "You see, I know everyone. I've lived here all my life. I grew up here. My parents grew up here, too." Then she said, "So, you and Ben are friends? How long have you been friends?"

"School friends. Yes. We've known each other for years."

"And your handsome little boy. May I ask, is he a friend of Ben's too? I mean, is he, well, you know?"

Suddenly, Margot realized that Frau Feiner was prying because she thought Erik might be Ben's child. She frowned. She was starting to dislike this woman. "His name is Erik. He is my son. My husband, who is at work right now, is also a friend of Ben's."

"So, you're married?"

"Yes, I am married."

"And your husband knows you are coming to see an old friend? A man?"

"Yes, my husband knows. Well, it was nice to meet you, Frau Feiner," Margot said as she picked up the cookies and walked away from the woman. Then she took Erik's hand and headed up the walkway towards Ben's house.

"Yes, it was very nice to meet you and your adorable little boy. I'll see you around here again, perhaps?"

"Perhaps." Margot was trying hard to hide her annoyance. *The woman is just old, and she's just a busybody.* There's no reason to get so angry. She thought as she knocked on the door to Ben's home.

A few moments later, Ben opened the door. When he saw her, a bright smile came over his face. "Margot! Come in. It's good to see you. And look who's here." He picked Erik up and held him up high. Erik giggled. But then a look of genuine concern came over Ben's face, and he said. "What brings you here? I mean, is Erik all right?" He put Erik down on his feet inside the house. Margot followed.

"Yes, everyone is fine. Please don't worry. I just came by because I just wanted to thank you for everything. So, I made you some cookies." She handed him the cookies.

"Well, it is always good to see you. And mmm. I love cookies. Don't you, Erik?" he asked, bending down to be at the same level as the child.

"Oh, yes!" Erik said.

"Well, that's good. Shall I make a pot of tea, and we can all have some?"

"Yes. Cookies!" Erik said.

Ben smiled at the little boy.

"I'd like that," Margot said.

Ben filled a pot with water and put it up to boil, then he picked Erik up and sat down, putting the child on his lap. "He looks good."

Erik giggled.

"He looks so much better. I'm so glad. For a while, I was worried," Ben said as he smiled at Erik.

"I know. Me too," Margot said.

"Me too," Erik said.

"You were?" Ben laughed. Then Margot laughed, too. Neither of them was certain that Erik knew what he was saying, but he was so cute that they had to laugh.

"By the way, on my way here, I met your neighbor," Margot said.

"Oh, which one?"

"The lady who lives across the street. Frau Feiner."

He laughed heartily. "Yes, I can imagine you did."

"What do you mean?"

"I mean, she is the neighborhood yenta. She probably asked you a hundred questions because she didn't recognize you. So, she had to find out all about you. Do you know what the word Yenta means?"

"No."

"She's a gossip. That woman is always in everyone's business. My mother can't stand her. She always comes over trying to find out news about our lives. She's a phenomenon. She has an unbelievable memory. I don't think she can tell you how old she is, but she never forgets anything she finds out about other people. And, let me tell you, she's a wealth of information. She knows everything about everyone in the neighborhood. She knows people's private business, like if someone is having an affair. Frau Feiner knows it. I don't know how, but she does. And she tells everyone. In fact, my father says she knows when two people are destined to marry each other even before they know it."

"That's quite a feat," Margot said.

"Like I said, that old woman is a marvel. But, I must admit, she's also a little irritating."

"I'll bet." Margot let out a little laugh. "She tried to find out how you and I know each other. And she seemed to be asking in a roundabout way if Erik might be your illegitimate son. Can you imagine?"

He laughed. "I know her. So, yes, I can imagine. I'm sure she wanted to know that. That would be some very juicy gossip for her. And considering everyone around here thinks I am too old to still be a single man. She figured maybe I haven't gotten married because I have a mistress and a child on the side."

"Well, I would never have spoken to her, but when I came around the corner, I saw she had spilled her potatoes on the ground. I felt sorry for her, so I went to help her, and she began asking questions. I meant to be nice. But you're right. She is irritating."

He laughed. "Don't let her bother you. She's harmless."

The tea kettle began to whistle, and the sound made Erik tremble. He put his hands over his ears and let out a shriek. "Here, give him to me. He hates loud noises," Margot said.

"Shhh, little man. Everything is fine," Ben said as he handed Erik to Margot, then he got up and turned off the stove. The whistle stopped, and Erik smiled as Ben poured three cups of tea.

Ben sat down and handed Erik a cookie. Then he blew on Erik's tea. "It's too hot for you to drink right now. I'm going to cool it off for you first. All right?"

"Yes," Erik nodded, gobbling up the cookie.

Margot stayed for the rest of the afternoon.

CHAPTER 11

The summer of 1938 was busy for all of Adelaide's daughters. Trudy became pregnant. And while her entire family was very excited, she was not. She had always been very careful to keep her weight down, and now she worried about how the pregnancy would affect her figure. Besides that, she didn't want to devote her time to a child. She was still obsessed with Max and wondered how she might use the shocking information she had overheard a few years ago about Margot to win Max's heart. So far, she had kept it a secret because she was waiting for the right opportunity to make the most of it.

Rudy was ecstatic about the pregnancy. And since they found out, he had been exceptionally nice to her. He had already set up a room in their home that would be a nursery for the new baby. And he was happy because, due to the pregnancy, the Nazi party had given him another promotion. He was earning even more than before.

As promised, Rudy introduced Mattie to a young man, Ebert

Cline. Ebert was a party member and worked for the government, but his position was not nearly as high as Rudy's. Even so, he earned a decent living. Mattie thought that although he wasn't handsome in the classic sense, he looked impressive in his uniform. He had not had a girlfriend before and liked her as soon as he saw her. He wore his uniform when they went out for dinner that night on their first date. Mattie had not been on many dates. Men never seemed very interested in her. But that night, as she sat with Ebert, she was thrilled by the respect people showed him. That had been two months ago. It was a whirlwind romance, and they had recently become secretly engaged. Plans were already made to invite everyone in the family to Adelaide and Leo's home for dinner, where the couple would officially announce their engagement.

Max and Margot were having a difficult summer. Erik was showing signs of problems in his physical development. He walked with a severe limp and had difficulty holding small things in his hands without dropping them. It seemed there were occasions when his eyes looked unfocused, and Margot wondered how he saw the world. Sometimes, when Max was at work and Margot was alone with Erik, she held her son in her arms and wept. But when Max was at home, she tried to be strong for him. Letting him see how afraid she was for their son would do no good. She knew Max would have moved heaven and earth to heal their little boy if he could. But he, like her, was powerless.

Ben, even though it was forbidden by law, went to check on Erik at Margot's apartment at least once every week. He tried to tell Margot that he believed that although Erik would never be normal, he would get along in the world. Ben promised Erik would grow up and adjust to his body's shortcomings. But Margot knew better. Her precious child had been damaged that day when the crow came to call. And now, he was living out his destiny, and there was nothing anyone could do to help him. She knew seeing Erik in this condition was almost as difficult for Ben as it was for her and Max. She saw the look on Ben's face when Erik fell as he tried to run, and she knew it broke Ben's heart. He often wondered if modern medicine might find a cure sometime during Erik's lifetime.

Although Margot never doubted that Ben was still in love with her, he was always respectful of Max, and neither she nor Ben ever openly acknowledged their feelings for each other. But Margot knew that although she loved Max, she would always have a special place in her heart for Ben.

CHAPTER 12

The following month, Mattie and Trudy came to visit Margot and Erik. They arrived early in the morning before Max left for work. Max was sitting at the kitchen table finishing his breakfast when they knocked on the door, and Margot was busy washing Erik's face and hands. But when she heard the knock, she stopped to open the door and was surprised to see her sisters. "What are you two doing here so early?"

"We've come to invite you, Max, and Erik, to Mutti's house for dinner."

"Hmm? Mutti's house for dinner? Why isn't she inviting us? This all sounds very strange," Margot smiled and winked. Erik caught a glimpse of his mother smiling, and he laughed. Mattie tickled him under his arms, but he wiggled away. Then, in a light-hearted manner, Margot asked, "Come on, tell me, what are you two up to?"

Mattie and Trudy were both smiling broadly. But they didn't answer. But from the way they looked, Margot wasn't at all worried. There was no doubt that this dinner was to announce something positive. And she already had an idea of what it might be. "All right, you two. Keep up the suspense for a few more minutes while

I finish dressing Erik," Margot said. Mattie followed Margot into the bedroom. But Trudy stayed in the kitchen with Max.

Trudy was dressed in a pretty white summer dress with a sunflower print. Her nails were polished red, and the shade matched her lipstick perfectly. She carried a batch of freshly baked cookies in her hands, which she put down in front of Max. "I baked these for you last night," Trudy said.

"They look good."

"Well, don't just sit there looking at them. Take one."

He did. It had been a while since Margot had baked for him. She was always busy with Erik and quite often with Ben too. Max knew Ben came by to see his son because he was trying to help Erik develop his motor skills, but it was hard for Max not to feel some twinges of jealousy. After all, Ben was often alone with Margot and Erik while Max was at work. And Max was not blind. He could see the way Margot and Ben looked at each other. But he tried constantly to remind himself that they were just good friends. And he had to remember that if he was to have a good marriage, he must trust his wife. Still, as much as he had come to like Ben, there were times he couldn't help but worry.

"Do you like them? I baked them for you," Trudy whispered to Max. "I know you love *Pfeffernüsse* spice cookies. I remember from last Christmas."

"Yes, I do. But you made Christmas cookies in the middle of August?" he said, smiling.

"I did for you," she smiled back at him.

He looked at her, and for the first time, he realized that over the years, she'd grown to be a pretty woman, but not as pretty as Margot. However, Margot was not as polished as she was before Erik was born. She had stopped taking care of herself lately. She was obsessed with their child. Max couldn't blame her. Erik needed constant attention. And Margot was a good mother. She gave Erik everything she could. So much so that she was exhausted at the end of the day, and often, she refused Max when he tried to make love to her.

"The cookies are delicious," Max declared. "Just delicious!"

"I'm glad you like them." Trudy smiled. Then, her face grew serious. "You know, Max, I would do anything for you."

He was stunned at her frankness. It put him at a loss for words. Max put his half eaten cookie down and looked at her. Trudy's eyes were shining. Her face glowed. For a single moment, he had a strong desire to kiss her. But then Margot and Mattie walked into the room, and the spell of the moment was broken. Leaving Max to feel ashamed.

"Guess what?" Margot said.

"What?" Max asked. He was glad for the distraction from the tense moment with Trudy.

"Mattie is getting married to a man named Ebert. You remember Rudy mentioning that he knew some nice men, don't you?"

"Yes, I remember that Rudy said he was going to introduce Mattie to some single fellows."

"Yes, well, Ebert is the fellow Rudy introduced her to. So, anyway, we have all been invited to Mutti and Vater's apartment next week because Mattie and Ebert will announce their engagement. And while we're there, you and I will have an opportunity to meet Ebert."

"That should be very nice. I look forward to it," Max said as he glanced at his watch. "I'd best be going, or I will be late for work, and my father hates it when I arrive late. Whenever I am late, he says it is because I feel I can take advantage of him because he's my father. He says if I had a real boss, I would be forced to come on time," Max laughed. "It's not true. I would never take advantage of him. In fact, I'm hardly ever late. My father is a good friend to me. He talks a good story, but I don't think he'd ever fire me."

"You're still apprenticing under him, aren't you?" Mattie asked.

"I am. I'm learning carpentry."

"Yes, I know. And you're very good at it, too," Trudy said. "You made this table, didn't you?" She pointed at the kitchen table at which he sat.

"Yes. I did."

"It's beautiful. Just look at this carving on the legs, Mattie. I think this is pine, isn't it?" Trudy asked.

"Yes, it is," Max said.

"He'd be a fool to let you go," Trudy smiled and ran her hand down the table leg suggestively. "Oh, Max, you are very talented. And your father is lucky to have you."

Margot cast an evil glance at Trudy just as Max stood up and wiped his mouth with his napkin. Then he kissed his wife and son. He walked over and hugged each of his sisters-in-law. Trudy held on to him just a moment longer than was appropriate. But he broke away, said goodbye to everyone, walked out the door, and headed to work.

CHAPTER 13

The following week, Ebert and Mattie officially announced their engagement after dinner. Adelaide and Leo were thrilled at the news. Leo got his bottle of schnapps out of the cabinet, which he saved for special occasions. Adelaide poured for everyone, and they all drank to the future of the newly engaged couple. Afterward, Erik handled things he had been told not to touch. Leo knew it was just a ploy for attention. The adults had been busy, and so they had been ignoring him. Leo left the table. He took Erik into the living room and sat on the floor playing with his grandson while his daughters and wife discussed wedding plans.

Rudy, Ebert, and Max left the table, too. They all sat down on the sofa in the living room. They were quiet at first, and the only sound was Erik's laughter.

Then Rudy said, "Max, Ebert, how about you two join me outside for a cigar?"

"Yes, sure," Ebert said.

"Max, will you join us?"

"I don't smoke," Max said.

"That's smart. The Führer says that smoking isn't good for us.

But I can't help it. I do love a good cigar. Let's hope he doesn't ban it, huh?" Rudy said.

"I agree," Ebert said.

"But won't you join us, anyway? We can get a little fresh air. And besides, I have something I'd love to discuss with you," Rudy said to Max.

"Yes, all right."

The three stood in the courtyard in the front of the building. Rudy handed Ebert a cigar. Ebert put the cigar in his mouth, and Rudy lit his and Ebert's. Rudy stretched, sighed, and then took a deep puff. "That's so good." The spicy smell of cigar smoke filled the air. Rudy turned to look directly at Max and asked, "Have you given any thought to what we talked about last time I saw you?"

"I'm sorry. I don't know what you're talking about. I don't mean to be rude, but Margot and I have been a bit overwhelmed. Erik has been having problems with his development, and to be quite honest with you, I've thought of nothing else."

"Of course. I completely understand. Who could blame you? It's difficult what you two are going through."

Max nodded.

"What I was referring to was, have you considered joining the party?"

"Oh, that."

"Yes," Rudy said. "Both Ebert and I are members, and I think it would be a good career move for you. With my influence, you could land quite the position. However, even if you decide not to work for the party, it might help Erik. Once you are a member, your son will have the best medical care."

Max considered this. "Well, I don't know."

"I have an idea. Why don't I arrange for all of us, you and Margot, Ebert, Mattie, Trudy, and I, to go to Munich for *Großdeutsches Volksfest?*"

"You mean the *D'Wiesn*, the *Oktoberfest?*" Ebert asked.

"Yes, exactly. Have you ever been?"

"No, actually, I haven't. I've never had the time or the money. But I've always wanted to go," Ebert smiled.

"What about you, Max?"

"I can't say that I've been there either."

"Well, I have been there, and I can tell you it's a lot of fun," Rudy said, smiling as he took another puff from his cigar.

"I'd love to go. So would Mattie, I think," Ebert said.

"Yes, I know Mattie, and she would really enjoy it. So, would Margot," Rudy said to Max, trying to appeal to his love for his wife.

"I hate to be the one to disappoint all of you, but Margot and I can't afford to take a holiday right now. We're trying to save money to buy a home, and so far, we can't because we have a lot of doctor bills."

"The party would pay for it. I would arrange it. It would be good for Margot. She could use the break." Rudy was insistent.

"Yes, she could. That's true," Max said. "But what about Erik?"

"You could bring him with us. But better yet, we could ask Adelaide if she would take him for a few days. It would give you and Margot a break. What do you say?"

"I don't know. I'm not comfortable accepting an expensive holiday like this from the party. If I do, they will expect me to join?"

"You wouldn't be taking anything from them. I would. You will be coming as my guest. So, they would not expect anything from you. The decision to join or not to join would be yours," Rudy said, then he patted Max on the shoulder.

There were a few moments of silence. The fragrance of cigar smoke wafted up in the air. Then, in his kindest and most sympathetic voice, Rudy implored Max again. "Think of how difficult things have been for Margot. It would be good for her to get away from all of this for a little while. Besides, we could take this time to celebrate Ebert and Mattie's engagement. What do you say?"

It might be good for our marriage. After all, Margot and I have been so busy with Erik that we haven't had time for each other for a while now. And, although Margot wouldn't want to leave Erik, she would trust her mother to watch our son. There is only one other person she would trust as much, and that is Ben. He thought of Ben and how worried he was that he might lose his wife to him. *No, not*

Ben. I think I'd prefer Erik to stay with his grandmother. And maybe Rudy is right. If Margot and I can get away for a little while and be alone together, we can bring back some of the passion that seems to have gone out of our marriage.

"I say, I'm not sure what to do. I think we should talk to the girls and see what they have to say about this. I can't commit to anything without discussing it with Margot first."

"Mattie will want to go. I can say that for sure," Ebert said.

"And as you all know, Trudy is always ready to have a good time." Rudy smiled.

"Yes, well, let's talk to Adelaide and see if she will watch Erik. Then I have to ask Margot if she will agree to leave him for a few days."

CHAPTER 14

"You want me to watch my grandson? You didn't have to even ask. Of course, I will. Leo and I would love to have Erik stay with us. Wouldn't we, Leo?" Adelaide smiled.

"Of course," Leo answered.

"Oh, this is going to be such fun," Mattie said as Ebert put his arm around her shoulders.

"Yes, it will. I can't wait. I've never been to Munich," Trudy said.

"Munich is lovely all the time. But it's a very special place during *Oktoberfest*. They have wonderful beer and a huge parade," Rudy said.

"I've heard all about that beer," Leo said, smiling. "But I must admit, I've never been either. I've talked to friends who've gone, and they said it's a lot of fun. You should enjoy it. And Addie and I will enjoy spending some time with our grandson."

"So, Margot? What do you say? Will you go?" Rudy asked.

"I'm sorry, everyone. I don't want to put a damper on your excitement. But I can't just agree to go. I have a son who needs me. So, I must take some time to think this over."

"Well, you have time," Rudy said. His voice was friendly. "Just don't take too long."

"Please come," Mattie said sincerely.

"Yes, won't you please come?" Trudy said, but there was a twinge of sarcasm in her voice.

CHAPTER 15

When Margot and Max got home that evening, Margot gave Erik a quick bath. Then she put him to bed. He was so tired that he fell asleep almost immediately.

"Shall I make a pot of tea?" Margot asked Max.

"Yes, sounds good."

Margot put the teakettle on the stove, sat across from Max, and waited for it to boil.

"I know how hard it is to leave Erik. I feel that way too. But, Margot, things have been strained between us since Erik got sick." He hesitated, then he went on. "I love you, and I don't want to lose what we have together. We have to put some focus on our marriage, or it's going to dissolve. I really believe that this trip would be good for us."

Margot looked at Max, and he saw that she was uncertain. He could see the worry lines on her forehead. And the more he looked at her, the more he realized she needed this trip. She had stopped wearing lipstick. She no longer styled her hair. The vivacious young woman he married was disappearing before his eyes, and he had to find a way to stop it. "We never had a honeymoon," Max said. "This would be, well, like our honeymoon."

"I don't know," she shook her head. "What if Erik needs us and we're not here? What if he gets sick, very sick? What if he has one of those seizures again, and we are so far away?"

"And if we were here in Berlin and that happened, who would we call? If Erik needed a doctor, would we take him to our doctor or call Ben?"

"Ben. Of course, we'd call Ben because we know he loves Erik. He would do everything in his power to take care of our son."

"So, if we are in Munich, we can leave Ben's phone number and the number to our hotel room with your mother. If she needs Ben, I'm sure he will come. But just to make sure, we'll tell Ben where we're going and that Adelaide will call him if anything happens. We'll give Ben the phone number of our hotel. So that if he needs us, he can get in contact with us. We're only going away for a week."

"I don't know. A week is still a long time to be away from our son."

"Margot. I had doubts, too, when Rudy first came up with this idea. But I can't say this enough. I believe that it will be good for us as a couple. We've been going through so much with Erik being sick that it's taking a toll on our marriage. Let's try this. Please, won't you? For me?"

Her shoulders dropped. "All right. For you. I'll go."

CHAPTER 16

O n the seventeenth of August, the Nazis enacted a new law. Every Jewish person was given a new name, a Jewish name that could be used to further identify them. Every woman was given the name of Sara, and each man the name of Israel. This was meant not only to identify these people as Jews but also to depersonalize and humiliate them.

And so, on this date, Ben became Benjamin Israel Weismann. He would carry this name with him for the rest of his life.

CHAPTER 17

T his was Erik's first time away from Margot for more than a few hours, and she wanted to be sure he had everything he needed. She hated it when she saw children with running noses or dirty faces. Margot took pride in caring for her child. She adored him; in turn, he was a loving and gentle little boy. She watched him playing on the floor as she packed his little bag carefully. There wasn't much money to spend on extras, so Erik's clothing was old and used, but Margot made sure that it was always scrubbed until it was spotless. In fact, she saw to it that everything that came into contact with her son was always clean and neat. She picked up his favorite blanket and held it up to her face, inhaling the essence of him. Tears threatened to fall. *How can I leave him? He needs me. He's used to being with me. I wish I had never agreed to go.* She forced herself to fold the blanket and place it in the bag. Then she went to his toy box and took out a stuffed rabbit that she knew made him feel comfortable because he'd owned it since he was born. She looked at the stuffed animal. One of its eyes was hanging off, and one of its feet was twisted. But she knew Erik loved it. Whenever he was sick or had a seizure, he always asked for his rabbit. "Get me Rabbit, please," he would say. And she would give him his rabbit. He would hold it close to his chest, and somehow, it comforted him. *My little boy. My darling, precious little boy.* Then she put his comb in the bag and gently closed the top.

Margot's stomach ached, and her head hurt when she dropped Erik off at her parent's home so she and Max could go to Munich for the *Oktoberfest*. She felt selfish, and although she knew she needed to work on her marriage and that Max deserved some of her attention, she found it hard to separate from her son. She'd already spoken with Ben about the situation. And she was surprised to find that he thought it was a good idea that she went with Max. He promised her that even though it was dangerous and against the law, he would find a way to go to her mother's apartment every other day to check on Erik. Margot knew that Ben meant to reassure her. However, now she was not only worried about Erik, but she was also concerned about Ben. If he were caught, the price would be very high. And she shivered just thinking about it. Besides, she and Erik were inseparable. Until this trip, she'd never left her child for more than a few hours to go to the market. Now, she would be away from Erik for a full week. *It just doesn't seem like a good idea. I know I must do it for Max's sake. But so much can go wrong. I wish I hadn't promised.*

When she arrived back at her apartment, Max was smiling brightly. He kissed her, then put his arms around her and whirled her in a dance until she had to laugh. He touched her face and whispered, "Thank you for doing this for me."

She nodded. Then she looked over at his suitcase. It stood in the corner of the room by the door. He was already packed and ready to leave. She had waited until the last minute to put her things together. "I'd better hurry and pack," she said.

He loosened his arms and let her go. "Yes, you'd better. They'll be here to pick us up any minute," he said.

Margot grabbed her small cardboard valise. She didn't have much, so packing didn't take very long. And after she finished, she put her suitcase next to Max's and sat on the sofa to wait. Margot wanted to cry. *I should be excited about this trip. We have never gone anywhere, and this is an opportunity for Max and me to become closer.* But the truth was she was fearful that something might happen, something terrible, something irreversible, something she would regret for the rest of her life.

"Are you ready?" Max asked, forcing her out of her terrifying thoughts and back into the moment.

Margot nodded and tried to smile, but her lower lip quivered. *I don't want to ruin this for him. I know how much he has been looking forward to it.*

Max noticed her lip quivering, and he touched her chin. "Everything will be all right. I promise you," he said softly.

"I don't know, Max."

"Don't be afraid," he whispered and kissed her forehead.

"How can you promise me? You don't know what the future holds. How will we feel if we've made a mistake? What if something happens and Ben can't get to Erik, or he gets to my parent's home too late? What then? Or what if he is arrested? Then what?"

"Ben is very smart. He won't be arrested. And your mother will keep a keen eye on her grandson. She adores him. Your father adores Erik, too. He's in good hands. Try to enjoy this trip, Margot."

"I will. I promise you. I will," she said, but she knew her voice did not sound convincing.

"Are you ready to leave? Because Rudy's driver should be here in the next ten minutes to pick us up."

"Yes, I'm all packed." Then she said, "It's such a long ride to Munich."

"It will be fine. Everything will be all right," Max said, kissing her.

The driver and Rudy, Trudy, Mattie, and Ebert arrived on time. Rudy sat in the front of the car with the driver while the rest crowded into the back seat. Mattie volunteered to sit on Ebert's lap because there wasn't enough room.

Margot could count the few times she'd been in an automobile on her fingers. It was a crisp fall day. The windows were open. Margot sat next to the window, and the breeze was lovely. But try as she might, Margot could not relax. She was consumed with thoughts of her son. Max reached over and held her hand. Then he winked at her and gave her a reassuring smile.

About halfway to Munich, Mattie got car sick. They had to pull off the road and wait while she vomited behind a tree.

"Do you think she'll be all right?" Ebert asked Rudy.

"Of course. She's just not used to riding in a car. That's all. Let her sit by the window and get some fresh air. She'll be fine," Rudy promised.

They all moved their seats so that Mattie could sit by the window. Now Margot was sitting on Max's lap. And just as Rudy promised, Mattie was fine.

CHAPTER 18

They arrived in Munich late in the afternoon. The hotel was a beautiful modern building with German flags on either side of the front door.

"All right, everyone. We're here," Rudy chirped. "I'll check us in, and then we'll go to our rooms and freshen up before lunch. All right with everyone?"

They all nodded.

Each couple had their own room with a private bathroom. Fluffy white towels embroidered with a black and red swastika had been supplied. And over the bed hung a picture of the Führer looking very serious.

"Would you just look at this room?" Max said. He was clearly impressed. "It's bigger than our whole apartment. And can you believe we have our own bathroom right here in the room, and it has a shower? This is very nice."

"Yes, it is nice," Margot agreed, but she frowned as she glanced up at the picture of Hitler and thought about Ben. "I can't believe the government will pay for all of this."

"That's what Rudy says. So, I have to believe him."

"What about food? I'm assuming we're going to have to pay for our own food."

"It will be all right. I brought some money from our savings," Max said.

Money we should be saving in case we need it for medical care for Erik. Margot was worried but said, "Good, that sounds good."

Margot waited while Max washed his face and combed his hair. Then she washed her face and attempted to neaten her dark curls. Once they were both ready, they went to the lobby to meet with the rest of the group.

Margot wore the same simple cotton dress she'd worn on the drive. But Trudy came down the stairs looking like a movie idol traveling incognito. She wore a tight wool suit with dark sunglasses.

"You look absolutely glamorous," Mattie exclaimed excitedly.

"Oh, thank you," Trudy said, shaking off the compliment. But anyone could see by how Trudy walked and talked that she lived for compliments.

When they gathered in the lobby, Rudy said, "There's a cute little café I know of down the street where we can grab a quick lunch. Then we'll do a little sightseeing, and tonight, we'll go to the oldest *Biergarten* in Munich. I've been there before, and it's extraordinary. I promise you will love it. We can get some good food there and enjoy some good German beer. What do you think?"

Everyone nodded in agreement.

"So, follow me."

Everyone followed Rudy to the café, where he ordered plenty of food for the table. He ordered sausages and sauerkraut, crispy potato pancakes, and spaetzle. There was plenty of delicious food, and everyone was hungry. They were all eating like they had never eaten before. All except for Margot.

As it turned out, Max need not have brought any money with him. When the restaurant owner took one look at Rudy's uniform with the SS band on the sleeve, he insisted that everything was complimentary. In fact, after they finished eating, the owner sent an apple strudel to the table. It was large enough for the entire group.

"You see what a pleasure it is to be a party member?" Rudy said as he smiled and looked directly at Max. "This is how you are treated everywhere you go. Especially if you know someone who can get you hired into a good position. And you do." He winked and added, "You know me."

They walked down the streets for a while, wandering through the little shops, and then they stopped to watch the giant clock as it put on its daily show in the center of town.

While window shopping, Trudy stopped in at one of the boutiques where she bought two dresses. Mattie was admiring a pair of faux pearl earrings. "Aren't these lovely?" she said to Trudy.

"They are," Trudy said. Then she took them from Mattie's hand and said, "Let me buy them for you."

Rudy saw his wife purchasing a gift for Mattie, and he said. "Why don't you buy something nice for Margot, too?"

Margot protested, "Oh, that's really not necessary."

"Of course, it is. I can afford to buy you anything you'd like to have. After all, my husband is wealthy," Trudy said, smiling and winking at Rudy. "What would you like, Margot?"

The gesture was kind, but Margot knew that Trudy's intentions were anything but kind. She wanted Margot to see that she had married a more successful man, a man who could give her the things she wanted. But Margot didn't care. These things had long since lost their luster for her.

"Oh, I don't need anything but thank you. It's very kind of you to offer."

Mattie glanced at Margot. She saw the wrinkles on Margot's brow, and she felt sorry for her sister. Erik's illness had changed Margot. She had been such a spirited girl, but this had taken the joy out of her. And Mattie couldn't blame her. After all, Margot had almost lost her only child, and he was still so sickly. But Trudy hadn't changed from the girl she was when they were young. She still wanted all the material things the world had to offer. And no matter how much Trudy had, she still seemed unsatisfied. And the way she looked at Margot, anyone could see that she still hated and envied her sister.

After returning to their rooms to change that evening, they all went to the *Biergarten,* as Rudy had promised. "This is the oldest one in Munich. It's very famous," Rudy said as they walked up to be seated by the host, a tall blond gentleman in lederhosen who stood at the front door.

Margot looked around the restaurant. It seemed to her that at least fifty or more tables were set up outside under large trees, and they were all full. People were singing traditional German songs. There was laughter and beer toasts. And most of all, there were lots of men wearing Nazi uniforms. They were accompanied by friends in uniform, women in fashionable dresses, or traditional German dirndl dresses with fitted bodices and aprons.

There was a young couple in line for a table ahead of them. But when the host saw Rudy's uniform, he turned to the couple and said, "I'm sorry, but we are all full right now. We don't have any open tables. Perhaps you can check back in a couple of hours."

The couple left, and the host turned his attention to Rudy.

"Good evening," the host said to Rudy. "How many are in your party?"

"Six."

"Follow me. I have a very nice table for you."

As they walked to the table, Rudy winked at Max. "You see?" he said quietly so only Max could hear. "It's the uniform."

Rudy strategically sat down beside Max.

It was only a few minutes before their waiter arrived. When he did, Rudy ordered a pitcher of the special *Oktoberfest* beer served for the occasion. He turned to Max and said, "Do you know that there is a purity rule here as far as this beer is concerned?"

"I don't know anything about it," Max admitted.

"Well," Rudy put his arm around Max and said, "the German *Reinheitsgebot* limits German beer makers to only four ingredients: hops, yeast, malt, and water. They are not permitted to add anything else."

When the beer arrived, Rudy poured Max's glass first. "Taste that."

Max took a sip. "It's good. It's very good."

"Yes, it is," Rudy agreed, then sipped. He held up his glass. "I am going to make a toast."

Everyone at the table grew quiet.

"To Hitler and to a bright future for our fatherland."

Everyone lifted their glasses. "To our Führer," Ebert said.

Then, other people at nearby tables joined in, raising their glasses and toasting the Führer.

Margot felt her stomach lurch as she looked around her. There were so many men wearing Nazi uniforms. She wondered what this might mean for Ben and his family in the future.

Then, the waiter returned to take the rest of their order. "May I take the liberty of ordering for everyone?" Rudy asked generously.

"Yes, of course," they all nodded.

Rudy ordered black forest ham with spicy mustard, Bavarian cheese, and thick, dark bread.

"Would you care for some spaetzle or sauerkraut?" The waiter asked.

"Of course, yes, we'd like both. And make sure there's plenty for the whole table," Rudy said.

And once again, there was no bill. Everything was complimentary.

After dinner, they walked around the old city, and as they walked, they saw vendors selling beer. Rudy stopped at several and ordered beers for himself and the other two fellows. Mattie and Trudy each had one more beer, but Margot refused.

"I can't remember the last time I drank so much," Max said, smiling. He was clearly a little drunk.

Margot didn't want to spoil things for him. It had been so long since either of them had done anything so carefree. And since he was having such a good time, she tolerated his excessive drinking. But she said gently when he stumbled and almost fell, "It's getting late. I think, perhaps, we should all get some rest."

"Yes, of course. I agree. But first, before we go back to our rooms for the night," Rudy said, "let's have some *Lubkechenherzen* gingerbread cookies. We can get them at the bakery right over there and then eat them on our way back to our rooms."

"Oh yes, let's get cookies," Mattie said. Her voice was full of excitement, like the voice of a child.

"Well, only if it's all right with Margot?" Rudy said.

Margot nodded in agreement, even though she preferred to return to her room. "Yes, of course," she said.

Rudy bought everyone a cookie from a vendor who was selling them. They were large and heart-shaped. Each cookie was beautifully decorated with icing. Max noticed that some of the cookies had messages written in icing. Some said, "My Angel" or "My princess." There were various messages to choose from. But Rudy, as he did this entire trip, took control and purchased cookies without messages. Then he handed one to Ebert to share with Mattie and another to Max to share with Margot. Rudy then broke off a tiny piece of the one he purchased for himself and gave the rest to Trudy.

They walked slowly back towards the hotel to get some rest. Once they were in the lobby, and before they went to their separate rooms, they decided to meet at nine o'clock in the morning for breakfast.

CHAPTER 19

Trudy was exhausted by the time she and her husband got back to their room. She was glad Rudy had too much to drink because she knew alcohol made him tired, and he would not try to make love to her. This pleased her. Now, she could take a hot shower and be free to get lost in her thoughts about Max. She knew why her husband wanted Max to join the party. He'd explained to her that if both of their families were party members, it would look very good for Rudy, and he would be considered for another promotion.

As she hung up the dress she'd worn that evening, she glanced over to see that Rudy had already passed out on the bed. He still had his boots on and was still in his uniform. But it didn't matter. He had brought another two uniforms with them; both were clean and pressed. In the morning, she knew Rudy would have her send this one out to be cleaned. But for now, she didn't have to worry about what Rudy wanted from her. He would sleep for hours. And that would leave her free for the whole night. It would be morning before she would be required to fulfill any of his demands.

Trudy went into the bathroom and turned the water on in the shower to let it warm up. Then she removed her undergarments and looked in the mirror. She was pleased with how her body looked as her eyes traveled over her ample breasts and slender hips. *I was afraid being pregnant would ruin my looks. But that's not the case. At least not yet. I hope not ever. Maybe pregnancy suits me. My breasts have grown so large and full. I wonder what Max would think if he saw me naked. My sister Margot looks so old and worn out. I'm sure he's got to be unhappy with her. She's not the pretty little thing she was when they got married. I wonder what he thinks when he looks at me. I wonder if he wishes he'd chosen me instead of her.*

Trudy stepped into the shower and let the warm water run over her body. She shampooed her hair and slowly spread the sweet-smelling soap over her skin. It was an expensive soap of good quality. It gave off the fragrance of roses in bloom and was nothing like the harsh soap their mother had made from lye when she and her sisters were growing up. The warm water caressed her skin as she reached up and embraced her ample breasts. "Max," she said, her voice barely above a whisper. "Max, I love you."

CHAPTER 20

Max was tired. He wasn't used to drinking so much. Even so, he wasn't too tired to make love to his wife. And Margot found it easier to make love to Max than when she was busy taking care of her son all day. This was because this trip was relaxing compared to her daily life at home. She wanted to give herself completely to her husband. She knew how much he loved her. But it was difficult because she was constantly worried about Erik and Ben. Still, she forced herself to hide her concerns and did her best to be lighthearted. Margot did what she could to please her husband. And Max was happy that she seemed to be letting go just a little. He was glad that she had stopped refusing his affection. Although she still was not wearing lipstick or doing much with her hair, he was stunned by how beautiful she was to him when he looked at her.

The following morning, Max awoke early on purpose. They planned to meet at nine, but he was awake by seven. He had an idea and wanted to carry it out before Margot awakened so he could surprise her. Quiet as a jungle cat, Max moved around the room quickly and slipped on his clothes. He was slightly nauseated and had a headache from drinking the night before. But he could not let this opportunity to see his wife smile pass him by. So, after turning to assure himself that Margot was still asleep, he left the hotel room. He walked all the way back to the bakery where they had stopped the previous night to buy the heart-shaped cookies. There was already a line in place, and he stood waiting for almost a half hour. When he finally got to the front of the line, he purchased one of the heart-shaped cookies and had it wrapped. Then, with his purchase in his hand, he ran back to the hotel. When he arrived back at the room, Margot was already awake.

"Where were you?" she asked, and he could hear the worry in her voice.

"I went to get you something," he said, handing her the cookie.

She looked at him and cocked her head. "What is this?"

"Open it," he smiled.

She opened it carefully. It was one of the beautiful heart-shaped cookies. But this one was different because "I Love You" was written on it with red icing.

Margot put her arms around his neck and whispered, "Oh, Max, you had me worried. Now, what am I ever going to do with you?"

"Love me?"

"I do love you," she answered.

CHAPTER 21

The following day, the famous *Oktoberfest* parade was scheduled to take place. Rudy found them all a perfect place where they would be able to see everything. They stood in front of the crowds of people on the street and watched. Everyone seemed to be at least a little drunk and very happy. The parade was exciting, and afterward, Rudy insisted that they go to an Italian restaurant called Osteria Italiana restaurant for dinner. It was located on Schellingstrasse. "You know, Hitler dines here," Rudy said proudly as he opened the door for his guests. Then he added, "So, of course, the food will be excellent. Only the best for our marvelous Führer, yes?"

"Yes!" Ebert said.

"I've never had Italian food," Mattie said.

"It's delicious," Trudy said. "Rudy and I go out for Italian food in Berlin often."

"I have no idea what to order. Will you order for us?" Ebert asked Rudy.

"Of course, I intended to," he said, then he turned to Max. "Would you and Margot like me to order for you as well?"

"Yes, that would be fine," Max said, not wanting to admit that he and Margot hardly ever went out for dinner. Whenever they did, they went to a small, inexpensive café that served traditional German food. So, neither of them had ever eaten Italian food before.

Rudy ordered a green salad, followed by spaghetti with garlic and oil and tiny *pepperoncini*. After that came a main course of chicken with rosemary. And for dessert, he finished with a light and delicious tiramisu with coffee accompanied by real cream and sugar. Margot and Max had never eaten so much food at one time. It was delicious and very rich.

Oktoberfest was scheduled to last for two weeks. But they had only planned to stay for one. And that week was going by quickly for all of them except Margot. There were still a few days left, and everyone was sitting in a restaurant having lunch and trying to decide what to do next. Margot was with them, and she tried to enjoy herself, but Erik was never far from her thoughts. Finally, she decided to speak to Ben and find out what was happening at home. So, as they all sat eating, drinking beer, and making toast, she excused herself. Margot told them that she needed to find a restroom and would be right back. Then she went to a public phone where she called Ben.

As the phone rang, her heart beat so hard that she thought it would fly out of her chest. He answered on the third ring. "Ben, it's me, Margot."

"Margot. It's so good to hear your voice. Is everything all right?"

"Yes, everything is fine here. I just had to call to find out how Erik was doing. Have you gone to see him?"

"Every other day, like I promised. He is doing well."

"You can't imagine how much it means to me to hear that," she said. "How are you? I've been so worried about you getting arrested. I would die if anything like that…"

"I'm fine," he said, but he sounded sad.

"You don't sound fine. What's wrong?"

"Oh, it's nothing. I'm all right. I promise."

"Please tell me if something isn't right."

"It's just that a young man I have known all my life was arrested last night. He and his family live just a few houses down from mine. I know this fellow. He's a good man, and I can't imagine he did anything wrong. He was always a shy, quiet fellow. Never got in trouble. My mother was his teacher, and he went to the Jewish school. I asked her to tell me about him, and she said he was a good boy, never a troublemaker. And last night, the Gestapo came and took him away. Now, everyone in the neighborhood is worried about him."

"Of course they are. I can't blame them," Margot said. But she closed her eyes and thought of how the people they met in Munich admired Rudy because he wore that SS uniform. *This whole country has gone mad.*

"Yes, well, it's not a good place for Jews here in Germany anymore," Ben said.

"I know. I wish it were not so."

"Margot," he said, hesitating for a few seconds.

"Yes?"

"I miss you. Be safe. Come home safely."

"You too, Ben. Please be careful."

CHAPTER 22

On the last night of their vacation, Rudy took everyone to a fancy steak house. Once again, the owner ensured that Rudy was given the royal treatment and that he was pleased with the restaurant and their meal. The owner insisted that everything was complimentary for Rudy, the SS officer. As they all sat at the table eating their dessert and coffee, Rudy smiled and said, "So, it's our last night. I had a wonderful time." Then he added, "And Trudy and I have something special planned for tonight. We have gifts for everyone."

"You shouldn't have," Mattie said, but her eyes glowed with excitement. "But I'm glad you did."

Trudy let out a laugh. "Of course, we did because we can afford it, right Rudy?"

He just smiled at her and nodded.

Trudy stood up and said, "All right, are you ready?"

"Yes," Ebert said.

"Go ahead, hand out the gifts," Trudy said to her husband.

"Well, this is for your new home," he said to Mattie and handed her a wrapped package.

"What is it?" she said.

"It's a handmade cuckoo clock. It was made here in Munich. You will always have something to remind you of our trip." He handed the clock to Mattie, who giggled with delight.

She tore the paper off the gift and said, "It's beautiful. Thank you so much."

"Yes, thank you," Ebert echoed.

"And for you, Margot, Trudy bought this lovely new dress," Rudy handed Margot a dressy black silk dress.

"You really didn't have to. I don't ever go anywhere I would wear such a fancy dress," Margot said. "But it's lovely. Thank you."

"Well, we are going to have to change that, won't we?" Rudy said. "We'll have to get you and Max to go out more in the future. I'll see what I can do." He winked. Then he took a long breath, put his arm on Max's arm, and said, "And for you, my friend, I bought this special watch. It's very good quality." Rudy handed a box to Max. Max opened the box and found a watch with a swastika on the face. "Do you like it?"

Max didn't know what to say. He knew it was expensive, and he also knew that Rudy had gone above and beyond to ensure that everyone had a wonderful time. But Max didn't want to join the party, and he didn't want to wear a watch with the Nazi party insignia, no matter how good the quality. Still, he said, "Thank you. It's really quite nice. I appreciate everything you've done for us."

"So, let me ask you, are you ready to join us now?" Rudy said enthusiastically.

"You mean the party?"

"Of course, that's what I mean."

Max shook his head. "I'm sorry, but I can't say I am. I just can't do it," Max admitted.

A flash of anger crossed over Rudy's face. But he immediately caught himself, and the look of anger disappeared. He smiled, and he was in control. "Well, you really should think about it. Didn't you see how well everyone treats me? That's because of my position. Wouldn't you like people to treat you like that?"

"I suppose," Max said, squirming in his chair.

Trudy could see that Max was uncomfortable, and since she

didn't want him to stop spending time with her and her husband, she smiled gently. Then she looked at Max and said, "Listen, we don't want to put you under pressure. You take your time and think it over. Let us know when you are ready. How does that sound?"

Max nodded.

CHAPTER 23

That night, as Trudy lay beside her husband in bed, he asked, "Why do you think he is so adamant about not joining the party? I can't imagine what is wrong with him."

"Don't you know?"

"I'm sorry, but to be quite honest, I don't have a clue."

"It's my sister, Margot. She is the one who doesn't want him to join. It's because she has a Jewish friend. He's a boy she went to school with. Now, he is a friend of her family."

"Why would they continue to have a friendship with a Jew? It's illegal, and besides, there's no point to it."

"My guess is that it's because this fellow is a doctor, and he has convinced them that he can help them with Erik."

"Hmmmm. That's rather interesting. I'm sure the Jew is manipulating them. They do that, you know. They do it to get what they want," Rudy said. "I'll have to find a way to put a stop to it."

"You do what you can," she said, cradling his arm in hers. *I'd love to tell him what I know about Margot, about her birth mother, but I can't. If I do, he'll make me sever all ties with her. Now I don't care if I never see her again. But if I cut ties with Margot, I would probably never see Max again. Even though the law would force them to get divorced if the truth came out about Margot. But what if Max was arrested for marrying a Jew? What if the police didn't believe him that he didn't know? I can't risk that. I know I still have a chance with him.*

CHAPTER 24

O*bersturmführer* Rudolf Schulze, or Rudy as his friends and family called him, sat at his desk smoking a cigar and thinking. He gazed out the window at the blanket of crisp, jewel-colored autumn leaves that covered the ground. The tree outside his window was almost bare. She had shed her leaves into a beautiful tapestry of color. He sighed as he poured himself a glass of whiskey and leaned back in his chair. *How am I going to explain why I want to be sure that Benjamin Weissman is targeted when the demonstration takes place on November 9? I can't tell them the truth. I don't want the Gestapo to start keeping watch on Margot and Max. Not because I give a damn about them, but if they are caught breaking the law, it will reflect poorly on me. And that could hurt my opportunities to rise in the party. Still, I want Ben and his family to stay far away from Margot and Max. And for that to happen, I must find a way to speak to him personally. I'll do what I have to do to make sure he stays far away from anyone related to me.*

Not everyone knew of the upcoming demonstration that had

81

been planned. It was a demonstration against the Jews of Germany, a way to let them know just how much they were hated by the German people. Only a select few in the Nazi party had been told about it. This was because the Nazi party would not openly accept responsibility for what was to come. They did not plan to go out as German soldiers or policemen in their uniforms. They put on a pogrom of unparalleled cruelty in a country considered civilized and as advanced as Germany. Instead, the top Nazi officials would hide behind their desks while they unleashed gangs of young thugs onto the streets of the Jewish neighborhoods. These hooligans had been given free rein. They grew up to hate Jewish people and were now told that they could do as they pleased without consequence. They were instructed to burn the synagogues, destroy the business, and beat up a few Jews. If any Jews died as a result, it was of no concern. As a reward, they were told they could keep whatever they could steal. Then, the Nazis planned to blame the Jews for what happened. They would turn this around and say it happened because the Jewish people had been causing trouble. This would allow the police to put as many Jews as possible under arrest.

Rudy took another puff from his cigar. The smoke had a faint hint of cinnamon, filling the air in Rudy's office. *I love these. I know our Führer disapproves of smoking, but a good cigar has a way of calming a man.* It had a way of helping him to think.

He had to admit that he didn't like Max or Margot. They were not the kind of people he would have chosen for friends. But they were family, and because of that, he had to put up with them. Anything that they did reflected on him. So, it would be best if Max would just join the party and behave himself. Rudy thought he should feel even a bit sorry for them because their child was so ill, but he didn't care. The child was not important to him. Still, he thought Erik was a boy, and because he was, Max should be more conscious of his actions.

Every action Max took would reflect on his son when his son grew up. This was another reason he felt Max was a fool not to join the party and make a better life for himself and his family. Rudy remembered that he'd been shocked when Trudy told him about

Margot's friendship with that Jew called Ben. He couldn't believe that Max hadn't stopped a friendship like that. *If it had been Trudy who was making friends with a Jewish man, I would have certainly taken matters into my own hands and ended it right away. And if she refused to listen to me, I wouldn't put up with it the way Max does. I would make sure she would be sorry and live to regret it. I would never allow my wife to embarrass me by having a Jewish doctor for a friend. It wouldn't matter to me that she knew him from school. I wouldn't care where she knew him from. Jews are not friends. It's like making friends with a pig or a dog. Oh yes, I can guarantee that nonsense would stop if it were my wife. Max's big problem in life is that he is faithful to one woman. No man should allow one woman to have that much power over him.* Besides, he thought that Margot was ugly. She was not blonde and blue-eyed like her sisters. *She's no beauty. She reminds me of those little brown sisters at the Lebensborn homes. They are not permitted to reproduce because, although they are of pure German blood, they do not have the desirable physical traits.*

Throughout his entire marriage, Rudy had always had a girlfriend on the side. Not only that, but as soon as he had risen high enough in rank to be permitted to go, he had been a frequent visitor to several of the Lebensborn homes. He adored the Lebensborn homes. The very idea that he was admired and put on a pedestal by the women made him smile. And there was no work involved. He didn't have to wine and dine with the girls. In fact, because he was an SS officer with blond hair and blue eyes, he could pick which girl he wanted to bed for the night.

Yes, the homes for the Lebensborn were fun. He was doing his duty to his country at the same time, spreading his very desirable Aryan seed. *Yes, that's what I like: lots of sex with no commitment.* The women all wanted him when he went. They competed for his attention. Thinking about his visits to the Lebensborn homes made him smile. He went as often as he could. And he didn't like being married. In fact, he would have stayed single if it was possible. He had only married Trudy because he was told by his superiors that it would help his career to have a good Aryan wife at his side. So that together, they could create plenty of blonde, blue-eyed Aryan children to help populate Hitler's new world. *Well, I've done my duty, and my higher-ups have already taken notice. They're happy that my wife is pregnant. I hope we have a son. I want a boy, a boy who I can teach and direct.* He sighed out loud. *But for now, I must deal with the situation at hand. My foolish sister-in-law and her idiot husband will not ruin my chances of rising by having a Jew for a friend.*

He picked up the telephone receiver and asked his secretary to put him through to his boss.

"What do you want, Rudolf?"

"I need to have a Jew family targeted on November 9."

"Oh? Why this particular family?"

"Because their son is a doctor, and he has convinced my sister-in-law that he can heal her son, who is a very sick child. I'm sure he's manipulating her, and because she loves her child, she is probably paying him a nice sum of money." He coughed, "And you know how cunning these Jews are. Well, this Jew is a wizard, just like Rasputin in Russia. He is a dangerous sort. And you know how foolish women can be when it comes to their children. They can be mindless."

"Actually, that is quite true," his boss gave a laugh.

"Yes, and so, I want to put a stop to this mess right now. And after the Jew is arrested, I want to speak to him. Once I get my hands on him, he will never speak to my sister-in-law again."

"Of course. I quite agree with you. So, I'll take care of it. Give me his information."

CHAPTER 25

T rudy was disappointed. She had hoped that when they were in Munich, she would have been able to find some time to be alone with Max. But try as she might, it was impossible.

I think he must be regretting his marriage to my sister. Just look at her. She looks so weathered and worn. And to make matters worse, she produced a sick child. All of this must weigh heavily on him. He sees that I am well put together when he looks at me. My hair is always done, my makeup is perfect, and my clothes are expensive and beautiful. I look young and vibrant, while Margot has aged. There are wrinkles on her forehead and around her eyes. Before she gave birth to Erik, she was a beauty. Even in her second-hand clothes, she was stunning. And I was so jealous. But now, she's far too thin. He must secretly wish he had chosen me for his wife instead of her. I think he knows he had the chance. But he doesn't know that he still has a chance with me. All he has to do is tell me he wants me. She sighed as she looked at herself in the mirror. *I am still quite beautiful, but I must admit that I do hate being pregnant. I'm terrified of getting fat and being unable to lose this baby weight. But as long as I don't eat much, I will be all right. So far, this preg-*

nancy has made my skin glow, my hair shiny, and my breasts larger than ever. It's taking every bit of willpower I have not to eat. I'm always hungry. But I can't let my figure go. Having a child is just not worth it.

CHAPTER 26

The trip to Munich did help Margot and Max ignite the passion in their marriage. And the magic lingered even after they got home. Since their return, Erik had not had an episode, which was encouraging. He seemed to be improving. And Margot and Max were trying to believe that maybe Erik might be outgrowing his condition. As Max was getting ready for work one morning, Erik said, "I love my Vater and my Mutti, and I am feeling much better." Margot heard him and gathered him into her arms, kissing his face as she broke into tears. Then she called out to Max, "Max, come here! Erik said, 'I love my Vater and my Mutti, and I am feeling much better.'"

Max ran into the room in his underclothes. He took the little boy from his mother and hugged him tightly. "Maybe it's all over. Maybe he's going to be all right from now on."

"Oh, Max, do you think so? I can only pray that you're right."

Max kissed Margot softly. "I am praying too."

Even though they could hardly afford it, Max brought Margot flowers that night. And she made love to him more enthusiastically than she had in years. They both believed that by some miracle, their son was healing.

They lay beside each other in their small bed. She gave him her hand. Max always liked to hold Margot's hand after making love. Outside the window, there was a hum from a night bird sitting contentedly in a tree. "Margot?" Max called her name in a soft, questioning voice. "Do you think I am making a mistake by not joining the party? Did you see how everyone everywhere we went reacted to Rudy's uniform? Life is obviously a lot easier for party members."

"Yes, actually, I did see that. It was rather amazing, and I must admit, it was also a little disturbing."

"I agree with you. But life is sometimes difficult for us. And I think we would have plenty of money if I joined the party. We could afford the best medical care for Erik. And, besides that, Rudy says he might be able to get us a house. A house we could afford."

"That sounds strange. How could he get us a house?"

"I guess because they have homes that belong to the party. He says they allow their officers and their families to live in them sometimes for free, sometimes for low rent."

"Would it be a home of our own? Or would the party still own it, and we would just live there?"

"I don't know. But I know there would be enough room for us to have another child, a sibling for our son. And Erik could have a swing in the backyard." He hesitated, then said, "We would never want for food or anything for that matter. Look at the way Rudy and your sister live. She has beautiful clothes, and they have such nice things. I want that for you. I want to buy you beautiful things, Margot. You deserve the best of everything. But right now, I am nothing but a poor carpenter. I work hard, and we live frugally. And, well, sometimes I feel like I am failing you."

She cleared her throat. "You have never failed me, Max. You're a good father and a good provider. We may not have all the luxuries, but we have what we need. I don't care about fancy clothes anymore. I did when I was young, but now there are more important things."

"Yes, I agree with you. But one of the most important is Erik, and there again, if I were a party member, he would have the best medical care. We would have access to the most current discoveries. Maybe even a cure."

"I know. I have thought about that. I just wish that the party wasn't so against the Jews. It makes me feel like a traitor to Ben. He's been a good friend to us."

"Yes, he has. And we would remain friends with him, but we would have to be even more careful than we are now about keeping our friendship a secret."

She was quiet.

"What are you thinking?" he asked.

"I am thinking that I don't know how much more we could keep this friendship a secret. It's already illegal for us to be friends with Ben. He only comes by to see us after dark. What more could we possibly do?"

"So, you don't want me to join? Because if you don't want me to, then I won't. I don't like the party or what it stands for, either. But I like the benefits. It's hard to walk away from the benefits. Don't you agree?" he asked.

"I don't know. I can't decide right now. I have to think about it," she said. Then, after a few moments, she asked, "Do you think that if you belonged in the party, we might be able to do something to protect Ben?"

"Oh, Margot. You know how much I like Ben, and to answer your question, I'd love to say yes. But the truth is, no matter how high up I get in the party, I doubt I would ever be able to help him. You and I know that the Nazis don't want us to have Jewish friends. It's illegal. If they discovered that you and I were friends with Ben, they wouldn't like it. And they certainly wouldn't allow us to do anything to help him. In fact, it would be dangerous for him and for us."

She nodded. "I know. I was just hoping that somehow, we might be able to do something for him."

"You and I are just two people. We dare not try to go against this terrible government. They could destroy us in an instant. And now that we desperately need their help with Erik, I have to do whatever they ask of me. Even if it means becoming a part of something I despise."

CHAPTER 27

t was unusual for Ben to drop by during the day, but he did. He came by on Wednesday afternoon of that week to visit Margot and see Erik. Margot told him how encouraged she and Max were about Erik's condition. "He hasn't had a seizure for a while. Maybe he won't have them anymore," she said excitedly.

"Maybe," Ben said. His lips were trembling. He was not as positive as she was, but he didn't share his fears. Instead, he smiled at her happiness and changed the subject. "So, how was the trip to Munich? Did you have a nice time?"

"It was nice. I have to admit, it was very impressive. Would you believe me if I told you the government paid for everything? Everything. And we had the best of everything."

"Please don't tell me they've seduced you and Max, and you're thinking of joining?"

"Actually, I wasn't as impressed as Max was. He mentioned to me that he likes the benefits the party offers. Believe me, we are both against this hatred of the Jews. But it would be nice to have all the good things the party provides its members." She cleared her throat, embarrassed by what she'd just told him.

"So, if you two were Nazis, that would be the end of my coming by to see you and Erik," he said with a hint of disgust.

"Not necessarily. Max says we could still be friends, but we would just have to be more careful."

He shook his head. "Careful? I'm always careful. My whole life has become about being careful. You can't imagine how things are for Jews right now."

"I only meant that we would have to be careful not to be seen together. And although Max doesn't think it's possible for us to do anything to help you, I am hoping we can find a way. I won't give up on you, Ben. I can't. You're too dear a friend to me."

"Oh, Margot. I wish it were that easy. I wish all we had to do was be careful not to be seen together. But this is bigger than that. It's bigger than you and me, and it's bigger than Max, too. Nazis are everywhere. They see everything. People I grew up with, people I once trusted, are now party members and are ready to turn me in for no reason. No, I can't go on the way we are if you and Max joined. It would be the end of our friendship," Ben said. Then he added, "But if it's what you want, I won't stand in your way."

"Even you said that Erik needs better medical care than you can provide. You said you are unable to get the right medicines. And even if you could, they are expensive. Max doesn't earn enough money to buy them. We are barely affording our apartment and all our expenses. It's not that we want material things. Although it would be nice to have plenty of food. But the real reason Max is considering joining the party is that if he were a member, they would provide everything for Erik. Everything our son might need. And with the way medicine is advancing, who knows, they may even have a cure in the future. Don't you see? Without them, we are always on edge, wondering if we are doing everything that can be done for Erik. Max hates the Nazis as much as I do, but he just wants to help our son in any way we can. I pray that Erik has outgrown this disease, but if he hasn't, then we will need aggressive medical care."

Ben nodded. "I can't blame you. I want the best for Erik, too.

So, tell Max that I won't come by here anymore. I think this is what is best. If you ever need me, you know where to find me."

There was a dead silence in the room as Ben took his coat off the coat rack. He put it on, then put on his hat and scarf. He walked to the door and turned around. He looked directly into her eyes and said, "Goodbye, Margot."

She was crying, but he didn't stop to comfort her. Instead, he just walked out and quietly shut the door behind him.

CHAPTER 28

t was a Wednesday night, and Ben's mother was coming home late from her teaching job at the Jewish school. This was happening more often these days because she had been staying after school to help one of her students prepare for his upcoming bar mitzvah. She had always taken a special interest in the students who needed extra help. And this one was a sweet boy who was just not very bright. He was just the kind of child who tugged at Frau Weisman's heartstrings. Ben was used to this. Every so often, his mother had to put in extra time to help a special student. So, although he and his father hated having dinner so late, they tried to understand. Leah Weisman was the type of woman born to be a teacher. She loved her students like they were a part of her family. And even though they grew up and were no longer in her class, she never forgot one of their names. Ben's father knew his wife very well, so he tried, although he wasn't the best cook. That night, Ben and his father attempted to prepare a dairy meal. Because they were religious, dairy and meat meals must be served on separate plates with flatware. They must also be prepared with separate pots and pans.

However, Ben and his father agreed that a dairy meal would be easier to prepare than a meat meal. They would have bread and cheese, a few cut carrots, and a couple of apples cut into slices. There wouldn't be anything that required actual cooking that night.

As Ben set the table, his father cut the loaf of challah that his mother had baked two nights prior. Ben's father hummed softly to himself as they heard a loud commotion coming from somewhere down the street. There was shouting, followed by an ear-splitting crash. The neighborhood where they lived was very quiet, and it wasn't often that there was a loud noise. Ben looked over at his father. "Sounds like there are some noisy drunks out there."

His father nodded. "Yes. I wish your mother were home already. I don't like the idea that she's going to be walking through town with this drunken group in the street. Anything can happen."

Ben looked out the window. He could see a group of young men singing. "It looks like a group of young men," he said. "They are either very secular Jews, or they are not Jewish. I would guess by what they are wearing that they're not Jewish. I wonder why they're here in our neighborhood."

"I can't imagine. This is mostly houses and a few stores, but no taverns here. Why would they come here?" His father looked at Ben.

Ben felt a shiver run up his spine. The word *pogrom* came to mind, but he didn't say it out loud.

His father turned to go back to the kitchen to cut the bread, and Ben followed, but there was a deafening explosion before they could get back to their work in the kitchen. "What was that?" His father's eyes widened as he turned to Ben.

The explosion was followed by another even louder explosion. Ben ran back to look out the window. The crowd of drunken men had grown much larger. In fact, it was very large now, and the syna-gogue, which was only a street away and could be seen from Ben's window, was on fire. Orange flames leaped from the building in a macabre dance as hefty billows of black smoke filled the sky. The Jewish school where Leah Weisman taught was right next door to the synagogue.

"There's something terrible going on. The synagogue is burning, and Mama is at the school right over there," Ben said. His face was as pale as his mother's China plates.

"I have to go and get your mother." Ben's father grabbed his coat.

"Let me go, papa. I'm younger. I can get through this crowd better." Ben tried to insist, but his father pushed him out of the way.

Then, in a powerful and assertive voice, his father said, "No, you stay here. You wait for me and your mother. We'll be back as soon as I can find her."

"Papa! I insist."

"Ben, I am your father, and I insist. You will do as I say," his father warned.

Ben studied his father. He'd grown up to respect him, and he could not defy the old man right now, even though he wanted to.

Ben's father turned to Ben and said, "I'll be back home soon with your mother. Make sure you are still here when I return. Do you understand me?"

Ben nodded.

Then Ben's father ran out of the house into the night and into the waiting hands of the dangerous, blood-thirsty crowd.

Ben sank to his knees in front of the window and continued looking through the drapes. The sound of glass shattering made him jump. He was worried about his parents, and he wished he'd forced his father to stay at home while he went out searching for his mother. It was hard to believe what he was seeing right outside his window. *Is this a pogrom? Could that be what's going on here?* He felt sick as he watched four young men with clubs beating up an old man across the street. Ben had never been much of a fighter, but he couldn't bear to watch this. He knew his father would be furious at him, but he had to find a way to stop it. He was afraid, but he sucked in his stomach and stood up as straight as he could. Then he walked out the side door of his home. Sitting on the stoop weeping was the fourteen-year-old girl who lived next door. He'd known her all her life. "Miriam, why are you sitting outside during all of this?"

"No one was home when I got home from school, and I forgot my key, so I can't get in. I'm scared, Ben."

She was a small, delicate girl. And Ben knew she was very vulnerable. He began to speak, but then he stopped himself when he noticed that the old man who had been beaten across the street was no longer screaming. *He's either dead or passed out. And my guess is that they killed him.* Ben thought. More drunken men came running by. They carried lit torches. One of them smashed the window of the tailor's shop across the street with a club. Then, they set the store on fire. Ben looked at Miram Glassman. She was so small, and her eyes were so wide with terror that he knew he couldn't leave her and go to fight against this mob. Besides, he was not a fool. He could see that he was outnumbered, and if he did try to do anything heroic, he was sure to end up dead. "Come on. Come with me," Ben said to Miriam.

She got up quickly and took his hand. He led her into his house. "We must hide. They might break the front window or the door, and who knows, they could come in here."

"Hide? Who are we hiding from? Who are these terrible men?"

"I don't know for sure," he admitted. "But I would guess they have something to do with Hitler."

"I'm really scared."

"I know. So am I," Ben said. "Now, listen to me. We have a secret attic room upstairs. That's where you and I will go. We'll stay there until this is over. We'll just wait it out. All right."

Miriam nodded and followed Ben up a hidden stairwell into a dark attic. "I'm sorry, but we can't turn on a light. If we do, they could see the light through the window, and then they'll know we're here."

Miriam cried softly.

"Shhh, it's all right. Come on now, don't be afraid. I'll take care of you," he promised.

They could hear screaming and explosions from outside as they huddled together in the darkness. Miriam covered her ears. It was best not to try to look out the window, even though it was unnerving not to be able to see what was going on. Ben was worried about his parents. He wanted to try to get to the school where he might find his mother, father, or both. But when he told Miram that he would leave her to search for his family, she began to cry and hold on tightly to his sleeve. "Please, Ben. Please don't leave me here alone in the dark. I'm so scared. I don't know where my family is. I can't stay here all alone. I'll go crazy. Besides, what good will it do your parents if you go out into this and try to find them? You'll only risk getting hurt. All we can do is wait and pray that our families are all right."

He nodded. *She is right. What good would it do anyone for me to leave this hiding place?* Even though he felt like a coward. Still, he knew the only thing that could come out of him going out into the madness would be his own demise.

CHAPTER 29

I t was difficult to determine how many hours had passed, but Miriam had fallen asleep on the cold concrete floor. Ben could not sleep at all. He sat beside her, awake through the night. He was listening to the chaos and hoping that his parents were safe. Perhaps they were somewhere hiding. The destructive crowd continued with wild abandon through the night and the following day. It did not stop until the thugs had exhausted their evil will, which was well into the next night. "Do you think they're dead?" Miriam asked.

"What are you talking about? Do you mean our families?" Ben asked.

"Yes, do you think they're dead? If they weren't dead, they would have come home."

"Not necessarily. I mean, maybe they're hiding."

"Hiding where Ben? I can't imagine my father hiding from anyone," her voice was hoarse with crying. Ben thought of Miriam's father, Herr Glassman. He was a large, heavy-set man who had found great success in the banking industry. Ben's parents had never cared for him because he was a loud and obnoxious man who demanded that others listen to him and obey. Frau Glassman, Miriam's mother, was petite and pretty like her daughter, but she, too, was outspoken to the point of being obnoxious. *Miriam is right. I can't imagine her parents ever hiding from anything. I could be wrong, but I think her father would stand up to this mob or at least try to. And although he is a large man, I don't think he is in good physical shape. But he is used to being a boss, and he is used to ordering people around. The results could be disastrous if he tried to stand up against a large mob of angry men. But I won't tell Miriam what I'm thinking. It would only worry her even more.* "I think that perhaps I should go out and try to find our parents. You'll be safe here."

"No, I am begging you, please, Ben, don't leave me here alone. I told you before that I just can't be here all alone." She tugged at his shirt sleeve. "Besides, they might kill you if you go out there."

"I'm no hero. And I'm no fool. But I am worried as hell about our families, and it's very hard to stay here and just wait."

"I know. I know it is. But if you leave me, I'll go mad with fear. I can't stay here in this dark attic all alone and listen to the sounds of people screaming. Please, Ben. It won't do any good for you to go out there and get yourself killed."

He knew she was right. It was hard for him to sit by and do nothing. Yet, he knew that it was exactly what he must do.

In the middle of the night, on the second night of the attack on the small Jewish neighborhood, Ben heard the front door of his house flung open. In the stillness of the attic, he heard the knob of the door hitting the bricks on the outside of his home. Miriam was sleeping soundly. He gently nudged her so she would not awaken and cry out. When he felt her stir in the darkness, he whispered in her ear, "Someone is here in the house. I heard them. You must be very quiet. I don't know who it is. It is probably a gang of hoodlums intending to rob us. But by some miracle, it could be my parents. For now, don't say a word or make a sound."

Then Ben heard a male voice. "Would you just take a look at this silver? It will bring a nice sum when I sell it."

"When we sell it," another male said.

"No, you're wrong this time. This is mine. I'm taking this silver. You go ahead and find what you can."

"Then I am going to check the bedrooms. Rich Jews like this will have jewelry."

"Ehh, they probably have a safe."

"Where do you think it is?"

"I don't know. But even if we find it, I don't think we can break it open."

"I'd like to try."

"All right. Go ahead and check the bedrooms first and see what you can find."

Miriam whispered in Ben's ear, "My heart is beating so fast. I'm terrified. They're here right here in your house, and they're robbing you."

He nodded.

"Do you think they'll find us?"

"I hope not."

"If they find us, they'll beat us. Maybe kill us. Ben, what are we going to do?"

"Stay quiet. Don't speak. Just let them take whatever they want, and then, with God's help, they'll go."

She was breathing hard. He could hear her in the darkness.

The thieves rattled around in the house for the better part of the night, during which Ben felt he had not drawn a single breath. Sometime near dawn, the robbers were joined by another group. These men were more than robbers. They searched for Jews, and they'd come to Ben's home looking for the owners. The robbers had been looking for things to steal, but this new mob was angry and destructive. Miriam jumped at the sound of glass shattering near where they were hiding. Ben thought it might be the sound of the windows breaking, but he couldn't be sure. He could hear them kicking doors in. They were screaming, "Come out, Jews! We know you're in there." A shiver ran down Ben's spine as he imagined this murderous gang finding him and Miriam in his mind. He closed his eyes to fight the image, but in his mind, he could almost hear the door to the hidden attic room being kicked in. Miriam seemed to hear his thoughts. She reached out and took his hand. They stayed that way without moving for what seemed like a lifetime.

A few hours later, it seemed the group of robbers had gone because it grew quiet in the house. Miriam squeezed Ben's hand, and then she asked in a voice that was barely a whisper. "Do you think they've gone?"

"I don't know for sure. It's very quiet. But there still could be a few downstairs who fell asleep. I say we stay hidden for a little longer."

"All right."

"You must be hungry," he said.

"I am. How about you?"

"Yes. I'm hungry, too."

CHAPTER 30

The silence was eerie. There was no way of knowing what was happening outside the confines of that dark and secluded little room. And it was the not knowing that was driving both Ben and Miriam crazy. But still, Ben insisted that they wait. He had no idea how long they waited. It seemed like days, but it was only late afternoon when Ben finally said, "It's been a long time since we heard any noise. I will go downstairs and see if they left any food behind. While down there, I'll glance out the window to see what is going on. I'll bring back whatever I can find to eat. Wait here."

"No, please don't go, Ben."

"I have to go. We must eat. Now, just stay here and be quiet. I'll be right back."

"Ben, I'm scared. Please be careful."

"I will." Ben's heart was pounding so loud he was afraid that if anyone was in the house, they might hear it. But there was no one there. The front door was wide open, hanging on one of its hinges, and all the windows in the living room were destroyed. The wool rug his father had given his mother for their anniversary a few years ago was covered in shards of glass. And the China cabinet, which had held all the family's valuables that had survived generations of Weismans, was now broken and empty. The only things left were the family's cherished photographs, which had been torn to shreds. Ben's stomach lurched as he looked around him at the destruction. He felt like vomiting, but he only gagged. His stomach was empty. *The story of my life in pictures is all right here, torn to bits and lying on the floor like trash.* He thought of Margot. At first, he wished he could talk to her. But then he got angry as he looked at the broken kitchen table and his mother's dishes shattered on the floor. Ben was angry at this mob, but he was also angry at Margot and Max. *This is the work of Hitler against the Jews. I know it as sure as I am standing here. My parents are missing. That poor girl upstairs has no idea where her family might be. I saw an old man murdered before my eyes last night. How can Max still be willing to join the Nazi party after all of this? I know he is doing it for his child. But if things continue this way, the world is going to be a mess by the time Erik grows up. What happened here was a pogrom against the Jews. And I am afraid that pogroms like this will start happening all the time in Germany. It's hard to believe that a country like Germany, a country so advanced, could do something like this to its citizens. How many of my Jewish neighbors put their lives on the line to defend Germany during the Great War? How could Germany forget them?*

Ben sighed. Then, slowly and carefully, he moved the drape just a tiny bit so he could look outside. The houses around his house were also in bad shape. There was blood on the street. And not one single soul was outside.

He searched the cupboard. It was empty, as he had suspected it might be. Then he saw the bread and cheese he and his father planned to serve for dinner before this began. The food was lying on the floor. The bread was smashed, and on its side was the footprint of a dirty boot. Ben picked it up, and then he picked the cheese off the floor. He searched for the water pitcher, but it was gone. So, he filled an old pot with water. Then, carrying the food and drink, Ben made his way back up to the attic.

"You found food?" Miriam asked.

"Yes, it's a little dirty, I'm afraid. They threw it on the floor and stepped on it."

"Oh, my," she said. "If I weren't so hungry, I wouldn't eat it."

"I know. But we're both hungry, and this was all that they left behind. It's better than nothing, so I'm glad we have it. Come on." He tried to smile. "Let's eat and not think about it."

At first, Miriam gagged when she took a bite of the bread. "Don't think about it," Ben repeated. "If you think about it, you won't be able to eat it. You must eat. And since I don't know when we are going to be able to get out of here, this is the best I can do. For now, I think it's safest to stay where we are. We can't risk going downstairs. They could come back."

He watched as she forced herself to swallow the dirty bread. "That's good," he said. Then he stuffed a piece in his mouth. He had not realized that the bread was wet. It smelled like urine. *Those animals urinated on the bread*. He thought. But he didn't mention it to Miriam. Instead, he forced himself to swallow.

Without windows, sitting in the black darkness amid the spider webs, it was impossible to tell whether it was night or day or how many hours had passed.

Miriam whimpered softly as she leaned against him. He had known her since she was born. She, like him, was an only child. He'd overheard his mother saying to one of her friends that it had been difficult for Miriam's mother to carry a baby to full term. After Miriam, her mother had been told not to try to bear any more children. Ben's mother had difficulty bearing children, too. Ben knew that his mother had miscarried twice. Once before Ben and once after. So, she was sympathetic to Miriam's mother's pain at being unable to bear any more children. The two families had been neighbors even before Ben was born. But they had said little more than "Good Morning" or "Good afternoon." Ben was several years older than Miriam, so they had different crowds of friends at the synagogue. In fact, until the previous night, there had been so little contact between them that Ben had never really noticed Miriam. And now, as they sat in the attic, it felt strange how close they had become in two days. He still didn't really know her. They had not talked about anything or shared ideas, yet the physical closeness of her head on his shoulder or her hand in his had made him feel protective of her.

"What am I going to do if my parents are dead?" she asked in a small voice.

"Let's try not to think about that. All we can do right now is pray that everyone is all right."

"I have been praying."

"That's good," he said.

There were a few moments of silence, then she blurted out, "I don't want to go back to boarding school. Did you know I've spent most of my life at boarding school? While in this attic, I realized that I hardly knew my parents. They have always been so keen on sending me away."

"Let's just wait and see what happens." He didn't want to discuss this right now. So, he just patted her hand.

Even though he'd tried to silence her, she continued, "But I've decided that if they're dead, I will stay here alone. I am not going to go back to boarding school. I hate it there. They're mean to me there. And besides, it's very expensive. I don't know how I will pay for it. I hope I don't end up in some orphanage. Can I be sent to an orphanage at my age? Or will I be permitted to stay here by myself?"

He hesitated. Then he said, "I don't know. I don't know much about it. But you won't have to go to an orphanage. If worse comes to worst, you'll move in with us."

"But Ben, what if your parents are…"

"Then you'll move in with me."

"I can't. I'm a young single girl. Can you imagine what people would say?"

"Actually, I can. And I don't care. I never cared what people said about me," he admitted.

"Would we get married?"

He let out a laugh. "What?"

"I mean, if we were married, it would be all right."

"Well, let's just wait and see what happens. I don't know about all that."

But she wouldn't be silenced. "Do you have a girl?"

He sighed. "That's a complicated question."

"Not really. You either have one, or you don't."

He thought of Margot. She'd been the only girl he'd ever loved. And even after she married someone else, he was willing to stand on the sidelines and be her friend just to be near her. But sitting in this attic, caged like an animal, he realized he was really angry with her. The things she'd done, in his opinion, were stupid. She'd married Max, who he liked and believed was a good person at heart, but she'd married him while she was in love with Ben. She'd admitted as much to Ben, but there was nothing he could do to stop her. Now, she was sanctioning Max's joining the Nazi party, even though she hated everything the Nazis stood for. *I understand she wants what's best for Erik, but I wouldn't trust the Nazis to care for my child. I wouldn't trust the Nazis with anything.*

Miriam shook him a little. She seemed to think he'd fallen asleep. "So, do you have a girl or not?"

"No," he said simply, "no, I don't."

"Well, I have always liked you, Ben. I think you're handsome. And I would love to be your girl."

He laughed again. "You're a bold one, aren't you?"

"You have to be in this life if you are ever going to get what you want."

He laughed a little.

Then, they sat silently for a few moments. She lay her head on his lap, and he heard her breathing slow down. As her breath became calm, he knew she had fallen asleep.

She is so young. She doesn't realize the impact this will have on her if her parents are dead. She's not thinking clearly. Poor thing.

It had been two whole days since Ben had last slept. Finally, he was so tired he could no longer keep his eyes open. He leaned against the wall and, still sitting up with Miriam's head on his lap, drifted off to sleep.

"Ben." It was his father's voice.

Am I dreaming? Papa, is that you? Are you alive? His eyes fluttered open. Miriam was asleep with her head on his chest.

"Ben, are you here?"

"Papa?" Ben called out, gently shaking Miriam until she was awake. "I think my father is here." She sat up and looked around, a little dazed. Then Ben stood up.

"Ben?" This time, it was his mother.

Ben took Miriam's hand. "Come on, my parents are here," he said as he led her out of the attic and down the stairs where his parents stood.

"Oh! Dear God," Leah Weisman said as she took her son into her arms. "You're alive."

"Yes, we're alive. And I can't tell you how good it is to see you and Papa." His voice was filled with emotion.

"This was a horrible thing that happened," his mother said, spitting three times on the floor.

"Where were you both all night?" Ben asked.

"*Oy* Ben, what a night it was. Those animals were running around outside. They burned the temple. They murdered a child. I can't believe the horror of it all. I was terrified. The little boy who I had been working with had already left. I was just getting ready to try to get home on my own when your father walked into my classroom in the school. He said it was too dangerous to go out into the streets. He asked me if I knew of any place we could hide. So, I took him to that little room in the basement where the rabbi sometimes went to study. You know that crazy little secret room where all the children like to hide when skipping class?"

"You hid there?"

"Yes, and we were so scared that the school was going to be set on fire. The synagogue was burning right next door. If that bunch of animals had set fire to the school, your father and I would never have been able to get out."

"I know about the synagogue. I saw the flames outside," Ben said.

Miriam was standing silently behind him.

"Where were you?" His father said.

"In the attic."

"Good thinking, son."

"Miriam, where are your parents?" Ben's mother said in a gentle voice.

"I don't know. I got home from school, and I'd forgotten my key. I was waiting for them to come home, but then this group of terrible men started beating up on Mr. Feinstein. Do you know him?"

"Yes, I know him. He is the old man living with his son- and daughter-in-law a few streets away from here."

"Yes, they beat him, and I couldn't stand it. I think he might be dead."

"Yes, he is. May his memory be a blessing," Ben's father said. "We saw his body across the street."

"Well, I had nowhere to go. My house was locked, and I was just sitting on the stoop. I was so afraid that they were going to get me next. But then Ben came out of his house. He saw me crying, and I begged him to help me. So, he took me into your attic with him."

"Have you been back to your house yet?"

"No, this is the first time I have been out of the attic since this started," she started to cry.

"Well, all right," Ben's mother said. "Why don't you and I see if your parents might have come home?" Leah said. Then she took Miriam's hand and led her out.

It was only after they had gone that Ben could take a good look at his father. The older man had a black eye and what looked like it might be a broken jaw. "Look at you, Papa. What did they do to you?"

"Ehh, nothing good," he tried to smile. Then he winced in pain, and his hand went up to his jaw.

"Sit down. Let me have a look," Ben suggested.

Ben was taking care of his father's injuries when his mother returned to the house. "Her mother was at home. She is pretty shaken up. She didn't know where Miriam was and still didn't know where her husband was. Miriam's mother was so happy to see her that she started to sob," his mother said. Then she added, "Your father and I were talking on our way home this morning. We were so worried about you. But we both said that if we found you safe, we should all try to get out of Germany. It's just too dangerous here for Jews."

"Where would we go?" Ben asked. As soon as his mother suggested leaving, Ben's thoughts turned to Margot. *If I leave Germany, I will never see her again. Even so, I must think of my own family now. She is not thinking of me, that's for sure. And I can't expect my parents to stay here. I want them to go somewhere where they will be safe until this madness is over.*

"Papa wants to write to his cousin in America and ask him to sponsor us."

"I'm sure he will help," Ben's father said. "I haven't seen him since I was very young, but from what I understand, he is doing all right in America."

"America," Ben said. "Where in America?"

"New York."

"New York," Ben repeated. *That would be a good place to study medicine. I could actually become a doctor there. And we would be far away from Hitler. But of course, if I left, it would mean saying goodbye to Margot forever.*

Ben's parents did not realize that their son was conflicted. "I'll write to him right now," his father said. "I want to get us out of Germany as soon as possible."

"Yes, that's a good idea," Ben said, but he wasn't sure how he felt about leaving.

CHAPTER 31

There was not a drop of food left in Ben's house, which had been ransacked during the two-day attack. Everything of any value had been taken, including the flour and sugar in the pantry. Ben's mother was too frightened to go to the market alone. So, Ben said he would go and buy whatever food he could get his hands on. Ben left early in the morning and made his way to the market. But when he arrived, the stores had been destroyed. And instead of being open for business, the owners were busy trying to clean up the mess.

Since his family desperately needed food, Ben boarded a bus and left the Jewish sector to go to the market where the Gentiles shopped. He knew this place well, as he had gone there several times with Margot and Erik to shop for food. As he walked through the familiar stalls, he purchased potatoes, cabbage, carrots, and whatever else he could find. Then he looked up from his bag of food to see a man standing in the corner with his arms folded across his chest, watching him. The man was tall and slender, with pock-marked skin, wearing a black SS uniform. Slowly and deliberately, the man walked towards Ben. Ben felt a shiver run through him.

Should I run? If I do, I am sure he will go after me. Right now, he suspects that I don't belong here, but he's not sure. However, if I start running, he'll assume I'm Jewish and breaking the law shopping here. I must be very careful when I present my ration cards. If the vendor says a word, that man will come running. I could just walk away slowly and hope he doesn't follow. But we need the food. I can't go home empty-handed. So, I have to try to buy whatever I can. Perhaps I am imagining that he's watching me. Is it possible that he is not coming towards me at all? Maybe he is just on his way to the bakery or trying to find a stall to buy some tomatoes.

Ben tried to remain calm as he walked up to another vegetable vendor. His hands trembled as he selected two loaves of thick, black bread. He paid the vendor and started to walk away, carrying his purchases. But then, there was no mistaking it. The Nazi walked right up to Ben and grabbed Ben's arm. Ben dropped his bag of vegetables. "I know who you are. You're Ben Weisman, aren't you?" he said. His voice was a threatening whisper.

How does he know my name? I don't know who he is. I've never seen him before. All I know is that he is a Nazi. And somehow, he knows I'm a Jew.

A head of cabbage fell out of the bag and began to roll down the street.

"Should you be shopping here? It seems to me that you've left your own neighborhood to come to ours." The man clicked his teeth. "Now," he said in a patronizing tone, "you should know better. Jews are not permitted to shop here. Do you know the law?"

"I'm sorry. I didn't realize that I had ventured so far out of my own neighborhood," Ben said, and even as the words came out of his mouth, he knew how foolish they sounded.

"Oh, so you're an idiot?"

Ben wanted to hit that Nazi right in his pockmarked face. But he saw the gun hanging from his side. "Yes, I made a mistake. I'm sorry."

"Ahhh, yes, you're sorry. Well, not quite sorry enough. Because I have a few important things that I would like to tell you." The pockmarked Nazi smiled. Then he took a wooden club that hung from his belt and hit Ben across the knees. Ben fell to the ground.

"There. Now that's better. You're on your knees to me. Now, this is as it should be."

Ben didn't say a word, but he glared at the man with hatred. *I am going to die here. I don't know who this man is, but I think he must have been following me. But why? How does he know me, and why would he follow me? And now, he's going to kill me right here on the street. My parents will never know what happened.*

"You don't know me," the Nazi said in a patronizing tone. He was smiling, but the smile was sinister. "But let me introduce myself. I am *Obersturmführer* Rudolf Schulze, the brother-in-law of a young couple with whom you are quite familiar. Their names are Max and Margot Kraus." Rudy kicked Ben in the stomach. Ben let out a short cry. "Now, it's come to my attention that you are a Jew doctor and have been treating their son, Erik."

A crowd of shoppers from the marketplace had gathered around them.

"Now, Ben, you really should know better. You've been told to stay far away from Aryans, so what are you doing playing doctor on an Aryan child? You're a fool. I could kill you here and now. But I won't. I will grant you your life. And believe me, you should be very grateful. But let this be a lesson for you. Should I find out that you have gone anywhere near the Kraus family again, it will be the end of you and your entire family, you dirty Jew. Do you understand me?"

"Yes," Ben said, his voice was weak. The blow to his stomach had knocked the wind out of him.

"And, by the way, you had better make sure that Max and Margot never find out about our little meeting today. Because if they do, they will tell me, and I will hunt you down and torture you until you pray for death. Do I make myself clear?" He kicked Ben in the stomach again, and Ben rolled into a fetal position.

"Answer me." His voice was no longer soft and patronizing. Now, it was loud and angry. "Do you understand me, Jew swine?" He kicked Ben in the back this time. Then he kicked the bag with Ben's vegetables, and the potatoes and carrots fell onto the street.

"Yes," Ben said. He looked down at the food on the ground.

"What? I didn't hear you?"

"Yes," Ben repeated. "Yes."

"Good. Make sure you don't forget what we talked about during our meeting today. And make sure you do what I told you to do, or you will be sorry."

The *Obersturmführer* put his club away and turned his back on Ben. Then he walked away, heading down the street.

Ben held his side, which throbbed with pain, as he slowly gathered his food purchases from the dirty ground and put them back into the bag. Then, as blood trickled down his lip, he walked back to the bus stop to go home.

CHAPTER 32

R
udy was lost in thought while walking home after his confrontation with Ben. He had gone to the Jewish sector of town looking for Ben, and it was just by luck that he spotted him at the bus stop on his way to the marketplace. Rudy thought that the opportunity to stop Ben's communications with Margot and Max without their finding out had passed. During the demonstration, his boss sent a group of men to seek Ben out and bring him to Rudy. They'd gone to the address Rudy had given them, but they hadn't found Ben.

Damned sneaky Jew. I'm sure he must have been hiding some-where. I would have preferred to have some ruffians take care of this situation during the demonstration in the Jewish sector of town. There, it wouldn't have mattered if anyone noticed or not. It would have been easy to kill him without Margot or Max knowing I had anything to do with it. But downtown Berlin, where so many people know my name, was not a good place to kill him. It could easily have gotten back to Max, who would probably have rejected the party. That would not have looked good for me. And besides, I certainly didn't want to dirty my hands with this. I don't want to discourage Max from joining the party. He is just about to join. I can tell. He's been more open to the idea each time we discuss it, and I can't afford for him to decide that it would be the wrong decision. After all, my superior officer would be very impressed if my entire family were party members of the Reich. Still, this situation with the Jewish doctor had to be handled. He needed to know that he dared not continue associating with my family. I would have killed him if we had been alone in an alley. That would have put a clean end to the whole thing. But I couldn't risk having Max or Margot hear that I had murdered him. Ahhh, what a dilemma. I need some comfort.

Rudy stopped at a phone booth to make a call. "Frieda, this is Rudy."

"Rudy, hello," she said.

"I wanted to let you know that I would like to come by to see you tonight. Will you be at home?"

"I had plans to have dinner with a lady friend. But since I know you are coming, I'll cancel my plans. I'll be here."

He smiled. Frieda was his latest flame. She was a sweet young woman who was living with two other female roommates. All of them were studying to be secretaries for the Reich. Rudy had first seen her at a café one afternoon when he went there to have lunch. She was much younger than he, and he was immediately attracted to her. So, he sat up straighter in his uniform and called the waiter over. He told the waiter to bring a round of beers to the young girl's table, compliments of the SS *Obersturmführer*. Then he watched for her reaction. Rudy could see that she was flattered. He smiled at her, and she blushed and smiled back. Then he stood up and walked over to her. "May I join you?" he asked.

"Oh, yes. Of course," she stammered, and he could see the awe in her eyes.

The three other girls sitting with Frieda excused themselves and changed tables, leaving Rudy and Frieda alone. They had lunch together that first day. That was when he learned that she was a student. During the conversation, Rudy leaned heavily on the importance of his job. He told her that he was in charge of several people and promised her that he would hire her once she graduated.

Then he winked and added that he planned to pay her very well. Her eyes lit up, and her face beamed.

After they finished eating, Rudy, knowing how important it was to be the first to leave, said he had some important work. He paid the bill and was about to go, but then he said, "Would you like to have dinner with me tonight?"

She agreed eagerly. And by eight that evening, she was in his bed. If she hadn't been so young and attractive, he would have lost interest already and been on his way to search for another conquest. But for now, her warm bed and supple young body were a comfort, so he would keep her around until some other girl caught his eye. Rudy had vowed to himself when he got married that he would never give all of his attention to one woman. He would never allow his wife to have that much power over him. And right now, he was glad he would spend the evening in Frieda's bed.

Rudy did not return to work. He went home that afternoon after his meeting with Ben and his phone conversation with Frieda. He walked into the house to find Trudy sitting on the sofa, looking through a movie magazine. He sat beside her, and in his most charming voice, he asked, "So, tell me, what are the movie stars doing these days?"

Trudy giggled. "You don't care."

"No, I don't. But I pretend to care because you do."

"I bought a new shade of lipstick. Do you want to see it?"

"Only if you plan to do that special thing you do." He winked at her.

She was in a playful mood. Being pregnant had increased her sexual desires. Trudy tossed her hair back and giggled again. "I suppose I could do that for you."

"Well then, let's get to it."

He took her hand and led her to the bedroom. Before removing her clothes, she took a tube of blood-red lipstick off her vanity table and smeared it on her lips. "Do you like it?"

"I'll let you know," he said suggestively as he undid his pants.

Once they were finished, he said, "I'm sorry, I won't be home for dinner tonight. I have to go in to work for an important meeting tonight."

"Well, if you have to go, you have to go?" She pretended to moan. But he could tell that she didn't really care.

"Yes, I am sorry. I do have to go."

"Well, all right. Perhaps we can go out for dinner tomorrow? Somewhere nice."

"Yes, let's plan to do that. Unless, of course, something comes up at work."

"Of course," she said

CHAPTER 33

Ben held his aching stomach as he limped to the bus stop. He was having trouble breathing but didn't think any of his ribs were broken. His face was smeared with blood, and he knew his mother would be horrified when she saw him. So, he decided to stop at the library in the Jewish sector and clean himself up in the bathroom before going home.

Ben boarded the bus and tried to take a seat without being noticed. But everyone looked at him in horror as he walked by them. A little girl who was sitting beside her mother began to cry. *I must look like hell. I probably should have tried to walk home, but I feel it would have taken me hours to get there.* He leaned back in his seat and tried to concentrate on his breathing as his mind returned to the encounter with the Nazi who had just beaten him up. *So, that was the Nazi who married Margot's sister. Margot told me about him once. Turns out he fits the uniform well. He sure is a sadistic louse. But they all are. It's obvious that he doesn't know that I don't see Margot or Max anymore. I have to admit I miss them, and I think about little Erik all the time. I hope he is doing well. But now, even if I wanted to go by their apartment to say hello, I can't. I wouldn't dare. That man would find out, and he would kill me. I have no doubt about it.*

The bus came to a stop, and Ben got off. Then he limped all the way to the library, but when he got there, the library was no more. He had forgotten that it had been burned down during the demonstration. So, he had no choice but to head directly for home. When he entered the house, his mother came out of the kitchen. She was about to say something, but no words came out of her mouth. She took one look at Ben and fainted.

CHAPTER 34

Since the demonstration, Ben's parents had become very reclusive. They hardly ever left the house. If it had not been for the doctor that Ben worked for, needing his help, Ben would have stayed at home, too. People needing medical care came by the house to see him, and he was more than happy to help as much as he could. However, with his limited supplies, there was very little he could do. Miriam dropped over almost every evening to see Ben. They played cards and sipped tea. Sometimes, he helped her with her schoolwork. Ben's mother said it was a *rachmones*, a pity that Miriam and her mother were alone. Miriam's father still had not returned, and although no one said it, they were certain he had been arrested or was dead. The night of the demonstration, which would come to be called Kristallnacht, or the night of the broken glass, had changed the lives of everyone in the Jewish sector of town. Now, everyone walked a little more cautiously. They spoke a little softer. And there was a general climate of fear surrounding them all. The Rabbi began to have services in his home because the synagogue had been destroyed. But fewer people attended. Many had lost their faith.

It had been over a month since Ben's father had written to his uncle begging for help to migrate to America. But there had still been no return letter. And there were so many documents and forms that had to be filled out, each within its own time frame. Ben's father, who had once been a patient man, was frantically trying to work all of it out, and it was taking a toll on him. He had become nervous, high-strung, and always on edge. Ben's mother, who had always been a strong woman and a fearless teacher, now cowered in fear.

Ben was worried about his parents and the rest of his community. But he was also very concerned about Miriam. He knew that Miriam was falling in love with him. And he knew that it was because she was so lost and uncertain about her future. With her father gone, she was looking for something or someone stable to hang on to. She brought up the subject of marriage to Ben more than once. And he'd avoided talking about it. The last time she mentioned it, she had even gone so far as to ask him to marry her. And he had gently refused. Ben felt sorry for Miriam. She was a pretty young girl who should have been going to dances and meeting prospective boys who wanted to marry her. Instead, she was hanging on to Ben, a boy who was older than her and who had no interest in marrying her. He was certain that her fixation on him was only because she needed someone. Even so, he sometimes wished that he was falling in love with her. It would have been nice to get married and have someone to come home to at night.

Miriam was a nice girl with a good heart. But Ben was not romantically interested. What he felt for Miriam was more of a brotherly bond. Sometimes he allowed himself to remember the days before the Nazis came to power when he and Margot were young, and it was not yet illegal for Jews and Gentiles to marry. He was openly in love with Margot then. It was a wonderful feeling. Sometimes, in the loneliness of his room, he wished he could experience that feeling again, and just thinking about it made him sad. But because he had experienced love, he knew that he could never marry someone he didn't love.

December arrived, and with it came Hannukah, an eight-day

celebration of the wonderful hero Judah Maccabee. It was a festival of lights. Ben's mother invited Miriam and her mother to dinner on the last night of the holiday. They agreed, arriving just before sundown. Miriam wore a lovely tan-colored knit dress. Ben had to admit she was growing up, and as she got older, she was becoming even prettier. Miriam had also recently started to bake. It was difficult to get sugar and butter, but she bought the ingredients she needed off the black market. When she visited Ben, she sometimes brought him and his family something she had baked.

For Hanukah, Miriam baked a loaf of Mandelbrot and gave Ben a scarf she knitted for him as a gift. He didn't have a gift for her. And he felt bad. So, he gave her a silver pin shaped like a hummingbird that his grandmother had left at his house when he was a little boy. It was nothing special, just a small pin, but she was so happy to receive it that Ben's mother had to smile. Ben's mother talked to him that night after Miriam left. She told him that she was hoping he would consider marriage to Miriam. She was from a good Jewish family, and Ben was getting older. But, as much as he wanted to agree to it, he just couldn't.

One evening, about a week later, when Miriam came to play cards with Ben, he tried to talk to her about her future. He was afraid that he might be leading her on by allowing her to come and visit him. So, he decided that he must tell her. He considered his words carefully because he knew it would be hard for her to accept. Still, he knew he must gently let her know he saw her as a friend, not a potential wife. He explained how he felt. But she refused to listen.

"I am afraid you want more from me than I can give you," he said earnestly.

"You need time," she said, smiling. "That's all right. I will wait for you to be ready. I'm young and don't care how long it takes, Ben. I am in love with you."

He shook his head. Hearing her say those words made him feel terrible. It was like a heavy bolder had just fallen on his back. "I don't want to hurt you."

"I am not hurt. I am willing to wait. I told you that."

"But you're waiting for something that will never happen."

"You don't know that for sure. You might not love me now, but no one knows what the future holds for them. Please don't push me away, Ben. Give me a chance. You're all I have."

"I can't be all you have, Miriam. You must go out and meet someone else. Someone who can love you the way you deserve to be loved."

"Ben." She hesitated. "Ben, if it's not you. I mean, if you are not going to be my husband, then I don't ever want to get married. I'll be satisfied with coming here and playing cards with you. If that's all you can give me, that's all I need."

He stood up and walked to the window. Absent-mindedly, he tapped on the glass with his fingernail. Then he turned to look at her. "You think you are in love with me because I was there with you during a traumatic time? But it's not love. It's need. I know you are missing your father, and that's hard for anyone. I'm sure you're feeling lost and looking for someone to cling to. But I am not the right man. I have never openly admitted this to anyone except the girl I speak of. But there is someone else, a girl who, l guess you could say, owns my heart. And as long as she does, I don't have love to give to anyone else."

"Who is she? You said you didn't have a girl? Did you meet her recently? Ben, are you planning to marry someone?" Miriam turned pale.

"My goodness, Miriam, so many questions. No, I didn't meet her recently. In fact, I haven't seen her for a while. And there are no plans for us to marry. I wish I could say there were. But, no, there are not."

"Why not? Have you told her? Or is it that she doesn't feel the same way about you?"

"It's very complicated. Maybe someday I'll tell you all about it. But right now, all you need to understand is that I am not available. I don't want to hurt you. And the longer you carry these feelings for me, the harder this will be on you."

"I don't care if I get hurt. You're worth it. Like I said before, I'll wait for you. And now that I know you are trying to get over someone else, I'll wait even longer. I wish you would talk to me about her. I am willing to listen. Ben, I want to share everything with you. I never want you to feel that there is anything you can't talk to me about."

"Maybe someday." He smiled wryly. "But not today."

CHAPTER 35

JANUARY 1939

Margot and Max were asleep at four in the morning when suddenly thrashing sounds were coming from Erik's bed. Since he'd become ill with whooping cough, Margot had insisted that he sleep in his parents' room in case he needed them during the night. In the beginning, this posed some problems in the marriage for Max because it seemed impossible for him and Margot to make love. But after they returned from their trip to Munich, they decided they needed to find a way to build their intimacy. So, after Erik fell asleep, they quietly went into the living room and made love on the sofa. It wasn't ideal, but Max loved Margot, so he put his own needs aside for his wife. Margot was so emotionally attached to her son that even in her sleep, she could detect a strange movement from his bed. Margot's eyes shot open. She jumped out of bed and turned on the light. Max woke up and got out of bed. They both ran to their son's bed. Erik was twisted up in his blanket and his eyes rolled around. "He needs the doctor," Max said.

Margot agreed, but she could not speak. She was breathless with fear.

The doctor lived a few streets away in a two-story house. Upstairs was his home, and the lower floor was his office. Max threw on his clothes and ran to the doctor's house. He climbed the stairs to the upstairs apartment and knocked on the door, but there was no answer. He knocked harder, assuming that the doctor and his wife were asleep. It was, after all, not morning yet. Max didn't know what to do. The next closest doctor was a bus ride away, and he didn't have the time to waste. He needed a doctor right now, desperately. He pounded on the door, yelling, "Please, I need a doctor for my son!"

An old woman in the house next door peaked out the window. "It's the middle of the night," she said. "Stop screaming. What do you want?"

"I need the doctor right away. Do you know where he is?"

"For this, you have the gall to wake up the whole neighborhood. I'm only the neighbor. I'm not the doctor's wife."

"Please, please, I'm sorry to wake you. But I am desperate. My son is very sick. He's just a little boy. Please, is there anything you can do? Is there anything you can tell me to help me find him?"

"I would help you if I could. But he's gone. The doctor was arrested last week. It seems he was really a Jew, and he was living a secret life as a Christian. So, the Gestapo came and took him away. That's all I know. Now, be quiet. There is nothing anyone here can do to help you." She returned to her house and closed the window.

Max leaned against the side of the building. He suddenly felt as if his knees might give out or he might faint. The woman had closed the window, but he had to ask her one more question, so he called out again. "Do you know of any other doctor in the area?"

"You again?" She opened the window. "I told you to be quiet. Now I am telling you to go away. Go home."

"Please, do you know of any other doctors in this area? Just tell me and I'll go. I swear it. I will."

"What do I look like, the neighborhood advisor? I don't know where to tell you to go. I'm going back to sleep. Don't wake me

again, or I'll call the police." The old woman sunk back inside her
house and slammed the window shut. Max sat down on the stoop
for a moment. All he could think of was Ben. He wanted to go to
Ben's house and beg for help, but he couldn't. It was too dangerous
because it was against the law. If he or Ben got caught, there could
be terrible consequences for both of them. *Just look at what
happened to this poor doctor. He was a Jew, and he was treating
non-Jewish patients. They came and arrested him. If Ben comes to
our house to help Erik and the police find out, Ben would be
arrested. And maybe they would arrest me and Margot too. I can't
take that risk.* He ran his hands desperately through his short blond
hair. *I only have one other option.*

Max ran all the way back home. When he arrived, he looked at
his son, who lay in his bed like a limp rag doll. He bent down to
kiss Erik's cheek. But although he didn't want Margot to know it,
he also checked to ensure the boy was still breathing. *He is alive.*
Max let out a sigh of relief. Then he went over to where Margot
stood on the other side of the bed and took her hand. In a gentle
voice, he told her what had happened to the doctor. She gasped. She
longed for Ben. Not only did she believe that he could help her son,
but she wanted the comfort of his voice and his presence.

"We need a doctor right away." She held back the tears, trying
to be strong for her husband's sake. "We need Ben."

"I know. You're right. But we can't risk it. He can't come here.
It's too dangerous for all of us. So, I am going to call Rudy. He
knows so many people and has so many connections. He'll be able
to help us."

Margot nodded, "Yes, you're right." She knew it was best not to
call Ben. She was certain Ben would come, but she cared too much
for him to put him in danger.

Max's hand was shaking as he picked up the phone receiver and
dialed.

It was several rings before Trudy answered the phone. "*Allo,*"
she said in a sleepy voice.

"Trudy, it's Max. I know it's late, and I'm sorry to call at this
time of night. But I must speak to Rudy."

"Is everything all right?" she said. Max had caught her off guard, and her feelings for him made her heart race.

"No, we have a serious problem here. It's Erik. He needs a doctor right away. I went to his doctor's house a few minutes ago, but the doctor was arrested."

"What? Why?"

"Apparently, he was Jewish, pretending to be Christian, and treating non-Jews. So, he was arrested. Now, Margot and I don't know who to turn to."

"Are you referring to that Jew who is Margot's friend? I think his name was Ben."

"No, I'm not talking about Ben. I'm talking about a doctor who lives a few streets away from here. Please, Trudy, I'd love to sit and talk with you, but we need help right now. Please, put Rudy on the phone."

"All right. Hold on a minute. I'll get Rudy."

She walked over to Rudy, who was fast asleep, and gently shook him. "Rudy, Max is on the phone. Their child is sick again, and they need a doctor. Max said their doctor was arrested."

"Damn that Jew doctor friend of Margot's. He must have gone over there even after I had that talk with him. Well, at least he's been arrested."

Trudy didn't bother to correct him. She watched as Rudy got out of bed and walked over to the phone. He had always been a slim, well-built man, but now she noticed he was gaining weight. She looked him over as he stood in the living room in his underwear. He had never been truly handsome, but he had been svelte. And now, his belly hung over his underwear, and his once taut muscles seemed to be getting flabby. She closed her eyes and thought of Max.

After Rudy hung up the phone, he got back into bed, and Trudy followed him. "What does he want you to do?"

"Well, Erik is sick again. It seems he's having some kind of seizure. Max is going out of his mind with worry. He wanted me to recommend a doctor. So, I sent them to see my friend Karl Gebhart. I promised Max I'd call Karl in the morning and give him an introduction."

"Doctor Gebhart," she repeated.

"Yes, I'm sure you remember him. We met him at a dinner party once."

"Of course, I remember him. He was a charming fellow."

"I wouldn't call him charming. His ego is far too big. He thinks the world of himself. But he is a good conversationalist."

She laughed, "Yes, I remember."

"Well, he's been working at Hohenlychen. It's not too far. They can take the train there first thing in the morning."

"Hohenlychen? Is that a hospital?"

"It is. It was a tuberculous hospital in the early 1900s, but the party used it for the athletes during the Olympics, and now the facility has been converted to a place for treating SS officers. I'm confident Erik will receive good treatment there if I talk with Gebhart. And, of course, that's what we want because this is what we have been waiting for."

"I don't understand."

"I need Max to feel indebted to me. Then he will feel obligated to join the party."

"You're right. And you're so smart," she said. "If Max joins the party, it will be very good for us. Good for your career advancement."

"Yes, my dear. It will."

"And you always seem to have the perfect plan."

She leaned over and kissed him. The room was pitch dark. Trudy thought of Max as she put Rudy's hand on her breast. He felt himself growing hard, but he wasn't thinking of his wife. Rudy was thinking of a girl he had met the day before and planned to have dinner with later that night.

CHAPTER 36

n the morning, Max called his father and told him he would not be coming to work that day. He explained that Erik had a seizure and how he and Margot were going to take Erik to see a specialist, a doctor who was a friend of Rudy's, at the Nazi party.

"Of course, you must take him. Don't worry about work right now. Just take care of the boy. And good luck, God be with you, son," Artur said.

Margot dressed Erik in warm clothes. Then she quickly dressed herself. When they were ready, they headed out into the chilly January morning.

Hohenlychen was located a little north of Berlin. Margot, Max, and Eric took a bus to the train, then rode the train to a small town called Lychen, where they got off and walked to the facility.

Eric was tired and crabby. He hadn't eaten that morning and hadn't slept well the night before. "I'm going to give him something to eat," Margot said. "He must be hungry." She took a hunk of bread from her handbag and handed it to Erik. He began to eat quietly. Margot closed her eyes for a moment. Neither she nor Max had slept much, and neither had eaten. Her head ached, and she was exhausted. But she was hopeful. Her brother-in-law had confidence in the doctor they were going to see. And she had prayed all night that he could help her son. As she watched her little boy eating, she couldn't help but remember how his eyes had rolled around in his head the night before. A sick feeling of fear came over her. Margot was worried. Terribly worried. But she didn't want to worry Max more than he was already. So, she glanced at him and gave him a brief smile and a look of confidence that she didn't feel. He reached over and patted her arm. Then he said, "Just remember that no matter what the doctor tells us, we have each other. We will face this together."

She touched his cheek. "You're such a good man, Max."

"I love you, Margot."

"I know. I love you too."

They arrived at the hospital a little before noon and had to wait two hours because the doctor had gone out for lunch. By the time they were told the doctor had returned, Erik was crabby. He was tired of sitting still, and although Margot had laid him down across the chair with his head on her lap, he couldn't fall asleep. "I think he's overtired," Max said, picking Erik up and rocking him in his arms.

"The doctor will see you now," the young female receptionist said. "Please follow me."

They followed her to an examination room. "Have a seat, please. *Sturmbannführer* Doctor Gerhart will be right with you."

A few minutes later, a doctor entered the room. He wore an SS uniform rather than a white doctor's coat. Margot didn't know why, but she felt a chill when he smiled at her.

"My old friend Rudy Giess telephoned me this morning and said you would come by. He explained that your son has been ill?"

"Yes, that's right. He had whooping cough about a year ago, and since then, he has had several seizures," Max said.

"I see. Are you sure he is having seizures? Who told you they were seizures? Did a doctor diagnose him?"

"Well, I guess we aren't exactly sure what they are," Max said, not wanting to mention Ben.

"That's all right. Can you tell me what happens when he has one of these episodes that you call a seizure?"

Max went on to explain while the doctor examined Erik. Margot stood beside her son. Erik looked and watched the doctor with his eyes wide with terror. The little boy wasn't used to strangers probing him. He began crying and kicking his feet. Margot tried to soothe him, but he wouldn't quiet down. After the doctor finished with Erik, Margot picked him up again and held him close to her until he stopped screaming.

"I never did like to treat children," Gebhart said with a half-smile. "They really are too difficult. But since you are the family of a good friend of mine, I will do what I can. Let me start by saying that I am fairly certain he has epilepsy."

"Epilepsy? What is that?" Margot asked nervously.

"It's a neurological disorder. I suppose you might call it a mental disorder. And I am sorry to have to tell you this, but we have no cure for it. He will be like this for the rest of his life."

Still holding Erik, Margot released one hand from her son and gripped the examining table to keep from falling over. Max saw her struggling, and he took Erik from her. Then, with his other hand, he put his arm around her to hold her up. He cleared his throat. "So, what exactly does that mean?" Max asked.

"It means that no matter what we do, Erik is going to continue to have those seizures. And as he grows older, he will be a burden on society. I'm afraid he will never be able to keep a job or contribute to society in any way. He won't be able to attend school. He will be what we call a useless eater."

"That's a horrible thing to say," Max said. He was angry and ready to leave. He thought the doctor was harsher than he needed to be. *Can't this man see that what he is saying is destroying my wife? What kind of bastard is he?*

"But what I am telling you is true, I'm afraid. And the sooner you face it, the better off you'll be." Then the doctor shook his head and continued, "It's really a shame because he's a beautiful blond boy with bright blue eyes. He could have had so much potential. I do hate to see this sort of thing, you know?"

"Excuse me," Margot said. She ran out of the room. When she

saw the nurse staring at her, she said, "Please, where is the toilet?"

The nurse pointed down the hall, and Margot ran. When she got into the bathroom, she vomited. Then she stood in front of the toilet, gasping for breath. Her eyes were watering, and her nose was red. Margot sat down on the toilet seat and wept. She wept until she could not cry another tear. *I must be strong, for Max's sake. He must not see me like this.* She was trembling hard when she stood up and turned on the cold water. She wanted to lie on the bathroom floor and die but forced herself to splash her face until the redness faded. Then she took a comb out of her handbag, straightened her back, and combed her hair. It was long before she left the bathroom to return to the examining room.

"Are you all right?" Max asked. He was concerned.

"Yes, yes, I'm fine."

"So, there's nothing you can do for us, then?" Max asked. His voice had a deep, angry, almost threatening tone.

"I'm afraid not. However, I can give you some medicine to make him more comfortable when he has a seizure."

"All right," Margot said. "We would be very grateful for anything you can do to help him."

"Of course," the doctor winked and then smiled at her. He cast a glance at her that traveled from the top of her head to the tips of her toes. He seemed intrigued and attracted, but she hardly noticed. Then the doctor handed Max a bottle of medicine and said, "Don't lose heart. I suggest you bring him back to see me in a few months. Scientific research is moving very quickly these days. And you know there is always the possibility that we might find a cure. Sometimes, miracles can happen in medicine. That's why I love it." The doctor seemed almost like a different man, as if he had flipped from an unnecessarily cruel bastard to a caring doctor offering hope.

"What do we owe you?" Max said he was trying to curtail his irritation. He didn't trust this man at all.

"Oh," the doctor smiled. "You owe me nothing. Rudy took care of it."

"Let's go, Margot," Max said. He was still holding Erik, who had nuzzled into Max's neck.

When they got outside, the temperature had dropped. It was even colder. Max put Erik down on his feet. Erik seemed to know that something terrible had happened, and he didn't complain about the cold. He stood stoically for such a young child while Margot wrapped a blanket around his shoulders that she'd brought with her in case it got colder.

Max and Margot held Erik's hand as they walked back to the train. No one said a word. They watched as a group of eight or nine-year-old children came rushing out the door of a small brick building that Margot assumed was a school. The children giggled and threw snowballs at each other as they walked home. *That will never be my son. My little boy will never laugh and play with the other children. He will never go to school or grow up and have a family.*

"I wish Ben were here," Margot said when they got home. "I wish we could talk to him about what the doctor said."

"I know, but we shouldn't bother Ben. But if you want, I will go and get him." Max's Adam's apple bobbed as he swallowed hard.

"No. I don't think we should do that."

"I'm not sure what to do about joining the party," Max said, his heart swelling with love for his wife as he watched her carefully remove his little boy's coat and hat.

"I suppose you are going to have to join. I mean, what if the doctor is right? I mean, who knows, they might find a cure. And if they do, we must have a way to get it for him."

Max nodded. *My poor, sweet wife. She loves our son; I love him too. But Margot loves him so much that she wants to believe someone will find a cure. I doubt it. But because I love her, I can't kill her dreams. I have to give her hope.* "Of course, you're right."

"So, perhaps you should join."

"Yes, I suppose so. I'll call Rudy tomorrow when I get home from work and tell him the news. I just don't feel much like talking to him today. After that visit with the doctor, I just want to spend the afternoon with you and our son."

"I understand," she said. "Tomorrow is soon enough."

"Yes, it is. And I'm sure Rudy will be very pleased."

CHAPTER 37

When Max told Rudy he planned to join the party, Rudy was elated.

"This calls for a celebration!" Rudy said loudly and cheerfully as he spoke into the phone receiver. Then, without waiting to hear Max's answer, he held the phone out as he turned towards Trudy, who had been sitting in the living room reading a magazine.

"What calls for a celebration?" She looked up at Rudy, who was holding the receiver out towards her so that she could speak to Max.

"Max is on the phone. He's going to join the party."

"Oh! My goodness! What good news! Max, this is wonderful," she said. Then she turned to Rudy, "Let me have the phone. I want to speak to him." Her heart was pounding.

Rudy handed her the phone.

"Congratulations!" Trudy said loudly. "I'm so happy to hear this."

"Thank you," Max said softly. He couldn't muster any excitement about joining the party.

Just the sound of Max's voice set a whole family of butterflies into flight in Trudy's stomach. "Rudy wants to celebrate. So do I. Let's all go out for dinner. When are you two free?"

"We'll have to check with Adelaide to see when she can watch Erik. But should you go out in your condition?" he asked shyly. "I mean, it's cold and snowy outside. It might not be good for you or the unborn baby."

"I'm fine. The baby is due in the spring. I have a few months left of this. I would surely go mad if I tried to stay in the house all that time. So, don't you go worrying about me. I say we should all go out for dinner and have a real celebration."

"All right. I'll speak to Margot, and she'll call your mother and see when she's available. Then, as soon as we get in touch with Adelaide, we can make plans. Just wait until you have your child. You'll see. It takes lots of arranging before you can plan to go out for dinner."

"Yes, I'm sure it does. So, call me as soon as you have spoken to my mother, and you know when she is available to watch Erik," Trudy said. *And I am not enjoying being pregnant. When I look at what has happened to my body, I just hate this child that's growing inside me.*

CHAPTER 38

Adelaide was excited to spend an evening with her grandson. She said that she was available at any time. Then she went on to tell Margot that she and Leo enjoyed Erik almost as much as his own parents did.

Margot called Trudy, and they decided that they would all go out for their celebratory dinner the following evening.

Trudy hung up the phone and began to search through the dresses in her closet for something to wear. She was miserable being pregnant. Trying to find a dress that fit her and looked good in spite of her extended belly seemed impossible. She tried every dress on, and most were too small. The others pulled and looked ill-fitting. How she looked tomorrow night was especially important because she would see Max. She stared at herself in the mirror, and it made her want to cry. Margot had grown thinner, and although that was not particularly attractive, she looked better than Trudy, who was certain she looked frumpy and bloated. After she took every dress she owned out of her closet and tossed them on the floor, she plopped down on the bed in frustration.

Rudy walked in. He had just come home from work. "What has

happened here?" he asked as he looked at all the dresses on the floor.

"I spoke with Margot. We have plans to go out with her and Max tomorrow night. But I'm so fat, and all my dresses look awful."

He laughed. "You're pregnant. It's the responsibility of every pure Aryan woman to produce Aryan children for our Führer."

"I don't care about that right now. All I know is that none of my dresses fit right."

"Why don't you go shopping tomorrow? How does that sound?"

"All right." She smiled.

"I'm sure you can find something suitable. By the way, I have to go out tonight for work. I'll be home late." He was thinking about the girl he was going to have dinner with and wondering how long it would take him to get her into his bed.

"Do you have to? I hate to eat all alone," she said in a sing-song voice. She wanted him to give her plenty of cash to go shopping in the morning, and she thought she had to make him believe she wanted to be with him. But in truth, she didn't care.

"I'm sorry, my dear. But I do have to go. You know how important my work is, so you must try to understand."

"I guess," she said, pouting.

He smiled and said, "Please clean this mess up. I can't stand to look at it."

The following day, Trudy went shopping. She usually brought a friend, but the way she was feeling about her looks made her decide to go alone. It took hours and visits to several shops before she decided on a dress. It was difficult for a pregnant woman to find something pretty. Almost everything she could fit into was matronly. And even after she decided on a dark blue suit, she wasn't really happy.

The following evening, before Rudy got home, Trudy took a shower and put on her makeup. Then she slipped on as much jewelry as she could. And although Rudy had forbidden her to wear a corset while pregnant, she forced her body into one, anyway. Then she put on the suit and looked in the mirror.

She heard the front door open and Rudy's boots clicking on the wood floor as he walked in. Trudy was busy combing through the pin curls and waves she set into her hair.

"Are you ready to go?" Rudy called out. He sounded annoyed, saying, "I wish Max had an auto. It's a real pain in the neck to drive to their apartment to pick them up, and then we must drop the child off at your mother's. So, I'd really like to get going. To be quite frank with you, I'm tired. It was a long day at work, and I was out late last night. So, I want to eat as early as possible so we can get home, and I can get some rest."

"I'm not quite ready yet," she said.

"What's taking so long?" he sounded frustrated.

"I'm almost ready."

"Perhaps you should call and tell them we'll be late picking them up?" she said.

"How dare you tell me what to do? You're the one who is late. Besides, I am the man of the house, and when I say it's time to leave, you will listen. Now, come on. I'm not in the mood for your primping tonight."

Lately, it seemed that Rudy was always annoyed with her. When he spoke to Trudy, he was short with her. And she was sure it was because she was looking so matronly. *I have a terrible feeling I am going to hate being a mother. I already hate being pregnant. And once this is over, I will go off on my own and find a doctor who can make sure I never conceive again. Then, I will starve until I get my figure back. Of course, I can't use a doctor who's with the party. He would tell Rudy, and Rudy would be furious. He wants me to make a good impression on his precious Führer, who thinks all women should embrace motherhood. Well, I don't want any more children, that's for sure. But I can't think of any doctors who would risk their license or, even more importantly, risk arrest by sterilizing a pure Aryan woman. Perhaps I will have to find a Jewish doctor, like Margot's friend. That might just be the perfect plan.*

CHAPTER 39

The doctor Ben worked for was convinced that if he behaved
and didn't break any laws, he would not get into trouble.
He refused to see that innocent people were being arrested
in their neighborhood every day. His need to delude himself that he
was safe was so strong that he made up reasons why people had
been arrested. When the laws forced him to stop treating non-
Jewish patients, he did so immediately. But Ben knew better. He
knew that what he did or didn't do made no difference to the Nazis.
They arrested Jews for no reason at all. And so, he refused to turn
gentile patients away. If a non-Jewish patient came into the office
needing medical help, Ben would help them. This caused a rift
between himself and the doctor. Finally, the gap between them grew
to a point where they could no longer work together. So, the doctor
let Ben go. However, over the time Ben worked at the medical practice, he had grown a large group of his own patients. Most of them
were Jewish, although not all. And most of them knew where he
lived. So, although Ben had not planned it, the patients began to
come to his home, and he continued to practice medicine there.
With his father's permission, he set up an office in his father's
study. After school each day, Miriam arrived at Ben's house to help

him organize his patient load. He needed a receptionist, and so he was glad for the assistance. And she was glad to be at his side. Still, whenever she asked him how he felt about her, and she asked every week, he told her they would never be more than friends.

Then, near the end of May, the family finally received a letter from Ben's uncle in America. He was willing, he said, to sponsor the family. With a sponsor behind them, the Weisman family could now get on a waiting list. However, it was still a long process to get out of Germany. There were lots of very expensive documents that had to be secured. Not only that, but all the papers had to be obtained in a specific order. It would take every penny of their savings to purchase the papers and then to pay for passage on a transatlantic ship. But Johnathan Weismann was determined to find a way to get his family out of Germany. So, each day, he worked diligently to put together all that was needed.

At first, Ben felt terrible about taking patients away from the doctor who had taught him everything he knew. But then, when he began to work long hours, seven days a week, he realized there were enough sick people for him to have his own practice and for his former employer to continue to be just as busy. Although he was always working, Ben was financially strapped. Very few of his patients could afford to pay him. But even when they had no money, he didn't have the heart to send them away. So, he found he was working day and night for very little return.

Late one night, a woman came to Ben's home. He'd never seen her before. She knocked on the door. He answered. The woman trembled as she asked for the doctor.

"Please, come inside," Ben said.

The woman wore old clothes, and her hair was uncombed. Her arms and legs were very thin. She looked at Ben and asked, "Are you the doctor?"

"Yes, I am."

"You look so young."

He smiled. "I am young. But I am the doctor."

"My name is Bertha Danner, and I am not Jewish. I know you are not supposed to treat non-Jews. But I am not a Nazi. I'm a

Christian. And I really need your help. My daughter is pregnant. She is not married, and the father of her unborn child is a Jew. The people in our neighborhood used to spurn her because they knew she was running around with a Jewish boy. That poor young man has since been arrested. And now, I am terribly afraid for her because people can count, if you know what I mean. They will guess that the child belongs to the Jewish fellow. I cannot take her to one of our doctors because if I do, he will ask who the father is. We could lie, but he would probably find out the truth, and then he would be forced to report that the child is half-Jewish. Who knows what the Nazis would do to my daughter if they knew? I'm terrified. I spoke to the pastor at my church. He has heard of you, and so he sent me here."

"The pastor of your church sent you to me?" Ben was surprised.

"Yes."

"I wonder how he knows of me."

"He told me that one of his parishioners is a friend of yours. She always spoke highly of you."

"Oh, who are you speaking of?"

"Her name is Margot Kraus. Do you know her?"

Ben swallowed hard. "Yes, I do know her. We went to school together a long time ago." He closed his eyes to hide his emotions. Then he looked away from the woman. *Margot, sweet Margot. She told her pastor about me. I never knew.*

"Please, Doctor Weisman, I beg you to please help me and my daughter. I can't let anything happen to her."

"Of course I will. But before we go any further. I will not lie to you. I want you to know that I am not a licensed doctor. I was forced to stop my schooling when Jews were no longer permitted to attend public school," Ben said.

"It's all right. You come highly recommended."

He was embarrassed by the flattery. So, he tried to smile, and then he asked. "How far along is she?"

"She hasn't been to a doctor or anything, so we aren't exactly sure. But according to our calculations, we believe she is due in late July or early August."

"I see." He cleared his throat. "So, tell me, what exactly do you want me to do for you?"

"I want you to deliver the baby. Then, I will keep my daughter hidden in the house until she can leave, and as soon as she is, she will leave during the night and take the child with her out of Germany. We have family in Belgium. She can live there with my sister. No one there will know anything about the child. So, they will be safe."

"All right. I'll help you. Come for me when your daughter begins to go into labor, and I will go with you to your house and deliver the baby."

"I'm so grateful to you."

After the woman left Ben's house, he sat alone in his father's study without turning on a light. The darkness gave him a momentary sense of isolation, and he needed this to reflect on all that had happened. He had promised to help Frau Danner and knew he would. However, it was difficult not to remember what happened the last time he'd ventured out of his neighborhood. It was very dangerous now for any Jew to be caught outside of the Jewish sector. The world, it seemed, was filled with cruel people who the Nazis had handed a reason to persecute any and all Jews. The Nazis were growing bolder and even more vicious every day. Ben had lost count of the friends who lived in his neighborhood and had been arrested for no reason. His parents were always nervous and jittery. Each time there was a knock on the door, his mother jumped. They were anxiously awaiting the next interview for the documents for their visa, but at any time and for any reason, the Nazis could come and take them all. Ben's parents had spoken to every non-Jewish person who had once been their friend. They'd begged them to hide the family. And most of them were sympathetic. They said that they hated what the Nazis had done to their Jewish friends, but they also admitted that they were afraid for their own families, so they refused.

No one Ben's parents had spoken to was willing to take that risk. And Ben couldn't blame them. Hiding Jews was an offense that was punishable by death. Once, when Ben heard his mother crying and his father trying to comfort her, Ben asked Margot and Max to help them. But he couldn't bring himself to put Margot in danger. In fact, he would rather have died at the hands of the Nazis than risk seeing Margot and her family suffer. So, the Weismans found themselves with no one to turn to, and each day, they were forced to live in fear and uncertainty.

Ben thought about the woman who had just come to see him. It had not been difficult for her to find him, which was probably not good. It meant that anyone looking for him could find him very easily. *I can't forget that terrible man who beat me up, the Nazi married to Margot's sister. I can't help but wonder why he hasn't had me arrested yet. Just the thought of him makes my skin crawl. But the only thing I can possibly believe is that he has left me alone so far because of Margot. Perhaps he promised her he would leave me and my family alone if she and Max never saw me again. Well, if that's the case, then he has accomplished his goal. Oh, how I miss Margot, little Erik, and even Max. I've come to like him. He's really a nice fellow.* He knew he had to turn his thoughts away from Margot or he would become depressed. So, he thought about this young woman who desperately needed his help, and he hoped she would not go into labor during the day. It would be safer for him to get to her if he could travel by night.

CHAPTER 40

The phone rang at Max and Margot's apartment at two o'clock in the morning. Margot jumped out of bed and ran to pick up the receiver. Max awoke and stood at her side.

"*Allo,*" she said.

"Who is it?" Max whispered. Margot didn't answer him.

"Margot. It's Mutti. I have good news. Trudy had the baby an hour ago. It's a beautiful little girl. Rudy telephoned us a half hour ago. Your father and I are leaving right now. We're on our way to the hospital."

"Trudy had a little girl," Margot said to Max. Then she spoke to Adelaide. "Max has to go to work, but I will be at the hospital first thing in the morning."

Rudy and Ebert stood outside the nursery in their Nazi uniforms when Margot arrived. A few feet away, her mother stood beside Mattie. Margot walked over to Rudy and gave him a hug, "Congratulations!"

"Why, thank you," he said, but she thought she heard a twinge of disappointment in his voice.

"Max will be here right after work."

"Oh, good. Very good."

Margot nodded. She wasn't sure why he seemed so unhappy. After all, God had just given him a lovely baby girl. *Maybe he's not unhappy. Maybe he's just tired. He's probably been awake all night.* Margot walked over and said hello to her mother and Mattie. Erik was holding his mother's hand.

"That one right there is her," Mattie said to Margot, pointing to one of the cribs. "Isn't she pretty?" Mattie said.

"Yes, she is," Margot agreed.

"Rudy, you should be so proud," Mattie said, smiling.

Rudy nodded.

Less than a half hour later, everyone was permitted to enter Trudy's room. "I'm glad that's over." She was exhausted.

Max was still in his uniform when he arrived later that day. He'd come directly from work. Although he made more money now, Margot liked it better when Max was a carpenter working for his father. But the purpose of his taking this position with the Nazi party was not to earn more money. It was to ensure good medical care for Erik. And when Margot thought about the sacrifices Max was willing to make for his family, she suddenly felt an overwhelming love for her husband. She walked over and kissed him. Then she left Erik with her parents and took Max to the nursery to show him Trudy's new baby.

Later that evening, Heidi and Artur arrived with a small box of homemade cookies for Trudy. Everyone ate the cookies as they gathered in Trudy's room. There was great excitement as the nurse brought the baby in. Adelaide was the first to hold her. Then, the rest of the family took turns holding the little girl whom Trudy had decided to call Luzie. Strangely, Rudy was the last.

"She really is precious," Heidi said. "Don't you think so, Artur?"

"Yes, she's a beautiful baby."

Rudy's father had been dead for many years. And he never went to see his mother. But he called her to tell her about the baby. She only spoke to her son- and daughter-in-law for a few minutes before the call ended.

"Is she coming to see the baby?" Leo asked.

"No, I don't think so. She's too old to travel." Rudy brushed off the question. But Margot thought she saw pain in his eyes. So, she changed the subject.

"What fun it's going to be dressing a baby girl," Mattie told Trudy.

Trudy nodded unenthusiastically.

"You can make such pretty clothes for a baby girl. Little dresses and hair bows." Mattie went on.

"Yes, all that is just lovely, but it really is too bad she's not a boy," Rudy said, and then everyone in the room grew silent.

Margot shuddered. *So, that's it. That's why he's not happy. He wanted a son. Poor little girl. Her mother seems disinterested in her, and her father seems disappointed. Where does that leave a child? And I never realized it before, but he has no real relationship with his mother. He and Trudy were married in a private ceremony at the city hall, and no one was invited. So, I thought that was why his mother never came. I think he has a sister, too, but we have never met her either. Now that I see how his mother reacted to his new baby, I think they might not have had a wedding because he was ashamed that no one from his family would have attended.*

CHAPTER 41

JUNE 1939

F inding a doctor who was willing to help Trudy sterilize herself was as difficult as she had imagined it would be. As soon as she was able to leave the house, she left her new baby with her mother and took a bus into the Jewish sector of town. She walked into every doctor's office she saw and waited for each doctor to speak with her. But when she told them what she wanted, no one was willing to perform such a procedure, especially on an Aryan woman. Finally, she walked to the University in Berlin, where she waited in the cafeteria to speak to the students. She asked every student who walked by her if they were studying medicine until she found a young man who was a medical student. She could see by his tattered clothing that he was poor, so she offered him a large sum of money to take care of her problem. At first, he refused. But she sat beside him while he ate his lunch and begged him. By the time he had finished eating and was ready to attend his next class, he had agreed to help Trudy. They arranged a time, and he gave her his address. Finally satisfied, Trudy returned to pick up her daughter and headed home.

On the day that Trudy had planned to have her procedure done, she brought Luzie to Adelaide's apartment. "I haven't been feeling well," she said, "but I don't want to tell Rudy because I don't want to alarm him. I want to leave the baby with you so I can go and see a doctor. Would that be all right, mother?"

"What's wrong?" Adelaide's voice was heavy with concern.

"I don't know. I am very tired all the time. And I think something is wrong with my female organs. Sex is terribly painful. And I am always bloated. So, I think the best thing to do is go to the doctor. I hope it's all right that I leave Luzie here?"

"Yes, of course. But are you sure you don't want me to go with you?"

"Yes, mother. I'll be fine."

Trudy was nervous about what she was about to do. She was sweating as she rode the bus to the apartment. The medical student she had met shared with a roommate. When she arrived, she knocked on the door. And when he answered, she looked at him nervously. He was trembling. He had already set up his living room as a makeshift operating room.

"Come in," he said.

She tried to smile, but her lips were quivering. *I don't want any more children. But I don't want to die either. I've heard so many horror stories about women who died from things like this.*

"Can I ask you a question?"

"Yes, of course."

"Is this your first time performing a procedure like this?"

"Yes," he admitted. "Go into the bedroom and remove all your clothes from the waist down, please. Then put on the gown I left for you on the dresser."

Her hands and feet were so cold that she felt they would never be warm again. She walked into the bedroom and began to remove her dress. A voice in her head was so loud that she couldn't ignore it, told her to run away. Trudy began to unbutton her dress. Her heart was beating hard and fast. *I could easily bleed to death. He admitted he didn't really know what he's doing.*

She called out to him from the bedroom, "Did you learn how to do this in class?"

"No, I told you, I am a first-year student. I didn't want to do this, but you made me agree to do it for you, so I read a book on how to do it. However, I'm sure you know that this is forbidden by law. So, I don't know how accurate the book was. I am just as afraid as you are," he admitted. Then he said, "Are you sure you want to do this?"

She sat down on the edge of the bed. Her stomach ached. *I can't do this.* Then she slipped her dress back over her head and put on her stockings and shoes. Trudy took a few reichsmarks out of her handbag and went into the living room. "Here," she said, handing him the money. "This is for your troubles."

"You've changed your mind?" he said, looking at her as she walked to the door.

"Yes. I gave you the money, so you will never tell anyone what we planned to do here. Do you understand? This must remain our secret forever."

"Of course," he said, tucking the money into his pants pocket and sighing with relief.

Trudy shivered all the way to Adelaide's house. When she arrived, Adelaide was on the floor playing with Luzie, who was lying on a blanket. "What did the doctor say?"

"He said I'm all right. It's nothing. It's just my body adjusting to things after giving birth," she smiled.

"What did he say to do? Is there any medicine that might make you feel better?"

Trudy shrugged. "He didn't give me anything. He just said not to worry. It will go away."

"Well, that's good. Will you stay for dinner?"

"I don't think so. Rudy will be home tonight."

"All right then," Adelaide said, picking the baby up. "We'll see you at Mattie's wedding in two weeks?"

"Yes."

"Mattie is so excited."

"I'm sure she is."

CHAPTER 42

Trudy didn't want to go to the wedding. She still looked fat and dumpy and hated herself and Luzie for it. What made things worse was that she was still eating like she was pregnant. She couldn't stop. Round and plump was attractive, but she was downright fat now. She looked in the mirror and chastised herself. Lately, she couldn't bear for Rudy to make love to her. When he touched her, she cringed. The truth was that she didn't want any more children. And he made it no secret that he wanted a son. It seemed that since their daughter was born, having a boy was all he could talk about.

When she finally decided upon a dress that she felt looked at least decent to wear to the wedding, she went into the living room. Immediately, she saw by how he looked at her that he was disgusted by her appearance.

"Is that your best dress?" he asked. "With all the money you waste on clothes, that's the best you can do?"

"I tried on all my dresses. I am going to have to lose some of this pregnancy weight."

"Yes, you certainly should. You gained far too much. You look as round as a barrel."

Trudy felt like she might cry. She turned away from him and took her light jacket off the coat rack.

"Well," he continued, "if that's the best you can do, let's go."

She had dressed Luzie in a tiny, ruffled pink dress with white lacy socks and shoes and carried her in her arms.

Rudy walked ahead of her, not beside her like he used to. Trudy felt the tears welling up in her eyes. *I don't know what to do. I can't seem to stop eating and lose this weight. I've tried, but for some reason, I just can't. And, when Rudy looks at me, I can tell he thinks I am ugly. I wish I didn't have to see Max while I am in this condition. I know he won't say anything. But I am sure he'll think I look awful. Margot lost all of her baby weight quickly. Everyone said she got too thin. I used to laugh at her because her breasts got so small, but I would rather be too thin than fat like this.*

CHAPTER 43

Bertha Danner appeared at Ben's door on a warm day in August. It was mid-afternoon, and because of the daylight, it was dangerous for Ben to travel through the non-Jewish sector of town. But Ben kept his promise. He'd vowed to Bertha that he would be there when her daughter went into labor. So, when she arrived at his door, he packed his bag and went to Miriam's home next door. He told Miriam where he was going and said to tell any patients who arrived at his home that he would return as soon as he was able. "I'll take care of everything, Ben," Miriam said. Her eyes glowed as she looked at him.

Ben thanked her. Miriam was very helpful, and he was glad to have her working with him. Lately, he had begun to think he might be developing affection towards her. They shared their thoughts and worries about each of the patients, and every day, they grew closer.

When Ben arrived at Frau Danner's broken-down little home with the chipping paint and leaking roof, her daughter, Elsa, lay on the bed sweating from pain. The sheets stuck to her body, and tiny strands of her light hair stuck to her face. "Hello Elsa, I'm Ben Weisman. I'm here to help you."

"It hurts."

"I know," he said sympathetically. He'd delivered plenty of babies. And he knew that it was painful. But, of course, he had never experienced the pain. So, all he could do was try to sympathize. He sat beside Elsa and held her hand while her mother read to her.

Elsa went through two painful days of hard labor. But in the end, with Ben's help, Elsa Danner gave birth to a beautiful and healthy little girl.

"We don't know where the baby's father is. Like I told you before, he's a Jew, and he was arrested," Bertha Danner said when Ben was getting ready to leave. "My daughter doesn't even know if he's alive."

"Yes, I understand. These are hard times," Ben admitted.

"You're Jewish. Maybe you should think about getting out of Germany. It's not safe for you here."

"I have thought about it. But where would I go? First of all, I couldn't leave my parents. My father is trying to get a visa to get us into America. But there are a lot of things that must be done before we can get out. Lots of documents and things like that. It's not an easy road. But we have a sponsor in America now, so hopefully things will work out."

Bertha nodded. "You have my sympathy. I don't know a lot of Jews, but the ones I do know aren't bad people at all. I wish I could help you," Bertha said.

Ben nodded.

"Thank you so very much," Elsa said as Ben prepared to leave.

"Yes, thank you, Ben," Bertha said. "As you know, I can't pay you. But someday I will have the money, and I will come to your house and pay you for this. I know it's hard for you to believe that. But I will, I promise you."

"Of course," Ben said, then he left.

It was mid-morning by the time Ben was on his way back home. He walked several extra blocks to avoid a group of Nazis he saw on the street. When he arrived at his house, he saw two Gestapo agents in long black coats coming out of Miriam's house next door. But Miriam and her mother were nowhere in sight. Ben felt sick to his stomach. As soon as the Gestapo agents got into their black car and drove away, Ben ran to Miriam's house and knocked on the door.

No one answered. A sense of dark and terrible dread came over Ben.

He knocked again.

Still no answer

So, he went home to his own house, where his father was sitting at his desk trying to assemble all the documents needed to migrate to the United States.

"Papa, I hate to bother you," Ben said.

"Ehh, I have everything but the exit and transit permission documents. I am going to have to go and speak to that idiot again," his father said in frustration.

"Papa?"

"What is it, Ben? What do you want?" His father, who had always been so calm and easy to talk to, was now short-tempered. Trying to arrange passage out of Germany was proving very difficult.

"Do you know what happened to Miriam and her mother? The Gestapo was at their house when I got home this morning."

"How would I know? I have enough trouble just trying to take care of you and your mother. I can't be bothered with the neighbors, too."

Ben's mother worked at the makeshift Jewish school the teachers had put together at one of their homes. They thought it might be safer than bringing the children to the original Jewish school, which was now a half-burned building. She was expected to return later that afternoon. So, Ben decided to wait and see if she had any information.

Ben was on edge. He didn't like the looks of this. So, he paced for an hour and then returned to Miriam's house. Again, he knocked on the door. Still, no one answered. Ben had a sick feeling in the pit of his gut. He was certain that Miriam and her mother were taken by the Gestapo. He was angry with himself for not being there to help them. But when he thought about it more deeply, he was just sad. He knew that he was helpless. There was nothing he could have done for Miriam. The Gestapo had guns, and he had nothing to defend himself. Ben sat in his father's study feeling lost and depressed when a patient arrived. It was Frau Feiner, the woman who lived across the street. He had known this woman his entire life. Everyone in the neighborhood had secretly called Frau Feiner a yenta because she knew everything about everyone in the neighborhood. But she could also be very annoying. She loved to talk and spread gossip. But right now, Ben was not in the mood for her chatter.

"What seems to be the trouble?" Ben asked, trying not to sound put out.

"I cut my finger," Frau Feiner said.

"Let's have a look."

"I wouldn't have come, except it's bleeding badly."

Ben unwrapped the bloody towel from her finger and looked at the damage. It was a deep cut. As he cleaned and stitched the wound, he asked her, "By the way, Frau Feiner, do you happen to know anything about my neighbors? The Gestapo was at their house this morning."

"I know plenty about all the neighbors. If you're talking about the one right next door to you. I saw the Gestapo, too."

"Yes, the ones right next door, Miriam and her mother. I saw the Gestapo leaving their house this morning, so I went there to see if they were all right. I knocked, but they didn't answer the door," Ben said.

"You haven't been home. I know this, too. I heard you were delivering a baby for a *shiksa*."

He frowned at her. *How does she know these things? I haven't told a single person.*

"Anyway, you were gone when I saw the Gestapo take them away two days ago. I was in my kitchen looking out the window, and I saw the Nazis force them into the back seat of an automobile. It was terrible."

"Are you sure it was them?"

"I'm very sure. They hit the mother with a club, and Miriam started to scream, so they hit her too."

Ben's heart sank. *Miriam was hurt, and she must have been so afraid. Poor thing. Now, she has been arrested. What can I do to help her? How can I rescue her? I feel so worthless.*

"Like I said, it was terrible. And as you know, the Gestapo always show up at the house a day or two after they arrest a family to make a list of all their valuables. That way, if anyone should try to steal anything, they will know about it. It's gotten so bad here. I am afraid all the time," Frau Feiner admitted.

"Do you know where they've taken Miriam and her mother?"

"Usually, when people are arrested, they take them to the police station, where they keep them until they can transport them somewhere by train. No one knows where these people are being sent. But I am sure it's not somewhere good. So, anyway, I was in town right by the train station early this morning, and I saw them."

"You saw Miriam and her mother?" Ben felt he should not be surprised. This woman had always been right in the middle of everything.

"Yes, that's what I am telling you. I saw Miriam and her mother. The Nazis made them march to the train stop, along with a large group of other Jews. There were so many Green police and Nazis yelling that I was petrified. I didn't want them to see me, so I hid and watched. That was when I saw Miriam and her mother. Miriam's head was covered with dried blood, and she was crying. The police ignored her. They just forced them into a cattle car on a train. I was still hiding behind a building when the train left the station. A lot of our other neighbors were on that same train, too. Things are getting bad here, *boychik*, young man. I am trying my best to find a way to get out of Germany. I suggest you do the same."

"Damn it!" he screamed.

She looked at him, and her eyes grew large. Ben was not one to use foul language. In fact, he was never heard using words like that. "I know how you feel. It's terrible. It's very terrible. If we don't get out, they'll come for all of us," she said.

"How can I find her? You must know something more." He grabbed her shoulders. Then he realized that he was holding her roughly, and he apologized.

"I wish I knew more. But I don't. I told you all I know. If I find out any information, I will come and tell you."

After she left, Ben laid his head in his hands and wept.

Ben couldn't eat at all that day. He was sick at heart. He was not in love with Miriam, at least not in the same way he loved Margot. He cared for her deeply. And he chastised himself for not being with her in her time of need.

CHAPTER 44

The following day, early in the morning, Ben's father got dressed after Ben's mother left to go to work. Ben was in the study with a patient who had arrived at his house at dawn.

Seeing that his son was busy, Johnathan left a note for Ben that said, "I'm going to the police station. I need to obtain police certificates for our visa. I will be back as soon as I can." Then he quietly left the house.

Ben's father was trembling as he entered the police station. This was the last place on earth that he wanted to be. But if he was going to get his family out of Germany, they needed these police certificates. "Excuse me," Herr Weisman said quietly to the green policeman behind the counter.

"What do you want?" The man was curt.

"I need to obtain my police certificates. Please, can you help me?" Johnathan Weisman said.

"All right. Go and see that man over there." He pointed to a rat-faced man in his early forties.

Johnathan nodded. "Thank you, sir." Then he walked over to the man. "Excuse me, sir. The officer at the desk said you might be able to help me."

"What do you need?"

"The police certificates for myself and my family. We have all of our other documents in order. We only need these."

"So, I can assume that this is for you to be permitted to pay for passage on a ship leaving Germany. And where are you going?"

"To America."

"To America?" he said, and Johnathan could not escape the sarcasm in the policeman's voice.

"Yes."

"Show me the documents you have so far."

Herr Weisman handed the policeman a pile of neatly organized papers.

"So," the rat-faced policeman cleared his throat as he looked through the pile of papers and then fixed his eyes on Herr Weisman. "You look like a Jew."

"Yes." Herr Weisman said.

"And you think you can come here and ask for my help?"

"Please, I hate to bother you. But we cannot leave without police certificates. Please, if you could just take a moment and give them to me, I will be on my way, and I won't bother you again."

Ben's father knew he sounded far braver than he felt. On the outside, he was trying to smile. But inside, he was terrified.

The police officer tapped a pencil on his desk and smiled. Then he asked Herr Weisman for additional information. "I need your address and the birthdates for you and everyone in your family. Write them all down here." He handed Herr Weisman a sheet of paper and a pencil. Johnathan did as he asked, even though all that information was already written on the documents he had previously handed to the officer. After Herr Weisman finished and handed the paper to the policeman, the policeman laughed a little under his breath. Johnathan Weisman squirmed in his chair. "Now that we have completed that, I need to know who your sponsor is in America. And why is he willing to put up so much money to ensure you and your family are safe? What kind of man would put up all that money for Jewish swine?"

Johnathan was offended. But he knew better than to say a word. And besides that, he was certain that the police officer didn't need all of this information but would not argue. "He is my uncle. He lives in New York City."

"Oh, no wonder. He is like you, another filthy rich Jew. Only that Jew is not here in Germany. He's living in America. The American Jewish swine are even worse than the ones we have here. I've heard that anyway."

Johnathan did not argue. He just sat quietly, waiting, hoping the officer would tire of toying with him and just give him the papers he needed. Once he had these documents, he and his family would all be set to leave. This was the last and hardest part.

It was as if the policeman had heard Johnathan's inner thoughts. He looked directly into Johnathan's eyes and said, "So, are you all ready to go? Do you have everything else you need? Can you afford passage?"

"Yes, this document is all I have left to acquire."

The policeman looked down at the documents again. There was a long silence as the officer slowly studied each of the papers. Then he looked directly at Herr Weisman and smiled. After he did, he picked up a small pile of the documents and tore them in two. A scream escaped Johnathan's throat.

"What's the matter, Jew?"

Johnathan was stunned. That pile of papers that now lay torn on the floor represented months of work. Not only had it been difficult to acquire all those documents, but that pile represented all the hopes and dreams he had for a future for his son and wife.

The Policeman laughed. Then, he picked up several more of the documents. Johnathan noticed the officer's fat fingers as he tore them up.

Something came over Johnathan. It was as if he had gone insane. His mind went blank, and he forgot who that man was and the power he held to destroy Johnathan. For a few moments, Jonathan Weisman lost all fear. He had never had a fistfight in his life, yet he stood up and punched the rat-faced man as hard as he could in the mouth. Then he flung himself over the desk and began hitting the policeman with both fists. All the anger that had been brewing inside of him was contained in each punch that he delivered to the policeman. Blood covered the torn documents. It covered the desk and the floor. The officer was so shocked that he had not attempted to fight back. For just a few minutes, the other policemen in the room stood by without moving. They, too, were stunned. They were used to Jews being compliant, but this one was fighting back.

Then, a young officer who had been watching came out of the trance, and without even walking over to see what had caused the Jew to go out of his mind, the officer pulled his gun and shot Ben's father in the head.

Johnathan fell to the ground. His bloody documents lay on the floor, surrounding his dead body.

Ben's mother was distraught when Johnathan Weisman didn't return home that afternoon or that evening. "I told him not to go to the police station," she said as she wrung her hands. "That's why he waited until I was at work to go. Now, he's not coming home, and I don't know what to do. Do you think he's been arrested?"

"I don't know, mother," Ben said, but he went to his room and dressed quickly. Then he returned and was ready to go to the police station. His mother saw him, and she went pale. Then she grabbed his arm and held on tightly. "Please, Ben, be sensible. I beg you not to go there. You're all I have. You're my only child. I can't let you go. If I had known your father was going to the police station, I would never have allowed him to leave. Please, Ben, listen to me and stay here with me. There is nothing you can do for us by going there. You can't help your father. All you can do is get yourself arrested, and then where would we be? Please, Ben, I'm begging you."

He nodded and sunk down on the sofa. "So, what can we do now?" he said, more to himself than to his mother.

"Wait. All we can do is wait."

Several long and stressful days passed without a word about

Johnathan. But then, a police officer came by to pick up some things from Miriam's home. When Ben saw him, he ran outside before his mother could stop him. The officer was young and didn't look like he enjoyed the power he'd been given. In fact, when he told Ben what had happened to his father at the police station, he looked almost apologetic. Ben wanted to strike out and to kill him. But there was no point. So, he turned and walked back into his house. His mother was standing in the living room, waiting. "Ben, are you crazy? Why did you go out there and talk to that Nazi?" his mother said, "you should know better."

But Ben shook his head, then went over to his mother and put his arms around her. "Mama…" he said softly, "Papa is dead." His mother let out a scream, then she collapsed in Ben's arms and wept. "*Oy vey*, my Johnathan is gone. My love, my partner. They took him away from us, Ben. They stole him away. And now we can't even bury him," she said, her eyes glazed over with tears and misery.

"I know," Ben said, knowing it was pointless to go to the police station to try to retrieve his father's body. He had been willing to risk his own life to save his father's life, but he would not do so just to retrieve a dead body. Ben's mother was filled with sadness, but Ben was filled with anger and rage. He wished he could blow up the police station. Until now, he had never had the desire to hurt any living thing. From the time he was a child, Ben had been a healer. But now, he had hatred in his soul, and he would have killed every last one of them if he had the chance.

As it was, there was nothing left to do except go to the rabbi and ask him to gather ten men for a *minyan*. Then, he and his mother began the shiva, the time of mourning. They tore the lapels of their shirts. They covered the mirrors in their home and sat on boxes in their stocking feet. Some of their neighbors and friends who had heard about the tragedy came by the house to pay their respects. But none of this mattered to Ben or his mother. They'd lost their beloved patriarch, and things would never be the same.

CHAPTER 45

SEPTEMBER 1939

Leah Weisman was not the woman she had been before her husband's death. She stopped teaching, which she had always thought was her life's purpose. In fact, she lost all of her passion for living. Leah had always loved to cook and truly enjoyed good food. Now, her appetite was gone, and most of the time, she refused to eat. And she went into the living room after dark many nights when she knew Ben was asleep. She sat in the dark without turning on a light and talked to her husband's spirit. Sometimes, she felt that he could hear her, and it was the only comfort she had. She often sat alone in the living room when Ben got up in the morning to begin his day. Ben was grieving, too, but his mother was utterly devastated. She separated herself from her friends and no longer did the volunteer work she had become known for at the synagogue. When any of her old friends stopped by to see how she was doing, she refused to see them. She told Ben to tell them that she was not at home.

Then, one afternoon, Ben went upstairs to his mother's room to ask if she would please come down and help him prepare soup for dinner. It wasn't that he wanted soup. He didn't care. What Ben wanted was to make his mother feel needed. But she was lying still on her bed when he entered her room. "Mama?" he said in a soft voice.

When she didn't answer, he gently shook her. But he already knew she was gone. He had seen plenty of dead bodies, and he knew by how cold she was that there was no point in trying to revive her. Ben turned on the light. There was no evidence that she had done anything to cause her own death. She just lay there on the bed, holding her husband's pillow in her arms. She seemed quiet, at peace, and Ben assumed her heart gave out. *My poor mama. She couldn't go on without papa. She died of a broken heart.*

He sat at her bedside and let the tears fall down his cheeks. *Now, I am an orphan. I have no parents. And my friends are all gone. I can't find Miriam, and I must not try to find Margot. How did things ever get this bad?*

CHAPTER 46

On the first of September 1939, Hitler invaded Poland, and the war began. With the war came food rationing for everyone who was living in Germany. The rationing was bad for the Germans. But it was even worse for the Jews, who were given far fewer rations. Now, Jews were strictly prohibited from entering some areas of the city and could only purchase supplies from certain stores and at certain times. A strict curfew was put into place for all Jewish citizens. The Jewish population was only permitted to live in certain areas in what the Germans called *Juden-häuser*, Jewish houses. And Jews could no longer appear in public without wearing a yellow Jewish star on their clothing.

Ben was resentful. He had always been calm and easy-going like his father, but he no longer had patience with anyone. When he went to the market, he sometimes said or did things that were far too bold, which could have gotten him arrested. So, he left the house as little as possible. He no longer made house calls, even if the patient could not come to him. If a patient needed to see him, they would have to go to his home for treatment. Each week, one of the women he had treated or whose family member he had saved would take his ration cards and purchase his food for him. Often, these women cooked for him, too. And those who were single or widowed would try to entice him into marriage. But Ben had no interest in marriage. In fact, he hardly had any interest in anything, even his medical practice. However, he continued to try to do what he could to help those in need. Frau Feiner dropped by at least once a week. She brought him a few slices of challah or a bowl of potato soup when she came. She was old and alone and very lonely. So, she tried to engage him in conversations by asking him questions about his patients' lives, but he was always evasive, and soon, she gave up.

One of the young women Ben had known all his life came to him with her mother, who had a rash. "I don't have the money to pay you to treat her, Ben. But she's so uncomfortable. This rash started when the Gestapo took my father away. Now, she's miserable, itching all the time. Please, can you help us?"

Ben nodded. It was a stress-related rash. He knew that, so he treated the symptoms as best he could and didn't charge her anything. He didn't care about the money. He wasn't greedy as long as he had enough to live on. In return for his help, the woman's daughter asked him if he had sewed the yellow star onto the front of his winter coat.

"I haven't had the time," Ben admitted.

"You must have that on your coat. If you don't and the Nazis stop you, they will arrest you."

"Yes, I know," he said softly.

"It will take me a few minutes. It would be my way of paying you back," she said.

He nodded, then he thanked her.

"Do you have a needle and thread?" she asked.

"Yes, my mother kept a little sewing kit somewhere in the kitchen. Let me get it for you."

Ben entered the kitchen and found his mother's sewing kit on the shelf. His hands trembled as he held the little box. It brought back so many memories. He closed his eyes and remembered when he was just a child and had torn his favorite shirt. His mother had fixed it using this very kit. He could envision her sitting there and sewing if he thought very hard. Running his fingers over the box, he felt the loss of his family all over again.

When the girl finished sewing the star on Ben's coat, she left. He picked up his coat and looked at the star. It wasn't that he was ashamed to be Jewish. In fact, he would gladly wear that star with pride. But he knew the real reason that the Nazis wanted him to wear it. It was because they wanted to know instantly who was Jewish and who was not. *Do they have a plan or a reason why they must have this information at their fingertips? Is it possible that they intend to arrest all the Jews in Berlin? Is that even possible? And if they did, where would they put all of us? What would they do with us?*

He poured himself a glass of his father's whiskey and sat at the kitchen table. *I wonder where the trains go, the ones that are filled with the people who have been arrested. I wish I knew where they took Miriam and her mother. I've asked everyone. But no one seems to know. I wonder if the rumors are true that Nazis have set up ghettos in different cities where they imprison Jews. But why? Why would they want to do that? The only thing I can think of is that they want Jewish people's homes and possessions, and this is the only way they can take them.*

Ben wished he could talk to his parents. He wished he could ask them what they thought would happen next. And even more than his parents, he wished he could speak to Margot. How he missed her. *She is so smart. I know she would have some insight.* But he was alone. There was no one he could turn to.

Only once, right after his father died, Ben tried to arrange passage for himself out of Germany. But it was very frustrating, and he found he didn't care enough about his own well-being to try that hard. So, each day, he did what he had to do to survive and little else.

CHAPTER 47

When Hitler plunged Germany into a war, things also changed for the non-Jewish population.

Margot, Mattie, and Trudy attended classes together where they were required to learn how to be good German house-wives. They were taught how to prepare *Eintopf*, the one-pot meal, using any ingredients that might be in abundance at the time. "A good German wife," their instructor said, "will know how to use any ingredients, no matter what they are, that are available to prepare a delicious meal that their husbands and children will love."

Max didn't want to bring Erik back to Dr. Gerhart's office, but Margot insisted. "I know he was a cruel louse of a man. But what if they've found a cure? He said to bring Erik back to Hohenlychen at the beginning of October to see him. We have to try. No matter what he said or did, we can't let our pride get in the way."

"I'll do whatever you want, Margot," Max said.

They made an appointment the following day and took Erik on the train again to see Dr. Gerhart. He examined the little boy and asked, "Any more seizures?"

"A small one last month," Margot said. "But he seemed to

recover quickly from this one. I am hopeful that he is outgrowing it."

"I see."

Margot was nervous. Her voice was shaking. "Max and I think that maybe he is outgrowing it. What do you think?"

"Not possible. I say, don't get your hopes up," the doctor said. "He is going to suffer from this for the rest of his life."

Margot gasped. She looked at Max. He looked away. He hadn't wanted to come and see this doctor in the first place. And now, Margot agreed. She didn't want to see this doctor again, either.

Max gave the doctor a look of disdain. "Is that all? Are we finished here?"

"Yes. Come back in six months," the doctor said.

Margot felt her blood boiling. "What's the point in us ever coming back if you can't help him? You say he will be this way for the rest of his life. How many times do I have to hear that? I'd rather not come back."

"Frau Kraus," Dr. Gerhart said gently, his voice soothing, "you must come back. You see, although I can't help him right now, I might be able to in the future. As I have told you before, we are always looking for cures. And new things are always happening in medicine. So, I suggest you bring him to see me. Yes?"

Margot nodded. But she hated Dr. Gerhart. He seemed to take pleasure in her pain.

Neither Margot nor Max said anything about what had happened as they walked to the train station. Margot picked Erik up and carried him as they boarded the train.

The train was crowded, but they found seats. And it seemed to Margot that everyone's eyes on that train followed Max in his SS uniform. Although he looked handsome, Margot knew what that uniform stood for, and she still hated that her husband was a part of it. Thus far, his involvement with the party had been good for them. It helped them financially. Their rations were better, and they could help Adelaide, Leo, Heidi, and Artur by giving them access to more and better food. The three families often combined their rations and made hearty stews or soups for dinner. Mattie and Ebert sometimes joined them.

Max's superior officer had said that Max would be considered to receive a house which would be free of charge. Max thanked his superior officer, but in private, he told Margot that he felt very strange about accepting a home from the party because he had heard that the houses awarded to Nazi officers had come from arrested Jews. Even so, Max found that he was excited about the idea of raising his son in a house of their own. Margot couldn't agree. She told Max that she would rather live in a tiny apartment than in a home that was not rightfully theirs. This sometimes caused an argument. And always in the back of her mind were thoughts of Ben. She missed him terribly. And she knew Max still didn't accept the Nazi ideology even though he was enjoying some benefits. Margot knew Max had joined the party because she asked him to, and he would do anything for her. She had been so optimistic that they might find a doctor who could help Erik. But so far, this doctor had done nothing but hurt her and Max with his cruel comments. Margot thought she could see fear in the eyes of the other passengers on the train, which made her squirm uncomfortably. *My husband is not one of them. He won't bother you. He would never hurt anyone.* She closed her eyes and hugged her little boy closer to her. *I love you. I love you fiercely. I love you despite everything: epilepsy and seizures. I love you in spite of your little arm and leg that are shorter than the other. You are the light of my life, and I will not give up on you. I will keep trying until I die to find someone somewhere to help you.*

Just then, an old woman boarded the train. There were no seats available. So, she stood in the aisle. Max noticed her and he immediately stood up. He walked over to her and gently said, "Excuse me, would you like to sit down?"

The old woman's eyes flew open. A Nazi in a uniform had offered her his seat, and the fact that she was shocked was all over her face. "Yes, thank you."

CHAPTER 48

A handful of well-dressed men found their seats as they gathered around the table. The attractive and vivacious young woman did not make eye contact with any of them as she placed a tray of pastries down, followed by another, a tray with a pot of coffee, real sugar, and fresh milk. Then, she quietly left the room and closed the door. One of the men, a tall, dark-haired man with flat, emotionless black eyes that matched his SS uniform, stood up. He did not greet the others or smile as he walked over and locked the door. Then, once the door was secured, he addressed the others who sat at the table and said, "The program I am about to speak of is of the utmost secrecy. Each of you has been hand-selected because of the purity of your blood and your true devotion to our cause. I realize that you may find this solution to an age-old problem abhorrent at first. But if you just listen, I'm confident you will realize that it is our responsibility to put this into action if our Aryan race is to thrive as the perfect race it was meant to be. Not only is it a necessary measure for our race, but it is also an act of mercy. Therefore, you must think of those who are suffering as being in need of a good death. And we are the angels of light that will bring it to them."

"Can you give us a more thorough explanation?" someone asked.

"Yes, I intend to. As you know, there are unfortunate creatures who are, well, shall we say, imperfect? They were born to pure Aryan parents. However, something has gone wrong. And they are, well, damaged, either during their lives or at birth. They can be physical misfits or mental. Either way, they are soiling our race and cannot be allowed to continue to do so."

"Are you suggesting sterilization?"

"Yes, of course. That is an option. However, the Führer feels we must do away with those who are not fit to live. It is best for them and best for our Aryan race."

"Where will we do this?" one of the men asked.

"We are currently setting up facilities for the program."

"But how will we find the patients who need this? Most people who have a child who is born a misfit hide that child. It might be very difficult."

"Yes, we've considered that. Therefore, it will be a law that every doctor and nurse must report anyone they think qualifies for this program. Should they not comply, there will be punishment."

"And what about the parents? They will not want to give their children up only to have them eliminated."

"We will encourage them to report their children. We will not tell them what we plan to do. Instead, we will tell them their children are being sent to a facility that can give them the medical care they need." Then he hesitated for a moment and then went on to say. "Have any of you heard of Case K?"

"No," they all answered in unison.

"I'm not surprised. It was not publicized very much. However, I will tell you a little about it right now." He smiled for the first time since he'd begun speaking. It was a half-smile, a smile that did not reach his eyes. A wicked smile. "Case K is the case of little five-month-old Gerhard Kretschmar," the facilitator said. "Sadly, he was born a defective misfit. But he came from good stock, pure Aryan parents who wanted the best for our country and for their son. So, they did the right thing by him. They contacted the Führer and asked that Gerhard be given a good death. They said they understood that it was for their son's own good. But they explained that they were also thinking of the fatherland. After that case, our Führer realized that the Kretschmars were correct, and that is how this program, referred to as T4, was born." He hesitated for a few moments, looking around the room and meeting the eyes of each of the men. Then he said, "If we are ever to achieve our dream of becoming a pure race, we must make sacrifices. It is just that simple."

CHAPTER 49

Margot was cutting up carrots and potatoes to prepare a pot of stew when the doorbell rang three times in a row, followed by a heavy knock. Erik, who hated loud noises, had been sitting on the floor playing with a toy train that Mattie had given him and began to scream. Margot picked him up and held him in her arms. He was getting older and much too heavy to carry around like this, but she knew it was the only way to quiet him. Still holding Erik, she looked through the peephole of the door. There stood a tall, slender SS officer. Her heart began to race. *Why is this man here? What does he want with us? Does this have anything to do with Ben? Oh, dear God, let Ben be all right.* The SS officer knocked again, and Margot knew she must open the door.

"Good afternoon," he said. He wore a nice smile, and his voice was soft and non-threatening. "I'm Dr. Eiker. I'm a colleague of Dr. Gerhart. He asked me to drop by your home and visit you."

Margot looked at the young man skeptically.

"Is this Erik? Dr. Gerhart said he was such a sweet little boy, and so he is," he asked as he reached up and touched the little boy's leg gently, almost affectionately.

"Yes," Margot said.

"And he certainly is a handsome child, isn't he? He has beautiful Aryan coloring."

She nodded.

"Anyway, I am sure you're quite busy. So, I won't take up too much of your time," the doctor said. Then he added, "Do you mind if I sit down?"

"No, of course not. Please sit."

The doctor smiled. "Do you mind if I smoke?"

Margot minded. She hated the smell of smoke but dared not say as much, so she said, "No, let me get you an ashtray."

Still holding her son, Margot went into the kitchen and returned with a small glass ashtray. She placed it on the table in front of Dr. Eiker.

"*Sturmbannführer* Dr. Gerhart has told me a great deal about Erik's case. It seems he has been afflicted with epilepsy. That's such a sad situation." He shook his head and took a puff of his cigarette. "But I have come to see you because I have some good news. Medical science is progressing quickly these days, especially under the direction of the superior Aryan doctors and scientists. And we have found what we believe to be a cure for Erik's condition."

Margot gasped. Tears came to her eyes. "A cure?" she whispered, shocked, surprised, and joyful. This was the answer to her every hope, every dream. "Are you saying that you can cure my son?"

"Yes. I am pleased to tell you that we can."

"How, what must I do?"

"Well, we have a facility for this sort of thing. It's called the NS-Tötungsanstalt Hadamar Center, and it's located in a lovely building between Cologne and Frankfurt."

"When can we leave? I will pack our bags and take him right away," Margot said.

"No, I'm afraid that would be impossible." The doctor smiled warmly. "I'm sure you are a good mother and would want to be

177

with him through all this. However, there are many patients in need of the facility, and because of this, we just don't have enough room for the families to join them. I hate to say this, but you would get in the way of the patients receiving the proper care. You wouldn't want to do that to other children who need our help, now would you?"

"No. No, of course not." She swallowed hard. "It's just that I would hate for him to be all alone." Tears began to sting the back of her eyes. "He's very attached to me."

"I understand, but you needn't worry. We have the finest doctors and nurses available to him. I will personally see to it that he is accompanied by a very kind and compassionate nurse who will stay with him for the duration of his treatment."

"How long will it take?"

"Well," the doctor put out his cigarette. "It's hard to say. This is a new treatment. And every case is different. However, we have been having very good results."

Margot nodded. *This is good news. But I hate to be separated from him. Still, I can't deny him this treatment. It could change his life.* "When would he be required to leave?"

"The first of January."

"Oh," she muttered. "That's only a few months from now."

"Yes, that's right." The doctor smiled. "So, of course, the choice is yours. However, if you want to help your son, you must sign these papers permitting us to treat him." He took a small stack of papers from his briefcase and put them on the coffee table in front of Margot. Then he handed her a pen and went on speaking. "If you decide to go through with this treatment, and I highly recommend you do, I will send a nurse to pick him up on the morning of January 1. The nurse will stay with him on the bus throughout his entire journey to the facility. Once treatment begins, the doctors will inform you of his progress every step of the way. And, of course, if for some unexpected reason we need you, we will send for you right away. However, I wouldn't worry about that. The medical staff at this center are very good, and they know exactly what must be done. I promise you; this is the best thing you can do for your little boy."

"Will he be normal when this is all over? He won't have any more seizures. Is that correct?"

"Exactly. That's what this is all about," he said, smiling at her. Her hands were trembling as she put Erik down on the floor and watched him begin to play with the train again. A bead of sweat trickled down her brow as she picked up the pen. "Sign here, Frau Kraus," the doctor said.

I should wait for Max to get home. I should talk to him about this before I sign. "Can I speak to my husband first? He will be home from work in a few hours."

"I'm sure that would be ideal. However, we only have a few spots left, and I can't promise we will have one open for Erik later this afternoon. I have one now. If you want it, you must sign now."

She did.

When Max returned home from work that evening, Margot was excited to tell him the news about Erik. He also had news to share with her. So, before he even sat down for dinner, he said, "Rudy was promoted today."

"Oh," she said, smiling. But Max was not smiling. His face was grim. "What's wrong? You look upset about something. Please don't tell me you're jealous. That's not like you, Max."

"I'm not jealous. Believe me. I'm worried. When I asked Rudy what he would be doing in his new job, he said he would be traveling to various places. He called them camps. But when he described them, I think they are more like prisons. He said that they keep Jews, Gypsies, and other people whom the government doesn't approve of in these camps. He's going there to work on data. Apparently, a large company called IBM has created a punch card machine and put these machines in each prison camp. From what he said, I think these punch cards have something to do with keeping track of Jews."

"Jews?" she said, and she thought of Ben. "A machine to track Jews?"

"Yes, a machine that tracks who is Jewish and who is not. From what I understand, these prisons are filled with Jews and others who are innocent of any crime. They've been arrested and sent to these camps. And, oh Margot, how do I say this? But I'm afraid these people have been arrested because the Reich wants their homes." He let out a sigh. Then he took down a bottle of schnapps and poured himself a shot. He drank it in a single gulp. "As much as I want a house with a backyard for our son, I could never feel right about taking a house stolen from someone else."

"I've always thought that was how the Nazis were getting these houses," she said. Then she hesitated for a moment. "What do you think they will do with all of these Jewish people? And all the others, too. Can they possibly keep them in these camps indefinitely?"

Max sat down at the kitchen table and poured himself another shot. Erik heard his father's voice and ran out of the bedroom. "*Vater!*"

"Come here, little fellow," Max said, and he picked his son up and put him on his lap. "How's my boy today?"

"Good," he said. "Will you play with me?"

"I will, of course I will, right after dinner. Why don't you go back and play for now? We'll be eating soon."

"All right," Erik said.

Max put Erik down on his feet, and Erik ran back to the bedroom.

Then Max turned to Margot and continued the conversation. "I can't imagine they could keep all these people in prison. I mean, with the war going on, food and other supplies are so scarce. But I have also heard from some of the men I work with that the Jews are being used as slave labor for the war effort."

"Slave labor?"

"Yes, I've heard they are being forced to work at some very dangerous jobs for no pay."

"But after the war is over, what will the government do with all of these displaced persons?" she asked, wondering if Ben had been arrested and was now working at some dangerous job for the Reich. The thought made her heart ache, and for a moment, she forgot the good news she had to share with Max. Ben's fate was consuming her thoughts.

"Who knows? This government has gone mad. I can't ask too many questions. Everyone is always watching everyone else. No one trusts anyone. Because I am Rudy's brother-in-law, they have given me a very menial job of pushing papers. And I am glad. I wouldn't want to be a part of all of this. I can't justify it. For now, at least, I am fortunate that no one pays me much attention. But believe me, if I start asking questions, they will watch me and look for things in my background to hold against me. Listen to this. There was a fellow I worked with. Sometimes, he would say things that were unkind about the Führer. One day, he was arrested for having a Jewish great-grandmother. No one has seen him since. I don't even know if it's true. They lie to further their own agendas. It's very dangerous in our world right now."

"What did he say that was so terrible?"

"It doesn't have to be so terrible. You can't say anything that might even be mistaken for a negative remark about the Reich or the Führer. I dare not speak too much. I have to weigh everything I say before I say it. Any wrong move could cause us trouble."

"I'm so sorry, darling," she said, standing up and touching his shoulders. "Please be careful."

"I am. I'm always careful, but sometimes it's unnerving."

"It terrifies me to think you could be in danger."

"Don't worry. I'll always be careful."

There was a long silence. Then he said, "What smells so good?"

"I made stew. I was able to get a hunk of meat from the butcher."

"I guess those are the benefits of wearing this terrible uniform." He tried to smile.

"Yes, I know. The butcher wanted me to tell you that his daughter would love to have a secretarial position at the Reich office if one ever opens."

"Of course, she would." Max shook his head.

"But at least we have meat tonight. Let's try to be happy about that. It's been a while since we had it."

"Yes, and it sure smells wonderful. I'm going to get undressed. I'll be right back," he said.

She nodded. He began walking towards the bedroom.

Then, hesitating momentarily, she added, "But I have some good news, too."

"Oh." He stopped and turned around. "Please tell me the news. I could use some good news."

"A doctor came by our apartment to see me today. He was sent by Dr. Gerhart from the center. He said that they have found a cure for Erik's epilepsy."

"What?" Max's face lit up. "Tell me everything."

She told him everything the doctor had said. He was pleased. But after she finished, she said, "The only thing that bothers me is, I just wish I could go with him. He's so young, and this medical facility is so far away. They said a nurse would be with him all the way there, but he doesn't know her. He will be scared, and he'll be looking for one of us."

"You signed already?" he asked her.

"Yes, I had to. There were limited spaces available. I didn't want Erik to be left out. Why do you ask?" She thought she heard doubt in his voice.

"Oh, no, nothing," he said, managing a smile. "I just wondered if you signed and if they might need both of our signatures."

"No. I mean, the doctor didn't say that they needed both. He said my signature was enough." Then she looked at Max's face, and a chill ran through her. "Why, Max? Do you think I made a mistake?"

"Oh, no. Not at all, my darling. I'm sure you did the right thing. I would have done the same thing if I had been here."

There was a short silence. Then Max forced a smile, and in a cheerful voice that sounded false to Margot, he said, "I'm starving. I'll be ready for dinner in a few minutes."

CHAPTER 50

That night, Margot couldn't fall asleep as she lay in bed. She wondered if she had acted too hastily. *Perhaps I should have consulted Max before signing. But then again, how could I have? He was at work, and the doctor was at the house. I feared the openings would fill, and Erik might never get help. I don't know why Max seems so skeptical. Perhaps I should invite my sister and Rudy over for dinner so that we can discuss our plans for Erik with Rudy. He might know more about this cure they've found because he seems to be in the inner circle. I don't like him much, and for that matter, I don't care for Trudy these days either. But I love my son. And more than anything in this world, I pray for Erik to be normal. I hate to see him suffer the way that he does when he has one of those seizures. It tears my heart out. Yes, I think the best thing to do is to invite my sister and her husband over to congratulate my brother-in-law on his promotion. Then I'll ask him to tell me everything he knows about this cure. Hopefully, he will be able to put Max at ease and me, too.*

CHAPTER 51

T he following day, after Max left for work, Margot telephoned Trudy.

"This is the Schulze residence," a young woman whose voice Margot did not recognize answered the phone.

"Who is this?" Margot asked.

"I am the maid. You've reached the Schulze residence."

When did my sister get a maid? Margot thought. She knew Trudy had a nurse for Luzie when she was born. But the nurse had been gone for a while now. And Margot didn't realize her sister had servants in the house now. "May I please speak to Frau Schulze?"

"Who's calling, please?"

"This is her sister, Margot."

"Can you hold the phone for a moment, please? I'll go and tell her that you're on the line."

"Yes, of course," Margot said.

A few minutes passed, and then she heard Trudy's voice. "Margot! How are you?"

"I'm fine. How are you?"

"Oh, just fine," Trudy said. "You know, Rudy was promoted. And he's doing so well. His latest promotion came with a lot more parties that I must attend. So, I've been swamped. Besides the parties, there is always the shopping for the right dress. You know how that is?" she laughed a little.

"Yes, of course," Margot said. *She's still so superficial. Ah, well, that's just Trudy, I guess.*

"I must admit, it is lots of fun, though. We travel a bit. And I have so many lovely friends. In fact, we are going east next month. Rudy must go to Poland for work. He travels all the time, but I wanted to go. And, of course, he just adores me. So, he can't say no to me. He never could actually…"

"Trudy," Margot interrupted her sister. Trudy could go on bragging for hours, and Margot just couldn't bear to sit and listen to her. Not today, not with all that she had on her mind. "I'm sorry to interrupt. But I have an appointment in a little while. So, I have to get right to the point. I called to invite you and Rudy for dinner to celebrate his promotion."

"Oh, how very kind of you. Dinner at your home?"

"Yes."

"How quaint. Even so, we'd love to come."

Of course, they would. Trudy would love to come and brag. "And we'd love for you to bring little Luzie. Max and I would love to see her."

"I'd much rather leave her with the maid. She's so troublesome these days. You know how much work a baby can be."

"Yes. I suppose. But I must admit, I always love having Erik with us wherever we go. But whatever you prefer is fine with us."

"If you had a maid to help you, you might feel differently. Besides, Rudy has a very important job and needs time away from our child. Babies are far too noisy, and they are too much work. Anyway, when would you like us to come?"

"How is next week on Wednesday?" Margot said, thinking she would never prefer to leave her son with a maid rather than take him to a family member's home for dinner. But she knew that Trudy would.

"Give me a minute, and I'll check our calendar."

Trudy disappeared for a few minutes. Then she returned and said, "Wednesday will be fine. What time shall we arrive?"

"How's seven o'clock? That will give Max a few minutes to freshen up when he gets home from work."

"Perfect. We'll see you then. And by the way, you can drop by anytime. I've recently redone all the furniture in the house, and I'd love for you to see it."

"I'll do that. I'd love to see Luzie," Margot said.

"Yes, she's quite the little Aryan girl. She's very healthy and robust, like an Aryan child should be." Margot felt the stab. She knew her sister said that because she wanted Margot to know her child was better than Erik. Margot didn't respond. So, Trudy went on to say, "And besides that, she has perfect looks too, with her blonde hair and her perfect blue eyes."

CHAPTER 52

Trudy had been working hard to lose the excess weight she'd
gained in pregnancy. Although she was not completely
down to her original pre-baby weight, she had lost enough
to fit into some of her clothes. However, to Trudy, seeing Max was
important enough to warrant the purchase of a new dress. So, she
called Mattie to meet her in town. Trudy left Luzie with the maid
and went to the shop. Trudy wanted Mattie to know she and Rudy
had been invited to Margot and Max's apartment for dinner. This
was because she assumed Mattie had not been invited. And Trudy
did what she could to put a rift between her sisters whenever she
had the opportunity. She wanted to assure herself that Mattie was
always closer to her than she was to Margot.

"I don't understand why Margot invited you two for dinner, and
she didn't invite us. This is a celebration of Rudy's promotion, isn't
it?" Mattie asked. By her tone of voice, Trudy could tell that Mattie
was hurt, which was what Trudy wanted. "I wonder why she
wouldn't invite us?"

"I don't know," Trudy said, trying to sound innocent. Then she
looked at Mattie and sighed, "Oh, don't be hurt, *Mein Liebchen*, my
dear." Trudy touched her sister's cheek and pretended to be sympa-

thetic, but she was hiding the fact that she was glad that Margot had insulted Mattie. "She's always been inconsiderate. But of course, you know that. We both know that."

"I suppose you're right."

"Of course I am," Trudy said as she ran her fingers over the rack of clothing in one of the boutiques where they were shopping.

"That one is so pretty." Mattie marveled at a sky-blue cashmere dress that Trudy pulled out of the row of dresses and held up.

"You think so?"

"Oh yes, I wish I could afford something like that," Mattie said.

"Well, someday perhaps you will," Trudy said. She liked feeling superior to her sisters. It made her feel special to know that because she'd married an important man, she could afford what her sisters could not. Then she added, "You know, I'd wager that Margot invited us to her house because she is trying to see if she can push Rudy to help Max get promoted."

"Can he do that?"

"Probably. He's wildly successful," Trudy bragged. Then she smiled and said, "You're right, this dress is lovely. It's the color of my eyes. Come with me. I want to try it on."

The dress was flattering. Instead of looking overweight and frumpy, Trudy looked curvaceous. *What's left of this baby weight is all in the right places.* She looked at her wide hips and ample bosom.

"What do you think?" Trudy asked Mattie.

"I think it's beautiful. But why do you need a dress just to go to Margot's house?"

"Yes, this is the dress," Trudy ignored Mattie's question.

"Please don't tell me you're still in love with Max."

"Don't be silly. Max is a nobody compared to my important husband," Trudy said.

"Trudy, I know you," Mattie said. "And from the look on your face when you say Max's name, I can see that you still have feelings for him."

Trudy sunk down into the chair in the dressing room. Her nose turned red, and she began to cry. "Because you're my sister. My favorite sister. My only real sister. I can't lie to you. I love Max. You know I always have. And I can't see what he sees in her for the life of me."

Mattie took Trudy's hands. "She's his wife. They have a son together. He loves her. You have a good husband who loves you. Please, Trudy, let Max go. Be happy with what you have."

"I wish I could. But, you see, I've never really tried to win Max. I mean, not really. When we were young, I was too shy, too afraid."

"Trudy, this is foolishness. You did try. You always tried. He has always been in love with Margot since we were little. You can't change that. So, please…"

"I must try just once more. I mean, really try."

"What does that mean, exactly?"

"You have to swear you won't tell anyone," Trudy said.

"I swear. You know I have always kept your secrets. I would never tell anyone anything that you told me in confidence."

"I'm going to try to seduce him."

"Oh no, no, Trudy. Don't do that. It will be a disaster, not only for him, but mostly for you. He won't sleep with you. Max isn't the type."

"I'll bet he will," she said. "I'll promise him plenty. And then he'll be mine."

"No, Trudy. I can't let you do this."

"You promised," Trudy glared at Mattie. "You promised you wouldn't ever tell anyone."

"And I won't."

"Well, don't try to get in my way either."

"I wouldn't do that. But you are making a terrible mistake."

"If I am, then it will be my problem. But I can't go on this way anymore. I have to try."

Mattie shook her head. "And what if he agrees? What if he sleeps with you, and you get what you want? What then? Are you going to leave Rudy? Would you really want to marry Max? Are you willing to give up this rich lifestyle you've been living? Max could never afford these things that you want. He is not rich. He's not anywhere as successful as your husband. If he left Margot and married you, you would have to live within his means. That is what you want, isn't it? You want him to marry you? Could you live within his means? Or do you want a casual affair?"

"No, I don't want anything casual. I want to marry Max. I want him to look at me the way he looks at Margot."

"If he did, you would have him, but you would have to give up cashmere dresses like this." Mattie touched the dress Trudy was trying on.

"I don't care. I would have Max for my very own, and that's all I really ever wanted."

CHAPTER 53

Trudy was as excited as a high school girl going to her first dance as she carefully applied her bright red lipstick. *Max. She thought of his deep blue eyes and what he would think when he looked at her. The first thing he'll notice is that not only have I gotten my figure back, but it's even better. My breasts are fuller, and my hips are rounder. He won't be able to resist me. Margot looks like a wet rat. She's too skinny. She can hardly eat because she's always consumed with worry about her little brat. And she looks weathered. There are lines around the corners of her eyes and sprinkles of gray in her hair. I pretend to feel sorry for her. But I don't. She always had everything. Men fell at her feet. Now, she is just a worn-out old rag, which is good for me. No man, not even Max, can resist a womanly figure. Besides that, I'm sure it weighs on his mind that I was able to give my husband a healthy child, and Margot gave him a son with some strange disease. Although Erik might be a boy, and every man wants a son, I'm sure that Max knows Erik has sickly genetics from his mother. He doesn't know why, but I do. It's because Erik is not a real Aryan. He has Jewish blood that comes from her. And that's why he's not well. I'd love to tell Max and Rudy that Margot isn't my sister. She's just a*

damn Jew born from a whore of a mother that my parents took in because they felt pity for her when she was a baby. I'd love to see the looks on their faces when they find out who Margot really is. But I dare not tell them. I can't trust Rudy. He doesn't like Max very much or Margot. So, if he found out the truth, he might decide to arrest Max for marrying a Jew. Rudy wouldn't want that in his family, and he would want to be the arresting officer just to show that he was perfectly loyal to the Nazi party. Rudy is the type of person who would turn on his own mother if he found out she was Jewish. I wouldn't care what he did to Margot, but I might never see him again if he arrested Max. It's best that, for now, Rudy doesn't know anything. But I'm just waiting for the right time to tell Max. A time when it will benefit me the most.

"Are you almost ready?" Rudy called out in frustration. "It takes you forever to get dressed these days."

"Yes, I'm coming right down," Trudy answered, hating his tone of voice. But nothing he said or did could spoil her excitement. She was, after all, on her way to see Max.

Trudy had a special spring in her step as she ran down the stairs. "Ready to go!" she said, smiling, her white teeth contrasting beautifully with her red lipstick.

"I can see that you are," he said, his eyes brightening with genuine admiration. "Why, you have really lost weight, and you look quite lovely."

"You really think so?" She glanced in the mirror by the door and ran her hand over her hair to make sure that not a single hair was out of place.

"Actually, yes, I do." He laughed. "But you are always competing with your sister, aren't you?"

"Don't say that."

"It's true. I'm not blind. Whenever we go anywhere with Margot and Max, you always take the utmost care of your appearance. Not so much with Mattie. But you are in fierce competition with Margot."

"And who wins?" she said haughtily.

He laughed, "Why you do, of course. She has dark hair and dark eyes. It is not very flattering, I'm afraid. You're blonde and blue-eyed, and of course, that's a sign of beauty. But I know how competitive sisters can be. Brothers can be that way, too."

"And how would you know?"

"Because I'm observant," he smiled as he took her cashmere coat with the silver fox collar off the coat rack and helped her to put it on. "I pride myself on being a good judge of human nature."

She smiled at him. *You think so. But you're not that good of a judge. You haven't figured out that Margot isn't our real sister, and you haven't figured out that I don't dress up for Margot. I dress up for Max.*

Rudy lit a cigarette and then opened the window of the automobile as they drove. A brisk wind filtered through the car, cutting through the tobacco scent.

When they arrived at Max and Margot's apartment building, Rudy got out and opened the door for his wife. Then he said, "I hate this apartment. I don't know why Max is so adamant about refusing to take a house from the Reich. This place is so run down."

"You wouldn't get them a house as nice as ours, would you?"

He laughed heartily as if he'd just heard the funniest thing, "There you go with that competition again." He shook his head. "No, of course not. I'll always make sure they never have anything as nice as ours."

They walked up the stairs and knocked on the door. Margot opened it and let them in. She wore a simple cotton dress. It was clean but well-worn. And Max, who had just returned from work, was still in his uniform. "Welcome to our home. I'm so glad you could come," Max said sincerely.

Rudy smiled.

"Please sit down. Can I get you a drink?"

"Yes, of course," Rudy said. "Whiskey?"

"Yes, I have whiskey. And for you?" he asked Trudy.

"Oh no, thank you, nothing for me," Trudy said as she smiled directly at Max. He returned her smile, and she felt a wave of heat travel through her. *I can see it in his eyes. He is attracted to me.*

Max is taken with how good I look. How could he resist me? Just look at Margot in that dress. She looks like a poor hausfrau.

"Congratulations," Max said generously to Rudy. "I'm not sure what your new job entails. But I hear it's something very important."

"Yes, I suppose you could say that." Rudy smiled.

"It's more money anyway," Trudy said, winking and nudging Margot with her elbow.

"That's wonderful," Margot said. "Congratulations to both of you."

They sat in the living room for a few minutes, and then Margot stood up and began to serve the meal. "Please, come and sit down. Dinner is ready. I don't want it to get cold."

"No, of course not," Rudy said.

Margot had put Erik to bed early that evening so that they could talk without being disturbed. But she had become used to listening for any sounds from Erik's room. And now, could hear him moving around, and she knew that Erik had awakened and was tossing and turning in his bed. "Excuse me for just a moment. I hear Erik. I'll be right back. Please, start without me." Margot's heart was racing. She prayed that Erik wasn't having a seizure as she ran to his room.

"Let me serve," Trudy said, leaning over Max so her breasts were only inches from his face. She smiled at him and served him a large helping of spaetzle and *sauerbraten.*

He looked up and smiled. "Thank you."

Max is attracted to me. I can see it when he looks at me.

Margot returned several minutes later. She was relieved, and Erik was fine. He'd just had a bad dream, and she'd rubbed his back until he went back to sleep. "He's asleep. I'm hoping he'll sleep through the night."

"That's why we have a maid. Otherwise, we could never have company. Luzie would demand our attention," Trudy said. "You could use one too."

"I don't mind taking care of Erik myself," Margot said. Then she said. "Actually. I have some news for you both. A doctor came by to see me about Erik's condition."

"The epilepsy?" Rudy asked.

"Yes. The doctor was very encouraging. He said he was a colleague of *Sturmbannführer* Doctor Gerhart."

"Oh, and what else did he say?" Rudy asked.

"He said that they've found a cure."

"A cure? Really? Well, that's phenomenal," Rudy said, genuinely pleased.

"Yes, Max and I are very excited."

"I can see why."

"There is only one problem," Margot said, "And I am hoping you might be able to use your influence to help us."

"What is it you need?"

"The doctor said Erik must go to a special clinic far from here. It's located between Frankfurt and Cologne. He is going to travel there by bus. And he will be accompanied by a nurse." She hesitated. "But I am finding it difficult to let him go alone with a stranger. He needs me, and I want to go with him. The doctor said that I can't. But I must. Please, Rudy, can you convince them to let me go with him?"

"When is he scheduled to leave?"

"January first."

"I see," Rudy said, putting his fork and knife down for a moment. "Well, I don't know how much I can do because, as you know, I am not in the medical profession. However, I will make some calls and do what I can. How does that sound? I'll see if I can speak with someone who has the authority to arrange this for you. It might take me a few days, but I'll get back to you by the end of the week."

CHAPTER 54

Margot didn't invite Mattie, her husband, or their parents to this dinner because she wanted to talk to Rudy alone. She wanted to ask if he knew anything more about this cure for epilepsy. She wanted to know what he knew about the hospital and how he felt about a nurse taking Erik alone on the bus. But most of all, she wanted to beg him to use his influence to arrange for her to accompany her son. However, after Rudy agreed to speak with his colleagues, he changed the subject. Margot felt she couldn't ask any more questions.

As she got ready for bed that night, Margot turned to Max. "It seemed to have gone well. I would have liked to ask him about so many things. But it seemed like I would be pushing him too hard. So, I didn't."

"I hope he can do something."

"Yes, so do I," Margot said. "It would be easier on Erik if I were there with him. He wouldn't be afraid."

"I know," Max said. Then he whispered, "Come here. Let me hold you for a while."

She cuddled in his arms, and he held her close as she listened to his heartbeat. Then she said, "You know, my sister has a crush on you."

"You're not jealous, are you?"

"Of Trudy? No. Not at all."

He laughed a little. "Trudy is not my type. She's too showy, and well, the truth is, she's not you. I hope you know that you're the only girl for me."

"I know. I love you, Max."

"I love you too, with all my heart."

CHAPTER 55

I t was a week and a half before Margot received a telephone call from Rudy. The phone rang just as Max and Margot were about to have dinner. Max got up and answered, "*Allo.*"

"*Allo*, it's Rudy. How are you?"

"Fine. How are you?" Max said. He was impatient to hear what Rudy had to tell him.

"Everyone here is doing well. I'm calling because I finally spoke with my friend Gerhart concerning Erik."

"Yes, and what did he say?" Max was anxious.

"He said that the program Erik has been enrolled in is very good. The chances of the doctors involved being able to cure Erik are excellent. Especially because he is so young."

"That's wonderful news."

"Yes, I agree, but I am sorry to disappoint Margot. She cannot go with Erik. The doctor said that if they allowed all the mothers to come and stay with their children, it would be too crowded, and the parents would only get in the way of the treatment. He said not to worry, though. Erik will be well cared for and attended to by the finest nurses and doctors the Reich has to offer."

"That sounds good, but Margot will be disappointed," Max said.

"I know. And I'm sorry. However, this is what is best for the child."

"Yes, I suppose you're right. I'll tell her," Max said.

"Please do," Rudy said, "and, by the way, you and I should go out for a beer or two one evening next week."

"Yes, of course. That would be very nice," Max said, dreading it and already trying to find a way out.

CHAPTER 56

On the first of January, it snowed just before dawn. Margot was awake, staring out the window and watching the snow cover up the front yard of her apartment building. *Today is the day. The nurse should be arriving to pick Erik up in a few hours. Erik hasn't even left yet, and I miss him already. I must keep reminding myself that this is what is best for him. If he can be cured, he will be able to live a normal life. This is a small price to pay for that.* Max must have felt her absence in their bed because he got up and took the blanket off the bed. Still sleepy, he walked into the living room. He laid the warm blanket over his wife's shoulders and sat beside her. Max didn't say a word in the stillness of the early dawn. He took Margot's hand in his and kissed it.

"Oh, Max, I hope he will be alright without me. Every time I close my eyes, I see his little face, and he's always so scared."

"Shhh, I know. I see it, too. But we must be strong. Try to imagine him growing up and getting married, living a normal life. Just think, we could be grandparents. Erik might have children of his own. Try to imagine him never having another seizure. This is what I do when I feel nervous about letting him go alone."

She sighed, "You're right. Only I can't help it. I still wish they would have allowed me to go with him. It would have been so much easier on all of us."

"Yes, I agree. And we tried. Even Rudy tried. However, it does make sense. Imagine the chaos if every patient had a family member with them at the hospital."

"I understand. It's just that he's so little and so small."

"Margot, please love, stop torturing yourself."

"You're right, Max. I must stop thinking this way. We are doing what we must do to help our son."

"Exactly," he said, squeezing her hand. There were a few moments of silence. Then he said, "Let's have a cup of tea. I'll make us a cup. You know, my mother always gave us a cup of tea when we were upset about something. She said it helped. And you know what?"

"What?"

"It did." He smiled at her, and she was comforted by his smile as she looked at him in the early dawn light that filtered through the window.

CHAPTER 57

The nurse arrived a few hours later, accompanied by a driver
in a black automobile. Margot was holding Erik in her arms
when the car pulled up in front of her building, and as soon
as she saw the auto, the hair on the back of her neck bristled. Max
had taken the day off to help Margot with the transition.

"They're here," she called out to Max, who was in the bathroom.
He came into the living room immediately. The two of them watched
as the nurse entered their building. The driver waited outside. Margot
closed her eyes and nuzzled her face into Erik's hair, taking in his
essence. She imagined that she could hear the nurse climbing the
stairs. Then came the knock on the door, and Margot felt her heart stop.

"Frau Kraus," the nurse said when Margot opened the door.

"Yes, that's me."

"Good morning." The nurse was a heavy-set, no-nonsense
woman with brown hair bound tightly in a bun at the nape of her
neck and thick glasses. "My name is Fraulein Vogel. I'm a nurse,
and I am going to be escorting Erik to the Hadamar center." She
smiled. "You needn't worry about him. I'll take good care of your
son."

Margot looked at the woman scrutinizing her. *She is smiling, but there is no sparkle in her eyes. Her eyes look dead. And she is trying to seem like she is warm and caring. But I don't feel warmth from her. Maybe I am crazy. Maybe she is a good person, and it's just me. I'm just worried because I don't know her, and she is taking my son on a long journey without me.*

It was as if Fraulein Vogel read her mind. "Please, Frau Kraus. Let me put your mind at ease. I am here to take your son to a hospital where the doctors can help him. You are doing what is best for your little boy. I assure you of this. Now, as far as the bus ride is concerned. I know you are apprehensive, but I have made this trip with several other children, and I know how to comfort them when they are away from their mothers for the first time. Erik will be fine with me."

Margot nodded. "Would you like a cup of tea?" she asked, hoping to prolong the time until Erik had to leave.

"I would love one, but unfortunately, we are on a strict time schedule, so I must refuse your kind offer. We must be at the bus in half an hour, or they might leave without us."

Margot nodded. She felt bile rise in her throat as Fraulein Vogel picked Erik up and held him for a moment. Then Erik turned to his mother and looked at Margot with terror. Then he began to scream. "Oh no, no, don't cry," Margot cooed as she reached out and touched her son, "It's all right. This nice lady is going to take good care of you." Margot was shaking as she handed a cardboard suitcase to the nurse. "Here are some of his things. I didn't pack much, just a couple of changes of clothes. And his favorite toy." Tears were running down Margot's face.

"Yes, that was a good idea. I'll take those things with us. In fact, perhaps we can give him his toy now. It might make this easier," the nurse said.

Margot opened the neatly packed valise and took out a stuffed rabbit Max had given Erik for his first birthday. Erik reached for the rabbit and pulled it close to him. But then, with his other hand, he reached for his mother. "Please, may I hold him just one more time before you leave? Just for a moment? Please? I know you are in a hurry, but I won't be long."

"Of course," the nurse smiled, handing Erik to his mother. The little boy stopped crying once he was in his mother's arms. He nuzzled Margot's neck, and she ran her hand over his hair, which was soaked with sweat because he had been crying so hard.

"Don't be afraid, my little love. You're going to be all right. This nice lady is going to take good care of you. And soon, you'll be returning home to your *vater* and me." Margot kissed Erik's head. Then she asked Fraulein Vogel, "Will you be with him even after he arrives at the hospital?"

"I will be with him during his entire treatment. I will take care of him. And I promise you, you are doing the right thing. This is what is best for him."

Margot nodded.

The nurse reached for Erik again. And once again, he began to cry. Then she picked up the suitcase. "Wave goodbye to *Mutti* and *Vatti*," she said.

"Nurse Vogel? May I write to you and ask you about Erik's progress?"

"Of course. I would be very pleased to keep you informed."

"Thank you. That would mean so much to me," Margot said sincerely. "I'll walk you both to the car."

"No, I've found it's easier on the child if you say goodbye here."

Max put his arm around Margot to give her support. "All right," Margot said softly, "all right." Then she waved with a trembling hand as the nurse carried Erik out the door. Margot stood in the doorway and watched the woman carry her son down the stairs. Erik's eyes were deep and dark. But he stopped crying and just stared at his mother until the nurse carried him out the door. Margot turned and ran to the window. She was shaking as she stared out. She saw Erik look up at the window for a moment, or at least she thought she did. *He's so young, so helpless.* A wave of panic overcame Margot, and suddenly, she wanted to run outside and take her child back. But she reminded herself she was doing what was best for him as the black car rode away.

Margot turned to Max. He was crying, "We did the right thing, didn't we?" she asked.

"Yes," he said softly.

CHAPTER 58

Margot was lost without her son. She couldn't get used to not having a child in the house. She missed Erik terribly. Every day, she wrote a letter to the Hadamar center and addressed it to Frau Vogel, asking about her son's progress. But a month passed, and she received no answer to her letters. Finally, she decided to visit Trudy to see if Rudy could get her some information about Erik's progress. She took the bus to Trudy's house early in the day, even though she knew Rudy would not be home from work yet. The maid answered the door with little Luzie in her arms. "Excuse me, please," the maid said in broken German, "But the baby has been crying all day. I know I should not answer the door with the baby in my arms. But the mistress can't stand to hear her screaming, so I am carrying her. I think she is maybe growing a tooth."

"Oh, that's all right. I'm Margot, and I'm here to see my sister, Trudy."

"Please, won't you come in?" the woman was shy and soft-spoken, almost as if she was afraid of something.

Margot nodded. She noticed the yellow star on the woman's chest. It had become commonplace to see these badges on the clothing of Jewish people on the streets of Berlin. Margot's mind flashed to Ben. *He must be wearing the star, too. It's the law.* The thought made her sad. But the baby smiled and cooed, and Luzie reached out for Margot. This grabbed Margot's attention. She reached for Luzie and said, "Can I hold her?"

"Yes, of course," the maid answered, placing the child in Margot's arms.

"There, there, now don't you cry. Your auntie Margot is here, and she's going to rock you until you fall asleep." Then Margot asked the maid, "You have an accent. Where are you from?"

"Poland."

"I see," Margot said. She knew that Germany had conquered Poland and wondered how Trudy had acquired the maid. But she didn't ask the maid any more questions.

"Shall I let my mistress know you're here?"

"Yes, please," Margot said, still holding the baby. *It is so good to have a child in my arms. It fills the emptiness I can't seem to fill with anything else.* Luzie must have felt the love as Margot rocked her because she stopped crying and fell asleep. It was almost ten minutes before Trudy came out of the bedroom.

"Well, well, if it isn't my sister. So, what brings you here?" Trudy asked.

Margot could see that her sister had taken a few moments to put on lipstick and comb her hair. Trudy looked as fresh as the morning in a white dress with a pattern of yellow roses on it. Margot smiled to herself. *Trudy never changes. She's always the fashion plate.* "I came by because I need to ask for a little help."

"Oh, what is it?"

"As you know, Erik went to a special hospital in January. I've been sending letters to his nurse. She said she would keep me informed, but I haven't received an answer so far. I want to know how he is doing. Can you please ask Rudy to see what he can find out?"

"Of course," Trudy said. "But he's out of town. He's somewhere in Poland. It seems he's been traveling constantly since he got this new promotion. Next time, I'm going to accompany him. I'm looking forward to it. Although I must admit, I would much prefer to go back to Munich, rather than east to Poland. I hear it's barbaric there." She shrugged. "Anyway, our trip to Munich was lovely. Wasn't it?"

"Yes, it was," Margot tried to have patience with her sister's frivolity. "I'm very worried about Erik. He's just a child, an innocent child. He doesn't know why he's been sent away. He has no idea that the doctors and nurses are trying to help him. All he knows is that his parents aren't around."

"Well, yes. But at that age, they forget quickly. So, I'm sure he's doing fine."

"But why would the nurse not answer my letters?"

Trudy shrugged. "She's probably very busy. I'm sure she'll answer you. But, in the meantime, I'll ask Rudy to see what he can find out. By the way, how's Max?"

"Oh, he's fine. He's working a lot. But he's worried about Erik, too."

"Well, maybe we could all have dinner next week. What do you think? Rudy should be back on Monday. I'll tell him about your situation and ask him to find out what he can. Then, once he does, we can all go out and talk. It would be good for you to get out of the house a little."

"How do you know I don't go anywhere?" Margot asked.

"Because I know you. And I know you are one to sit at home and worry. However, going out for dinner would be good for both you and Max."

"All right, we'll go out. Just let me know when."

"I will. As soon as Rudy gets home, I'll ask him."

"Trudy," Margot said wistfully. "Would you mind if I came by a few times a week to play with Luzie?"

"Really, you want to come and play with Luzie?"

"I do. I miss having a child in my arms. I feel so empty."

"Well, it's fine with me, but I won't always be home when you're here. I have a lot of social engagements. I hope that's all right. The maid takes care of Luzie when I'm gone."

"I know that. But she's such a sweet little girl, and I need to hold a baby in my arms."

Trudy shrugged. She was thinking of Max. "Perhaps on the days you come to see Luzie, you can have Max meet you here after work, and then we can all have dinner together. It will be nice to get together a few times a week. I'll tell the maid to prepare something special on those nights."

"Oh, Trudy, that would be so kind of you," Margot said.

"Well, after all, you are my sister," Trudy smiled slyly. Then she shook her head. "Aren't you?"

"Of course I am."

"Yes, of course, you are," Trudy said.

CHAPTER 59

The following week, Rudy returned home from Poland, where he had been invited to see the new camp being built. It was called Auschwitz, and *Obersturmbannführer* Rudolf Hoss was to be in charge. Hoss was an important man, and Rudy had been nervous about meeting him for the first time. When they finally met, Rudy laughed at Hoss's jokes about ridding the world of Jews. He listened patiently to Hoss's heroic tales of his service in the great war and how he'd become so important to the Führer. By the time he left, Rudy was exhausted. His new job was mentally taxing. It required him to flatter his superiors constantly. No matter what they said, he was required to agree with them. And he must always be willing to do whatever must be done to further the cause of the Reich. No matter what he witnessed or what he was asked to do, Rudy knew he must never show a single drop of fear or doubt. He forced a smile, no matter what he was feeling inside. Rudy would never have admitted it, and he never let on, but he found that he didn't really care for Hoss. Hoss was a braggart, fat, vain, and self-centered. But that didn't matter. He complimented Hoss until Hoss smiled contentedly.

Rudy walked into his home in the late afternoon. He longed for a hot bath, a good dinner, and a little sex before a good night's rest. But when he walked into the living room and hung his coat, Trudy came out of the bedroom and put her arms around him. "I'm so glad to see you," she said. Trudy wore a dark maroon colored dress. It was fitted, and it showed off her curves. "How was your trip?"

"It was fine." He always told her everything was fine. It was easier than trying to explain his feelings. He sat down on the sofa and began to remove his shoes. "You look good," he said honestly.

"I lost a little more weight," she said.

"It shows. You're looking very sexy, my dear. But now you can stop losing weight. You look perfect."

She smiled at him. "Don't get undressed. I promised Margot and Max we would meet them at a steak house for dinner when you got home tonight."

"Oh, Trudy. I'm so tired. I've been traveling all day."

"But you have to eat, don't you?" she rubbed his thigh. "Besides, I already promised them."

"All right. I suppose I could use a good steak."

"Perfect. I'll call Margot and let her know you are home. We agreed tentatively to meet at five. But that's only an hour from now. Do you want me to tell her that we need to make it a little later?"

"No, five is fine. I'd rather eat early so we can get back early. I need to get some rest tonight."

"Are you going in to work tomorrow?"

"Actually, no. I'm going to take the day off."

"Oh, but I have a shopping date with Elke. Do you want me to cancel it? I could do that, and we could spend the afternoon together?"

"No, it's all right. I am just going to lie around and rest. It's been a hard week. You keep your plans with your friend for tomorrow. I'll see you when you get home for dinner."

"All right," she said. Then she picked up the phone. "*Allo*, Margot. It's me."

"Trudy," Margot said.

"Yes, it's me. Rudy got home a few minutes ago, and he said five o'clock would be fine. Is Max home yet?"

"Yes, he just walked in the door."

"Is five alright with him?"

"I'm not sure. Let me ask him. Max," Margot called out, "Rudy is home from his trip. He says he can meet us at five at the steak house around the corner. Is that too soon for you to be ready?"

"No, it's fine with me," Max said.

"Max says it's fine. So, we'll be there."

Margot hung up the phone. She was eager to see Rudy to ask him if he had any way to make direct contact with Erik's nurse. She was hoping that perhaps he could call the facility after dinner.

Max walked into the room. He'd washed his face, brushed his teeth, and combed his blond hair. Margot smiled at him. He had grown more handsome as he'd gotten older. "You and Erik look so much alike," she said.

"Of course we do. He's my son." Max smiled. "But he looks like you, too. That's the part that makes him good-looking."

She laughed a little. "I miss him so much."

"I know. I do, too. But I keep telling myself that at least he's in a place where they can help him. I used to go crazy when he had a seizure, and I couldn't do anything to stop it. I felt so helpless and was always terrified that he might not come out of it."

"I know, me too," she admitted.

Max and Margot walked hand in hand to the steak house, where they planned dinner. It was only a few streets away from their home. Trudy and Rudy had not yet arrived when they entered the restaurant. So, Max got a table for four, and then they held hands while waiting.

"I'm hoping Rudy will be able to get in touch with Nurse Vogel. He has a lot of pull. Maybe he'll try to call Hadamar tonight. I hate to bother the doctors and nurses, but Nurse Vogel still hasn't answered any of my letters, and I am getting anxious. I need to find out how Erik is doing."

"I know, darling. I knew that was why you wanted to have

dinner with your sister and Rudy as soon as he got home. That's why, even though I am very tired, I agreed to come tonight," Max said.

"You don't fool me, Max. I know you hate those nights when I spend the day with little Luzie, and you meet me at Trudy's house for dinner, right? You don't like her or Rudy, and neither do I. But I adore Luzie."

"I wouldn't say I hate going there, but you're right, I don't really like Rudy. I know he has been nothing but nice to us, but there is just something about him that makes my skin crawl. I know there is no logic to it, but he does."

"It's not that he is higher up in the party than you, is it Max?" she asked gently. "Because if you think that impresses me, it doesn't. I hope it doesn't mean anything to you either."

"It's not that. It's just something about him. I can't put my finger on it."

"Well, I know he hates the Jews. And that bothers me. I think about Ben and how kind he was to us and Erik, and I feel bad. But then I tell myself that Rudy can't help it. It's just the way he was raised. I am trying to understand and not condemn him for it." Margot said. "I mean, he does such nice things for us. After all, he took us to Munich. He always pays for dinner when we go out. And he did get you a good job that pays well and helps to get us better food rations. I mean, he really wants us to like him."

"Yes, it's true. I just don't like the Nazis, but I will try harder to tolerate him. Does that make you happy?"

She smiled. "I will tell you the truth. I don't really like him or my sister. But I am trying, too."

Max let out a laugh. Then he and Margot laughed just as Trudy and Rudy entered the restaurant.

Rudy walked up to the table where Max and Margot sat. He raised his hand in a salute. "Heil Hitler." Trudy saluted too and said, "Heil Hitler."

Max and Margot stood up, and unenthusiastically, they both saluted. "Heil Hitler."

They all sat down, and Rudy let out a sigh. "I just got home from Poland."

"Yes, so I hear," Max said.

"It's been quite the week," Rudy said. "I spent some time with *Obersturmbannführer* Hoss."

"Oh, and what's he like?" Max asked, trying to show some interest.

"He's really a very interesting man."

"I'm sure he is," Margot said, trying to act as if she cared about Rudy's job.

The waiter arrived, and they all placed their order.

Rudy ordered a special Riesling wine he had tasted at a dinner party a few weeks ago. "Bring the wine to the table right away," Rudy ordered the waiter.

"Yes, of course," the waiter said nervously.

"You're going to love this wine. It's one of the best I've ever had. I tasted it at a party that I attended for the *Reichsführer*."

"Oh yes, that was quite the gala. And I remember that wine. It was wonderful. You're going to love it," Trudy said. Then she turned to Margot and bragged, "We went to a party for *Reichsführer* Himmler. It was a very lavish event. Everyone wore the latest fashions, and the food was so delectable. They were served in the most exquisite China, and we drank from the finest crystal. It's really a shame you and Max weren't invited."

Margot smiled at her sister. *She thinks I care about meeting Himmler and who wore what. I couldn't care less. All I care about right now is finding out what is happening with my son.*

The wine arrived, and the waiter poured Rudy a glass. He tasted it and nodded. Then, the waiter served the rest of the table.

"To the Führer," Rudy said, raising his glass.

"To the Führer," the rest of them repeated, Trudy's voice being the loudest.

Everyone sipped their wine.

"So, how do you like it?" Rudy asked Max.

"It's good," Max admitted.

"I knew you'd like it," Rudy winked, then he patted Max on the shoulder.

There were a few moments of silence as everyone savored the wine.

Margot cleared her throat, and then, in a quiet, almost apologetic voice, she asked, "I hate to bother you, Rudy. As I know, you are very busy these days. And you have a very important position. But," Margot smiled as sweetly as she could manage, "I was wondering if you could get in contact with Erik's nurse. Before she and Erik left for the hospital, she gave me permission to write to her. She said she would keep me informed as to Erik's progress. I've written several letters to her, but she hasn't answered. I am worried about him. I would just like to hear from her. You're a father. I'm sure you can understand."

"Of course," he said, smiling. "I understand perfectly. And it just so happens that I'm not working tomorrow, so I'll make some calls during the day and let you know what I find out."

"I would really appreciate that so much. It would mean the world to me," Margot said. Her hands were trembling as she took a sip of the wine. *I wish he would have called tonight. But I can't push him. At least he has agreed to call.*

After they finished eating, Rudy said, "I'm so sorry to cut this lovely evening short. But I'm terribly exhausted. As I said, it's been a long week with traveling and all. So, I'd like to get home and get some rest."

"Of course," Max said.

Rudy insisted on paying the entire bill. Then they all stood up, and Max helped Margot with her coat.

"Is it all right if I call you tomorrow? Will you have some information for me by evening?" Margot asked Rudy as he opened the door for them to leave.

"About what?" Rudy asked.

He's forgotten. How could he forget? This is so important to me. Margot wanted to scream, but she forced herself to keep calm. "I realize that you're exhausted and that you are an important man," she said, "so I'll refresh your memory quickly. You were going to call some people to see if you could contact Erik's nurse at the Hadamar Institute."

"Ahh, yes, yes. I do remember. I am terribly sorry for forgetting. I'll take care of it in the morning. Why don't you call me tomorrow night and I'll let you know what I can find out. All right?" he said sweetly.

"Thank you again," Margot said.

"Would you two like a ride home?" Trudy offered.

Max looked at Margot. "Would you, dear?"

"No, it's not a far walk, and I enjoy walking in the evening, even though it's cold. It helps me relax. But thanks for offering."

Trudy smiled. "I can imagine it must be nice to walk in the evening with a loved one. Rudy and I hardly ever have the time for such things. But I must admit, it's nice to have our own auto, especially on cold nights like this."

"Yes, I'm sure it is," Margot said.

Then Rudy opened the door for his wife, who climbed inside. She smiled sweetly at Max as Rudy walked around and entered the automobile on the driver's side. Rudy started the car, and they pulled away.

As Margot and Max walked back to their apartment, Margot said, "He can be quite charming when he wants to be. But you're right. I am not fooled by him. I realize that behind all that charm is a real Nazi. I can tell."

"Yes, I'd have to agree with you. And that's what I am talking about. It's the real Nazi that he hides but that I can sense, and that makes my skin crawl," Max said. Then he hesitated for a moment. "Do you think I'm a real Nazi underneath all my charm?"

She laughed. "Who said you were charming?"

"Oh, so you don't think so?"

"I do. And I think you're as far from a real Nazi as possible. But I also think you are like me because you would do anything for our son. And that's why you wear that uniform and play by their rules."

"You know me so well," he said. "By the way, when was the last time I said I love you?"

"Right before we left our apartment to go to dinner," she said.

He smiled.

Then she added seriously, "I can't wait to hear from Rudy tomorrow. I'm really hoping he will be able to get us in contact with Nurse Vogel. I am praying that Erik is doing well."

"Yes, so am I. I am praying for it every day," Max said.

CHAPTER 60

R udy purposely stayed in bed, pretending to be asleep until his wife left for her shopping date with her friend. Whenever he returned from a trip, she seemed full of mindless chatter. He assumed she'd missed him, which was why she talked incessantly, but he wanted to avoid it. So, once she was gone, he got out of bed and went into the kitchen, where he demanded that the maid make him some breakfast. He cursed under his breath when he heard Luzie crying in her room. *Little monster hardly ever sleeps.* Then he turned to the maid and said, "Shut her up."

The maid nodded and ran into the bedroom to quiet the child. Rudy was annoyed. He hoped to have a quiet morning, and now Luzie was awake and bothering him.

The maid prepared Rudy's breakfast while holding Luzie on her hip. But the child was still fussing. And Rudy was livid.

After Rudy was served his food, he told the maid to dress the child and take her to the park for a while. Then he went into his room and waited until they had gone. Once Rudy heard the door close, he came out of his room and picked up the telephone receiver. *Margot is going to call later tonight. I might as well find out what I can now while I am alone in the house.*

Rudy called Dr. Gerhart at the hospital. And since Rudy was of a higher rank than the doctor, the doctor got on the phone quickly.

They made small talk for a few minutes about Rudy's recent promotion, and then Rudy asked how he might find out how Erik was doing.

There was a long silence. Then the doctor said, "You don't know?"

"I don't know what?" Rudy said.

"You don't know about the program?"

"I know that Erik was sent to the Hadamar Institute to get help for his epilepsy. His nurse was Nurse Vogel. I need to speak with her."

There was a long silence. Then Rudy said, "Are you still on the line?"

"I'm here. Yes. I'm here," the doctor stammered. "I can't tell you anything more, but I can tell you who to contact for more information."

"All right. Who?" Rudy was losing patience.

"There is a house located at Tiergartenstrasse 4. Go there and knock on the door. Tell them who you are, give them your rank, and then tell them what you want to know."

"What is all of this mystery about?" Rudy said he was a little annoyed but also rather curious.

"I am not at liberty to tell you anything else. I'm sorry."

Then the doctor hung up the phone. *I should report him. He was rude to me.* Rudy thought, but he did enjoy the idea of solving a mystery. It intrigued him. So, he took a quick shower and put on a clean uniform. Then he drove to Tiergartenstrasse and parked in front of number four.

CHAPTER 61

That evening at seven o'clock, Margot asked Max, "Is it too
early to telephone Rudy?"

"No, I think it's probably a good time," Max said.

Margot's hands were trembling as she telephoned Rudy. He and
Trudy had just sat down to a late dinner. But when the phone rang,
he turned to Trudy, and in a gruff voice, he said, "Answer it. I'm
sure it's your sister."

Trudy did as she was told.

"Allo," Trudy said.

"Trudy, it's Margot. I'm calling to speak to Rudy about Erik. I
hope this isn't a bad time."

"Well, we are just about to have dinner."

"I'm sorry. I'll call later if that's better."

Rudy stood up. "Give me the receiver," he said rudely.

Trudy said, "Rudy wants to talk to you now." She handed him
the receiver.

"*Allo*, Margot. I've been expecting your call." Rudy's voice was
exceptionally cheerful.

"Did you find out anything?"

"Yes, yes, actually I did. I found out that Nurse Vogel has been meaning to write to you, but she is very busy. It's not that she's avoiding you. She's just busy with patients."

"And Erik, how is he? How is my son?" Margot asked nervously.

"Fine, fine. He's actually doing very well on the program."

"That's good. That's so good. Did they say when he might come home?"

"No, I'm afraid he is not ready to return quite yet. But you can rest easily. They are taking good care of him."

"Thank you, Rudy. Thank you for finding all of this out for me."

"Well, of course," he said.

After Rudy hung up the phone, he took a bottle of whiskey from the shelf and took a long drink right from the bottle. Trudy looked at her husband. Rudy never drank from the bottle. "What's wrong?" she asked.

Rudy shook his head and walked away from the table and his uneaten meal. He picked up the bottle of whiskey on his way and headed into the bedroom.

Trudy knew something was not right. She could hear it in his voice, and he behaved oddly. She followed him into the bedroom, where she found him sitting on the edge of the bed drinking the whiskey. "Please, Rudy, tell me, what's the matter?" she asked.

He shook his head, "Nothing."

Trudy sat down beside her husband and rubbed his arm. "You can talk to me. I'm your wife, your partner. I'm on your side."

He turned to look at her, and his face was crumpled into a map of worry wrinkles. "It's the child. Erik," he said. "You know, no matter what happens, the doctors are doing what's best for him at that center."

"Of course they are," Trudy said. "And if he doesn't make it, that's not your fault. He's a sickly little boy. He always has been."

"You know, over time, I've had to perform some difficult tasks to get where I am."

"Yes, I know."

"And rarely does any of it affect me. I've seen Jews die. But they're Jews. And less than human. So, it doesn't really matter. I can watch them die by the hundreds and not feel a thing."

"Yes, I know all that, but I don't understand what you're trying to say."

"The program Erik is in is called T4, and it's top secret. I shouldn't even be telling you about it."

She touched his face softly. "It's all right, just tell me. It will be our secret."

"Maybe if I do talk to you, I'll be able to release these worthless feelings of guilt. Can you believe that even I feel sick about what I learned today?"

"What did you learn?"

"Well," he sighed. "T4 is a good program. It's good for the fatherland and for the Aryan race." He took another swig of whiskey. "But unfortunately, a sacrifice must be made if we are to become the most powerful nation in the world."

"I still don't understand."

"It's a good death. It is a good death because it is good for our country. Do you understand?"

She shook her head. "Not really. Who is dying?"

"Erik. Erik, and all the rest of the little children, German children. I wouldn't care if they were Jews or gypsies, but these are German children who were born deformed. Erik probably carried that epilepsy gene in his body from the time he was born. It is simple. If we are to be a master race, misfits like that cannot be permitted to live, and more importantly, they must not be permitted to reproduce."

"So, he died? I really don't understand."

"Euthanasia. He is being euthanized. It must be done if we Aryans are to be the master race. We must weed out the weak and the sick. Do you understand now? We must produce a strong and healthy race."

"Is Erik in a hospital? Is that place a medical facility?"

"Yes."

"Who is doing this euthanizing?"

222

"The doctors and nurses. They know what must be done. You see, no one wants to do it."

She gasped. For a second, Trudy, the girl who cared about nothing but her creature comforts, was shocked. "What about Margot? You told her that Erik was doing fine. Can you imagine how she will react when she finds out he's dead?"

"She will never know the truth. She'll never find out that this was a mercy killing. After a month or two, the Hadamar Institute will send her a letter saying that her son has died of some disease or something. It will be a disease that has nothing to do with his treatment. They will say it was something like typhus or scarlet fever. None of the parents whose children are euthanized will ever know what happened in the T4 program."

"My goodness," Trudy said. She was shocked, but her emotions were mixed. It was distasteful to think of little Erik dying at the hands of his doctors. But at the same time, she hated Margot because, even though Margot had less than she did, Margot had Max. However, this was not the most important reason she was glad Erik would not be returning. When Margot and Max lost their son, she was certain it would break their bond. While Max is grieving, Trudy will be there to comfort him.

"It is rather disturbing. But we must realize that this is for the best. When trying to create a master race, you dare not consider the needs of the individual. It is important that we see the broader picture if we are ever to see our fatherland become the world power it was meant to be."

She smiled at him. "I'm glad to have such a strong man for a husband. You are the kind of man the Reich needs."

"So, they tell me." He patted her arm. Then he sat up straight and said as proudly as he could. "I am willing to do whatever must be done to perpetuate our Aryan race."

CHAPTER 62

Luzie loved Margot. In fact, she became so attached to her that as soon as Luzie saw her aunt, the child would reach out her fat little arms to Margot, begging to be picked up. For Margot, these visits with her niece helped to fill the emptiness inside of her while she waited for the return of her precious son.

On the days when Margot came to visit, Trudy always insisted that Margot invite Max to come for dinner after work. "It will be easier for you if you both have dinner with us. If you have to get home and cook, you won't have Max's dinner on the table until late."

"That's so kind of you, Trudy," Margot said.

On one such occasion, Rudy was not available to have dinner with them. He called his wife to say he had to work late. So, he was not at home when Max arrived.

"Poor Rudy, he has to work long hours sometimes. But, of course, that is how it is when you have a very important position," Trudy said. "We'll have our dinner now because there is no telling when he'll get home. I'll have the maid keep his food warm."

As the food was served, Margot began to feel nauseated. "Excuse me," she said and ran to the bathroom, where she vomited.

I'm sick. Then fear gripped her. *I hope I didn't give whatever I have to Luzie.*

A moment later, Max knocked on the bathroom door. "Are you all right?" he asked, and she could hear the worry in his voice.

"I'm sick to my stomach," she said.

"Please, open the door."

"No, I'll be all right. Go and finish eating. Then we can go home."

"I'm not hungry. I want to come in and see you. I have to see you to be sure you're all right."

"Max, please. I want to be alone for a minute. Go back and eat."

"All right, if you insist."

"I do."

He returned to the table and sat down, but didn't speak. He pushed his food around on the plate.

"What's wrong with her?" Trudy asked, trying to sound sympathetic.

"I don't know. She says she is nauseated."

"It's probably just something she ate," Trudy said, then in a gentle voice, she whispered. "Don't worry. She'll be fine."

Max glanced back at the bathroom door. He nodded. "Yes, I'm sure she will." But he was still concerned.

"Max," Trudy said, his name pulling him back to the present moment. "Do you ever feel bored?"

"Bored?" he asked, but he was distracted by his concern for Margot. "I don't know what you mean."

"Well, I mean, it's the same old thing every day."

"Excuse me? I don't understand."

She managed to smile, "How can I put this? Sometimes, I crave excitement. Romance. You know?"

"Sure," he said, but he was not paying attention.

"I was thinking, you and I, we go way back, right?"

"Yes."

"We were children together. I'm sure you remember those days."

"Oh yes, sure. Of course, I do."

"Well, we can trust each other, right?"

"Yes."

"So, I was thinking that you might want to consider having a little side thing. Do you know what I mean?"

"Not really," he said. Then he whispered almost to himself, "Margot has been in that bathroom for a long time."

"I mean, well, I see how you look at me, and I feel the same way about you. So, I thought maybe we could make arrangements to meet at a hotel in the afternoons. No one would ever find out."

"I'm sorry. I can't concentrate on what you're saying. I am very worried about Margot. I'll be right back." Max went to the bathroom door and knocked. "Margot. Please let me in. I'm worried."

Margot opened the door. Her face was flushed. "I am sick to my stomach," she said. "It's probably nothing, just something I ate."

"Let's go home." He took her arm, and they walked into the dining room. Trudy was sitting at the table, fuming. Their conversation had not gone well. Max wasn't even paying attention when she laid her heart on the line for him. Now, he was holding Margot's arm and helping her to put on her coat. She was angry and couldn't believe Max hadn't noticed. "I'm sorry we have to leave. We didn't mean to ruin dinner," Max said sincerely. "But Margot isn't feeling well, so I'll call you tomorrow and tell you how she is doing. Thank you for having us. And again, I'm sorry."

"Yes, I'm sorry too," Margot said. "Please keep an eye on Luzie to make sure she didn't catch this from me. I'm worried sick about her."

"Yes, of course, I will," Trudy stood up. Then she turned to Max and said, "Yes, please call me and let me know how she is in the morning."

"I will."

After Max and Margot left, Trudy was furious. She had just exposed her hopes and dreams to Max, and he ignored her. He wasn't even paying attention when she told him what she wanted from him. Trudy yelled for the maid, "Rebecca, get in here and clean up this mess right now."

"Yes, ma'am," the young girl said, keeping her eyes down.

"Clean up this table. I don't care what you do with this food," Trudy said, then she stood up and began walking towards her bedroom. "Make sure that Luzie doesn't disturb Rudy when he gets home. Make sure you keep her quiet, or there will be hell to pay. That child can be so annoying sometimes."

Trudy was in a terrible mood as she undressed for bed. She tossed her diamond bracelet into her jewelry box and stepped out of her dress, leaving it on the floor. Then she sat down at her vanity table to remove her makeup. As she frosted her face with cream, she felt her eyes sting with tears. *I love him, and he doesn't know it. I offered myself to him. Openly. And he didn't even hear me. How can he still be in love with her? She is so skinny, scrawny, and plain. When she was young, she was beautiful. And I could see what he saw in her. But since Erik got sick, she is not the same. It took all the sparkle right out of her. Maybe he feels guilty because he gave her the child. Maybe that's why he's so devoted to her.* She threw the glass jar of cream against the wall, and it shattered. Then she began to cry. *It's not true. It's not guilt that Max feels. Max loves Margot. He loved her since we were little children. And somehow, he still does. Well, I hate her. I'd like to see her suffer the way I do. I can't wait for them to tell her that Erik is dead. I want to be there to witness her suffering.*

CHAPTER 63

Max got up early the following morning. He dressed for work quickly, then made a pot of coffee and some toast for himself and Margot. He brought it to her in bed, but she couldn't eat. He had brewed her a cup of coffee, and as soon as she smelled the coffee, she ran to the bathroom and vomited. "That's it. I'm calling my superior officer and telling him I can't come in today. I have to take you to see a doctor."

"I don't need a doctor. I'll be fine," Margot tried to assure him.

"I won't be able to work. I'll be worried all day. You never get sick like this. This is very unusual for you."

"I know," Margot said, "but I'm sure it's nothing." She smiled at him.

"Humor me, please. Just come with me to see a doctor so I can stop worrying. Will you do that for me?" he asked.

She nodded. "Do you want to go now?"

"Yes. As soon as possible. I'll call in to work while you get dressed."

She washed up and put on a clean cotton house dress. Then she went into the living room. "I'm ready."

They had to take the bus, and the motion made Margot feel even sicker. When they finally got off the bus, she vomited on the side of the road. Max turned white with fear. "Sweetheart," he said and took her into his arms.

Then, with his arm around her waist, they walked the two streets to the doctor's office. When they walked inside, the waiting room was packed. But no one in the waiting room wore a Nazi uniform. So, because of Max's uniform, Max and Margot were taken in to see the doctor before any of the patients who had been waiting. The nurse led them into an examination room, and within minutes, the doctor appeared.

"So, what seems to be the problem?" he asked.

Margot explained how she was feeling. The doctor listened. Then he asked Max to leave so that he could examine her. "Please, wait in the waiting room. I will only be a few minutes. Then, once I finish the exam, I'll have the nurse bring you back so we can discuss the problem."

"Are you all right alone?" Max asked.

"Of course," Margot smiled. "Go on. I'm sure this exam will be quick."

Max paced while he waited until, finally, a nurse in a white uniform came out and told him to go back to the examining room. When he entered, the doctor was smiling, and so was Margot. He was puzzled.

"I have good news for you," the doctor said. "Your wife is going to have a baby."

Max looked at Margot. Then he took her into his arms and held her tightly. "Oh, sweetheart. I had no idea." He turned to the doctor and said, "But she was never sick like this when she was pregnant with our son. Why is she so sick?"

"Every pregnancy is different. And Margot has all the symptoms. She told me that she often has heartburn. She's nauseated in the morning and evening. I examined her, and I would say she is about four weeks into her pregnancy."

"Are you happy?" Max asked Margot.

"Very," she answered, smiling.

CHAPTER 64

That night, Max telephoned Trudy. "I know I said I would call in the morning to let you know how Margot is doing. But when we woke up today, Margot was still not feeling well, so I took the day off from work, and we went to the doctor." He hesitated, then excitedly said, "I'm thrilled to tell you that I have good news."

"Oh," Trudy said, trying to sound as enthused as he did.

"Margot is pregnant. She's going to have another baby."

"That's wonderful," Trudy said, trying to sound sincere.

"I was very worried during dinner last night," Max admitted. "I was afraid she might be really sick."

He didn't hear a word I said. He doesn't even know that I put myself in a compromising position for him. "I noticed that you were very concerned." Then her eyes narrowed, but she went on. "I was very worried, too. However, you probably don't remember that I was trying to talk to you about something rather important to me, and you weren't paying attention."

"I'm sorry. I would never ignore something you were trying to tell me. But, like I said, I was worried about Margot, so my mind was on her wellbeing. I'm sure you understand."

"Yes, of course," she said, trying to sound sweet, but her voice came out bitter. "You're always worried about Margot. She's a delicate flower, isn't she?"

"She's my flower," he said sincerely. "I don't think she's very delicate, though. Margot is a fighter. Anyway, Margot wanted me to call and tell you the news right away because she wanted to assure you that Luzie was not in any danger of catching any contagious disease. As you know, Margot adores Luzie, and when she was feeling sick, Luzie was her biggest concern."

"Well, that's good to know. And thank you for the reassurance," Trudy said.

"And before we hang up the telephone, I want to say once again that I'm sorry about ruining dinner last night."

Trudy didn't answer. She hung up the phone.

CHAPTER 65

Trudy was furious with Max. After she hung up the phone on him, she made a promise to herself that she was going to give up on him forever. But as the night wore on, she couldn't get him off her mind, and she began to make excuses for him. Trudy refused to believe that Max had rejected her affections. She longed to believe that he had not heard her. If he did, he had not comprehended what she was offering him. That night, Trudy lay beside her sleeping husband and thought about Max. *I can't blame him for how he behaved. Of course, he was distracted. Margot made a spectacle of herself, demanding his attention and pity. How could he even listen to what I had to say? He was too worried about her dropping dead in my bathroom. I can't blame him. She's always had a way of stealing all the attention of everyone around her. Even when we were just children, she was always the center of attention. Then, once she had that mentally deficient child of hers, she grew even needier. She's still needy and demanding that everyone feels sorry for her, even after Rudy reassures her that everything is alright. However, I know the truth. She hasn't begun to suffer because it really isn't all right. Her precious misfit will never return from that hospital, and she will finally deserve all the pity she has*

been begging for. Trudy snickered out loud in the darkness. Rudy turned over; he was still half asleep when he said, "What do you want?"

"Nothing, go back to sleep. I am fine. I just coughed a little."

He didn't say another word, but in a few moments, he was snoring lightly again. And then her thoughts of Max and Margot resumed. *I can see it all very clearly now. After Rudy tells Margot that her child is fine, she can't evoke everyone's pity for that child anymore, so she conveniently gets sick to get attention. I'm sure she knew she was pregnant, so she probably faked being sick. I've heard that some women get sick, but she didn't when she was pregnant with Erik, and I never got sick like that when I was pregnant with Luzie. That performance last night was all for attention. But even so, what bad luck to learn that she's pregnant again. I am almost rid of Erik, who is nothing but a little pain in the neck that keeps Max tied to Margot like a dog on a leash. Now, she is having another one. Damn that sister of mine. I wish I could tell everyone the truth about her, what she is, and where she came from. I'm sure it would change Max's mind if he knew. And Rudy would throw her in prison, that's for sure. But I have to remember to keep my head because I know Rudy. He will arrest Max, too. He doesn't like Max, and he's told me time and again that Max lacks ambition. Rudy knows Max is not as dedicated to the fatherland as he should be. But if Rudy had Max arrested, I would never see Max again. I just can't take that kind of risk.* She looked up at the ceiling. *The only thing I can do at this point is to take a risk and try to talk to Max again without Margot there to distract him. I know what to do. I'll go to his office and ask him to have lunch with me. I'll tell him I need to talk to him because I am worried about Rudy. I'll have to think of some reason why I would be concerned about Rudy. I know Max, and he'll want to help. Then, once we're alone, I'll seduce him. I'll wear something extremely provocative. Something I know he won't be able to resist. We can rent a room for a few hours. And I am sure that after he has come to my bed, he will be mine forever because I'll make sure that I give him the best sex he's ever had.* She smiled in the darkness. *Yes, this is exactly what I'll do. I'll get ready and go as soon as*

Rudy leaves for work tomorrow. Trudy felt better. She closed her eyes and sighed. Then, she fell into a restful, satisfying sleep.

The next day, Margot called in the morning. "I'd love to come by and see Luzie today. Would that be alright with you?"

"Oh," Trudy said, trying to sound cheerful, "of course, it would normally be fine, but I am taking Luzie to see a friend of mine who has a daughter her age. I thought it might be good for her to spend some time playing with another child. Perhaps another day this week might be better."

"Of course," Margot said. Trudy could hear the disappointment in her sister's voice.

"I am sorry. I'd love to stay on the phone and talk, But I am in a bit of a hurry, so I have to get going. I've got to get ready, and then I have to make sure that the maid has Luzie ready to go. That maid is so lazy sometimes." She laughed a little. "Anyway, I'll phone you sometime later in the week."

Trudy hung up the receiver. Then she stood in front of the bathroom mirror and carefully pin-curled her hair. She took a scarf and covered it. Then she ran the water and took a hot shower, hoping the steam would set the curls. Afterward, she carefully put on her makeup. Dark, sultry eyes and blood-red lipstick with a touch of matching red rouge. Smiling at her reflection. Trudy went to her closet and pulled out a low-cut red dress. One that was cut deep enough to show off her cleavage. It was more of an evening dress, but she didn't care. It had a small slit on one side that she wished that slit was higher. Careful not to ruin them, she pulled silk stockings up her legs, then slipped on black high-heel pumps. The final results were perfect. Trudy looked just as seductive as she hoped she would.

Rudy had taken his car and his newly hired driver with him when he went to work. Trudy wished he hadn't because she hated taking the bus, especially so dressed up. *But even if he'd left his auto at home today, I couldn't trust his driver not to tell him where I went, so it's just as well that I go alone.* She walked over to the coat closet and ran her hand over her coat. But even though she was going to take the bus, and it was not a good idea to look so wealthy, she didn't care. Trudy decided on her most beautiful but impractical coat. The one she wore only on very special occasions. It was a white cashmere with a large ermine collar. She slipped it on and looked in the full-length mirror. The woman who looked back at her took her breath away. *When Max sees me dressed like this, he will forget all about that little mouse he calls his wife.* Trudy thought. Then she walked into the kitchen, where the maid was cutting potatoes.

"I'm going out. I'll be gone for the entire afternoon. I might not be home for dinner. If Rudy calls or he comes home first, tell him that I went to visit a lady friend and that I might be late."

"Yes, ma'am," the girl said, her eyes cast downward.

Trudy took her house key off the key ring in the kitchen and walked out the front door without saying goodbye to Luzie.

CHAPTER 66

O nce she got off the bus, she was only a few streets away from the office where she knew Max worked. She went to a public phone to call him. *I will ask him to meet me at the café around the corner. I think this is the best way to do this. Just in case someone who knows Rudy is there at Max's office, it's probably better if I meet Max outside his office. Especially the way I am dressed today.* The phone rang.

"This is Max Kraus," Max said when he answered the call.

"*Allo* Max, it's Trudy." Her heart was pounding nervously.

"*Allo* Trudy. Is everything all right? You never call me at work. Is Luzie all right? Rudy?"

"Oh yes, everyone is fine." She cleared her throat. "I'm calling because I'm in the area, and I really need to talk to someone I can trust. I have a problem."

"Oh? What are you doing in this area so early in the day?"

"Never mind. It's a long story. Let's just say I am desperate and need to talk."

"I would love to help you, but I'm at work right now. I could speak to you later. But if you need someone this minute, perhaps you should call Margot or Mattie?" he said.

She cleared her throat again. "They couldn't help me. You see, Max, I need a man's point of view. I would have called Ebert, but I have to be honest with you. I don't think Ebert is very smart, and I don't think he would know what to tell me in my situation. But you would."

"Trudy, what's wrong? Go ahead and talk to me. I'm sorry. It was insensitive of me to refuse you. Please tell me what is it? Has something happened? I'll help you in any way I can."

"Yes, I know you will. But I can't talk about this on the phone just in case someone is listening at your office. You see, it's about Rudy. And some of the people you work with know him. And I'm sure you know how people are. They can be nosey. And well," she hesitated for a few moments, "someone in your office might be just nosey enough to be listening. So, can you please just meet me? I'm at a café just a short walk from your office."

"I suppose if it's really that important."

"It is Max. Please. Will you come? Will you help me?"

"Yes, all right. Go ahead, tell me where you are, and I'll be there in about fifteen minutes. I have some work to do before I can go."

CHAPTER 67

T rudy was so nervous she was sick to her stomach as she waited for Max to arrive. She ordered a cup of coffee because it was still too early in the day to order wine, but she couldn't drink it. Instead, she tapped her fingers on the table and watched out the window until she saw Max crossing the street and approaching the café. *He's here.* As he walked through the door and gave her a quick smile, Trudy melted.

Max sat down across from Trudy and ordered a cup of coffee. Then he said, "I hope you didn't have to wait too long. Now, tell me, how can I help?"

"It's Rudy," Trudy said, looking down at the white tablecloth, and then she picked up the spoon and stirred her coffee.

"Is he ill?"

"No, no, he's not sick. But, well," she hesitated, then she said in the softest voice she could muster, "I don't think he loves me anymore. He hardly gives me any attention at all. He always seems to be distracted. I think he has been seeing someone else."

"Oh no, I doubt that. I'm sure it's just that he has been working very hard. This promotion seems to be getting to him. I'm not even sure what he does anymore. But he has made it clear that it's something important and very time-consuming."

"Max," she said his name softly, "I don't know what to do. Rudy doesn't make love to me." She blurted out the words. "That's why I know he has another woman he has been seeing." It was a lie. Rudy was often willing to have sex with her. It was Trudy who was constantly avoiding it by pretending not to feel well.

"Have you tried to talk to him about it?"

"I've tried. But he won't discuss it. And he gets so angry when I try." She let the crocodile tears flow a little.

"Please, don't cry," Max said, patting her hand. Trudy's heart leaped at Max's touch. Then Max continued, "Would you like me to speak to him?"

She shook her head. "Absolutely not. I would rather he never know that I told you."

"So, how can I help you?" Max asked sincerely.

"Max," she whispered his name, which tasted like sweet honey on her tongue. Trudy looked into Max's eyes as she ran her finger down over the skin between her breasts, drawing his eyes to that area. He looked at her ample cleavage, but he didn't flinch. "I want you, Max. I want you to make love to me. It will be our secret. Margot and Rudy never need to know. We can comfort each other. I have always cared for you. In fact, I can get a room this afternoon and..."

"Oh, Trudy." He shook his head. "I am sorry that you are feeling unloved by Rudy, and I can understand that you are hurt," he said nervously. Then, a moment later, he continued, "I want you to know that I think you are a very beautiful woman. So, I am flattered by your offer, but I am sorry, I could never do what you are asking me to do. I love Margot. She's my life. Margot and my son are the most important things in the world to me."

"But you wouldn't have to separate from Margot. Nothing would change. The only thing that would change would be that we would have a special relationship. It would be just a moment of joy that we could share every so often. Margot and Rudy would never find out."

"I'm sorry, but I am happy with my wife. I can't do this."

"My sister looks like a ragamuffin. She doesn't take care of herself anymore. You must get tired of that."

"I never get tired of Margot. And to me, she's the most beautiful woman in the world," he said sincerely.

"Even now that she's let herself go?"

"We've been through a lot together. And sometimes, she's too worried about Erik to fix her hair or wear lipstick. But that doesn't matter to me. She's always been the love of my life, and she still is."

Trudy felt foolish. Suddenly, her fancy dress looked garish to her. She imagined how her dark red lipstick and black mascara looked in the bright daylight that shined through the window of the café, and she was ashamed. *I must look like a prostitute. Max has openly rejected me. He knows what I want. I made it perfectly clear. And I know he heard every word this time. So, I must accept the fact that he doesn't want me. I must leave. I must get out of this restaurant. I must go home and take off this dress and this makeup. I just can't bear to be here any longer.*

She stood up. "I'm leaving."

"Trudy, listen to me. Talk to Rudy. Tell him how you feel and try to work things out together. Like I said, if you want me to speak to him for you, I will. Just let me know."

She didn't say a word. She just picked up her handbag and walked out the door.

As she headed towards the bus stop, it began to rain hard. Her white coat was drenched. Her perfectly curled hair now fell limp at the sides of her face. The rain washed the black mascara she wore down her cheeks, and it mingled with her tears.

CHAPTER 68

When she got home, Trudy ran into her bedroom and undressed. As she tossed her dress onto the floor, she caught a glimpse of herself in the mirror. Trudy was appalled when she saw the black eye makeup and red lipstick smeared all over her face. Her wet hair was thin and hung limp around her cheeks. She'd lost weight and was slender, but her body was not the same since she'd given birth. The skin was no longer taut, and her stomach was now rounded where it had once been flat. *I'm ugly. No wonder he doesn't want me. He saw through my pretty clothes and freshly curled hair. He saw the real me.* The way she looked when she saw herself in the mirror made her feel sick to her stomach. When Trudy could no longer bear to look at herself, she got into the shower and scrubbed the makeup off her face until her skin burned.

Trudy finally got out of the shower and put on a robe. Then she sat down at her vanity table to apply some cream on her face. She thought about Max and Margot as she rubbed the expensive balm into her neck and chin. She had to admit that even though he had just spurned her, she still loved him. Perhaps even more than before. He was everything she'd ever wanted. A man who was completely devoted to his family and, most importantly, to his wife. Trudy did not delude herself; she'd always known that Rudy was more interested in his career than in her or Luzie. It was true that he often nagged her to try to get pregnant again, but that was only because he wanted a son. And she was convinced that he wanted a son so he could present his child like a trophy to the party. He would often mention that Aryan women who had lots of children were rewarded by the Nazi party. They received medals called the Cross of Honor and were celebrated by the party. Hitler was said to love German women because he needed them to produce more Aryan children. Rudy would have been proud if she had received one of those medals. But to even be considered for the bronze Cross of Honor, which was the lowest of the awards, a woman had to have at least four children. And as far as Trudy was concerned, that was out of the question. One child had taken a terrible toll on her looks, and she refused to even try to imagine the damage that four would do. Besides that, Trudy knew that it was only the recognition her husband wanted, not the child.

And even now, as much as she loved and admired Max, she hated Margot. The jealousy towards her sister was eating away at her like cancer. *I can't wait until the hospital lets her know her child is dead. She loves that little misfit brat. So, it will kill her. She'll just shrivel up and die. Well, it's about time she felt some of the misery I feel every day being married to a man I don't love who doesn't love me either. Rudy thinks I don't know that he is always cheating on me. But I know it. The other wives in our crowd have seen him at restaurants with other women, and they take pleasure in telling me. I'm humiliated, but I pretend I don't care. I must. It's my only defense. I want to scream and tear his hair out for making me look like a fool. But I don't dare say anything to him because I like my lifestyle. I like the material things he can give me, the money, the pretty clothes, the parties, the large sprawling home with the fancy artwork. And if I complain, he might divorce me. So, I endure the shame and keep my mouth shut. However, I know the truth. I know that when he comes home late and smells of perfume, he's been with another woman.*

Margot doesn't deserve Max. He is a good man, an Aryan man, and she is a Jew. She should never have been in his bed. It's illegal, and well, it should be. But, if I want to, I have the power to punish her. I can make her suffer. And I can do it so innocently that no one will ever know it's intentional. She smiled a half smile. I know she has put all her love and affection into Luzie. Every week, Margot comes here to see my daughter. And she spends more time with Luzie than I do. Well, I have the power to stop all of that. I'll take Luzie away from her. Whenever she calls and says she'd like to drop by, I'll tell her that Luzie and I are busy and to try again next week. Since I can't punish Max for how he treated me, I'll punish him through Margot. Since he loves her so much, it will hurt him to see her so lonely that she is going crazy.

CHAPTER 69

When Max walked into his apartment after he'd finished work that evening, he found Margot in bed. She was sick again. He asked her what was wrong, and she said she was nauseated and had terrible heartburn. He asked her if she had eaten that day, and she admitted she hadn't. He knew it was difficult for her to eat. But she agreed to try to eat as much as she could for the sake of the unborn child she was carrying.

"You stay here in bed while I go and put something together for dinner," he said softly as he sat on the side of the bed.

She nodded.

He could see she'd been crying. Running his hand over her hair, he said, "Don't cry. I know you don't feel well, but the doctor said you won't be sick the entire pregnancy. He promised that you should be starting to feel better soon."

"It's not that," Margot said, "I'm worried about the baby, Max. What if this child is sickly like Erik, and this is just nature's way of telling us?"

"You were not sick when you were pregnant with Erik. Remember?"

"Of course, but I am worried."

"I know. However, the doctor said that many pregnancies can be this way. He said not to worry. Your feelings of nausea don't mean that there is anything wrong." Then he squeezed her hand and said, "I wish I could have the baby for you. I wish I could go through this instead of you."

She laughed a little. Then she laughed a little more.

"What's so funny?" he asked.

"You are. I just got this picture in my mind of you being pregnant, and it struck me as funny."

He was so happy to see her laugh that he laughed, too. Then he bent down and kissed her gently.

"My breath must be awful," she said. "I've been vomiting all day."

"Your breath is fine. You are beautiful, and we are in this together."

She reached up and touched his cheek. "You're a good man, and I am very lucky to have you as my husband."

"Flatter me more. I love it."

"Oh no, I'd better stop. After all, we can't have you strutting around here."

He leaned down and kissed her again. Then he whispered, "I'm going to see what's in the kitchen, and I'll put something together for us for dinner."

"I can get up and help."

"No, you just lay there, princess. I'll take care of everything."

Max left the room and walked to the kitchen. There wasn't much to eat. But there was half a loaf of bread, some cheese, and some potatoes. He quickly cut up the potatoes, put them in a pot of water, and then boiled them on the stove. While they were cooking, he returned to the bedroom to change his clothes.

Margot was up and out of bed. He heard the water in the bathroom running, and he assumed she was trying to clean herself up for dinner.

As he removed his uniform and hung it on a hanger in his closet, he thought about Trudy and what she'd said earlier that day. Her intense feelings for him made him nervous. He wasn't worried about himself; he was worried about Trudy. She was clearly unstable. He could see that she was by the way she looked that day. She had been wearing far too much makeup, and her dress was an evening dress and far too revealing. He knew things were not as they should be between Trudy and Rudy. It would seem to any outsider that they had everything, but Max knew it was all a façade. He also knew that Trudy and Rudy were very different people than he and Margot. Rudy was a ruthless Nazi, and if it hadn't been for Erik needing that medical care, Max would have wanted nothing to do with Rudy or Trudy. He often wished he could go back to working with his father at the carpentry shop. It was less money, but it was an honest living.

Max knew he couldn't tell Margot what had happened with Trudy that day, at least not in the condition she was currently in. Still, he hated keeping secrets from his wife. In fact, he had never kept one before. Margot was feeling weak, and this would be a terrible time to cause trouble between the two sisters. Besides, Max knew that because of Erik, he and Margot could not afford to get on Rudy's bad side. At least not now, not while Erik was still under treatment, a treatment that would cure him of his illness. Rudy was a powerful man, and if he made one phone call, Erik could be kicked out of the program. No, Max decided that he would keep his mouth shut. Maybe in the future, he would tell Margot, maybe not. But either way, he would not tell her right now.

As they sat at the table, Margot broke off tiny bits of the bread and tried to eat it.

"Is there anything special I can get you to eat?" Max asked. "I'll go to the market if there is anything you want."

"No, this is fine," Margot said. "I am trying to eat as much as I can for the baby's sake."

"I know," he said.

She lay in his arms that night, and he softly sang her a lullaby.

"Did I ever tell you that you have a beautiful voice?" she said.

"You didn't, but did I ever tell you that I was going to be an opera singer before I started apprentice for my father?"

"Really?" she asked.

"No," he laughed. Then she laughed, too. "I can barely sing. But my voice is perfect for singing lullabies to you and our children."

"Sing me another?" she whispered.

And he did.

CHAPTER 70

T rudy didn't have to wait very long before Margot telephoned to ask if she might drop by to see Luzie.

"How are you feeling?" Trudy pretended to care.

"I've been very sick."

"Sick? How so?"

"Nausea. Heartburn. Just not feeling well."

"Are you worried about the baby? If I were you, I'd be afraid I might miscarry."

Margot gasped. She was overly sensitive these days. "The doctor says not to worry. He says that some pregnancies are like this, and it doesn't mean anything. I mean, it doesn't mean anything wrong with the baby."

"I hope he's right," Trudy said.

Margot felt her hand trembling as she gripped the phone receiver. "I was wondering if I might come by and see Luzie today." With her other hand, Margot rubbed her belly.

"How can you possibly try to take a bus in your condition?"

"Well, lately, I've been feeling better in the afternoon. I'm sick mostly in the morning and in the evening."

"So, every day, you get a few hours of reprieve. That must be nice."

"Yes, it's getting better."

"Anyway, I'd love to have you come by and visit with Luzie today. And I'm sure she would love it too. But we have a birthday party to go to. A child of one of Rudy's coworkers is having a birthday."

"I see."

"Perhaps another time."

"Yes, perhaps another time."

CHAPTER 71

The following week, Rudy was promoted again. He was now a part of the death head unit and was given a death head badge to wear on the lapel of his uniform. His superior officer explained what would be required of him with this new promotion. "You must prepare to move to Munich. You will no longer be traveling from camp to camp. You will be stationed at the oldest camp we have established; it's called Dachau. Because you have shown such devotion and your service to the Reich has been exceptional, you and your family will be awarded a beautiful home right on the grounds in the officer's section."

"Thank you," Rudy said.

His superior officer continued, "I realize that moving is difficult. You will be leaving your friends and family. But at Dachau, you will find other SS officers and many death squad officers. So, there will be no lack of friends for you and your wife. The ladies have plenty of groups that I am sure your wife will want to join. This will keep her occupied during the day. And it will be nice for you too, as they have special classes for the women to teach them how to use the most available foods during these difficult times in the most delicious ways."

"That should certainly keep her busy," Rudy said. "And I can't thank you enough for this wonderful opportunity. I am very honored." Then he thought, *my wife never cooks. But that's all right. I'll see to it that we have a Jew maid. Besides, I believe this move will also be good for little Luzie. As she grows up, there will be plenty of pure Aryan children for her to play with and eventually to marry. And, once we are settled, I am going to have a serious talk with Trudy. I really want to attempt to have a son. I've given her a very good life. She should be more grateful. After all, she is my wife, and she owes it to me to have more children.*

"At the camp, you will be in charge of keeping records on the prisoners. It's not an easy place to work. I'll admit. It's a bit dirty, and it smells. But that's because of the Jews. They are filthy, you know. And recently, we've started imprisoning large numbers of Jews at the camp. Need I say more? But the pay is good, and so are the benefits. Besides that, you'll find that there is plenty of room for job growth," his superior officer said. "I've always liked you, Rudy. That's why, even though I hate to lose you here in Berlin, I recommended you for this position."

"How soon would you like me to be ready to move? We will have to pack up our things," Rudy asked.

"Of course. That's understandable. So, I expect you to be ready to move by the first of June. Your new home at Dachau will be ready for you by then."

"Yes, sir."

His superior officer dismissed him, and Rudy left.

It was late afternoon and time for Rudy to leave for the day. He walked to his car, feeling very pleased. Not only would he be promoted, but he and Trudy would soon move away from Berlin. They wouldn't be living there when Margot received the news about Erik. So he would not have to deal with her hysteria and could avoid the entire mess. She would probably telephone. He would pretend to be sympathetic, but he planned to cut the call short, saying he was busy. And she wouldn't have enough money to call back again. The fact was that once the child was dead, Margot would not have any reason to bother him anymore. *She will finally realize there will be nothing I can do for her. She and Max will remain in Berlin. And since Max is earning a decent living, I assume he would stay with the party and not cause me any unnecessary problems. And occasionally, if Trudy and I are sent back to Berlin for some reason, we might have dinner with Margot and Max. Of course, we would act as if we were so very sorry about what happened. It will be a delight to be rid of their constant requests for help.*

Besides, I am truly excited to move to Dachau because it's only a short drive to Munich. I will be very important there because I will be a part of the death head squad. I've always loved Munich, and I am growing tired of traveling. Besides that, Dachau isn't far from the Hochland home for the Lebensborn in Steinhoring. I won't have to worry about pursuing women anymore because when the need comes upon me, I can go to Hochland and have as many sexual encounters as I please with no messy strings attached. I will be done with crying girls whose hearts are broken. No more women carrying on and threatening to tell my wife. The women at the Lebensborn know that they are doing a service to the Reich. They bear pure Aryan children for Hitler and would never expect me to leave my wife and marry them. All they want from me is my pure Aryan seed to father more children for the Reich. He smiled. *I am more than happy to provide that.* Rudy hummed an old German folk tune as he drove home.

CHAPTER 72

Trudy was happy that her husband was to be promoted because that meant more prestige and more money. Still, she wasn't as thrilled about the move as Rudy had anticipated she would be. "Moving?" she asked. "But why? I don't want to move."

"Because we must go where my new job is located. That's why."

"But I love our home. We have such a beautiful home."

"Yes, and we will have a new home at Dachau. I've been promised a house right on the grounds. It will be so much easier. All I must do is wake up in the morning and walk to work." He smiled at her, "And I won't have to travel as often anymore, either."

"Oh Rudy, there is so much packing involved in moving. And we'll be so far away from my parents, Mattie and Ebert. And from Margot and Max, too." Her heart was pounding. If they left Berlin, Max would be far away. She would never see him. Although she knew she should give up on Max, Trudy was still not ready to give up on him. She just couldn't let him go. But she also couldn't let Rudy know that it was Max who she dreaded leaving. She didn't care about leaving any of the others.

"I know, dear. But you will make plenty of new friends. And Luzie will have friends, too." He lit a cigarette. "As far as the packing is concerned, you don't have to worry about that. Just have the Jew maid do it."

"I keep her busy enough with housework and with the baby. She doesn't have time to pack up this whole house."

"Tell her to make time. I'm sure she wastes plenty of time. Tell her she can expect a beating, or worse, if she doesn't get the packing done. I'll dispose of her and get another one. That's all. I've seen how these Jews behave. They're lazy and notorious time-wasters. But if you can't handle her, I will. You see, I've found that Jews don't respond to kindness, but they understand beatings, and they respond well to those."

"Oh Rudy, I don't want to leave Berlin. Must we accept this promotion?"

"I'm afraid so, dear. Besides, you always tell me how much you loved our trip to Munich. And we would be very close to down-town. In fact, we would be able to go to the *Oktoberfest* celebration every year. You always ask me if we can go to *Oktoberfest*," he said he said gently.

"But Rudy, I want to visit Munich, not live there."

"You must go where I tell you to go," his voice was no longer gentle.

"I could stay here in Berlin with Luzie, and you could visit us."

"That would not look good to my superiors." His tone was firm, and she knew he was getting angry.

"All right. If you say I must go, then I must. How long do we have to pack up our things?"

"We will leave at the end of May and arrive at Dachau by the first of June."

Trudy knew there was no use in arguing with him. He had his mind set, and he wasn't going to budge. *How will I ever see Max once we leave here?* She thought as she watched her husband change out of his uniform. When he had changed into comfortable clothes, he turned back to look at her and said, "It won't be so bad. You don't really like either of your sisters, anyway."

CHAPTER 73

The packing was as overwhelming as Trudy thought it would be. Rebecca, the young Jewish maid Rudy brought from one of the camps he visited, was required to pack as much as possible each day. She began working on the daunting task as soon as she put Luzie down for a nap. Trudy was tense. She dared not take out her frustration or anger on her husband, so she took it out on Rebecca by being exceptionally mean and demanding. She sat on the sofa and watched as Rebecca wrapped each piece of glass wear in a newspaper. Trudy looked at the young girl with disdain. Trudy wanted to beat the pretty Jewish girl. She wanted to make Rebecca suffer for all of her pain. Sometimes, when Rudy was at work and Trudy was bored with reading her movie magazines, Trudy would slap Rebecca, demanding that she move faster. Rebecca tried to do as she was told. But there was so much to pack. There were boxes everywhere: in the middle of the living room, in the dining room, in the kitchen, and in each of the bedrooms. One afternoon, as Rebecca finished wrapping a very expensive vase, Trudy yelled at her to hurry up. She tripped and fell as she ran to place the vase in a box. Rebecca stared in horror as the vase slid out of her hands. It was a special vase because Trudy had purchased it when she and Rudy had gone to Nuremberg for a rally. It was expensive and had sentimental value.

Trudy turned to look when she heard the glass shatter. Her mouth flew open as she eyed the broken pieces of the vase lying on the floor and her Jewish maid's shocked and terrified face. Trudy was filled with rage. "Get up!" she yelled. Rebecca tried to rise to her feet as quickly as she could. Some of the glass had sliced into her leg, and she was bleeding. "Damn you. You're getting blood all over the rug. That's a wool rug." Trudy ran over to the maid and slapped her across the face as hard as she could. "You are nothing but a clumsy idiot. You can't even do this right," she said. "Look what you've done."

"I'm sorry," the girl stammered. "Please, I'm sorry."

The noise of the breaking glass woke Luzie, and she began to cry.

"Go and get her," Trudy demanded, "then come back and scrub this blood out of this rug before it stains."

Trudy walked upstairs and into her bedroom. She sat at her vanity table and put her head in her hands. *How am I going to live without Max? At least right now, I can see him whenever I want. And if I can continue to see him, there is still a chance for us. Things might go sour between him and my sister. Especially after they get the news about their son.* She heard Luzie crying in the other room. Rebecca was quieting Luzie by singing to her. The song sounded like it was in Yiddish, and if Trudy felt stronger, she would have gone in there and slapped the maid for singing to her daughter in that miserable language. But she felt weak and defeated. She had tried everything to convince Rudy to turn down this promotion, even using sex as a bargaining tool. He didn't care. Nothing she did seemed to affect him. *I'm surprised Max doesn't blame Margot for Erik's disease. Most men would. I know Rudy would blame me if there was something genetically wrong with Luzie. However, my sister is quite the manipulator. I'm sure she convinced Max that the epilepsy had nothing to do with her. I'm sure she told him that it was caused by that whooping cough Erik had. Max, being a good-hearted man, chose to believe her. He is one in a million. And I am going crazy because he's hers and not mine. How could I get stuck with such a lousy husband while Margot gets a man like Max? It's not fair.*

A few minutes passed, and Trudy's anger turned to exhaustion. She was tired, but she knew her time was limited, and if she wasn't completely packed, Rudy would make her leave her possessions behind. So, she forced herself to stand up and walk back down the stairs. At first, she hid in the powder room so she could watch Rebecca. She wanted to make sure that the girl was working even when she was not being supervised. She saw Rebecca on the floor scrubbing the rug with Luzie sitting beside her, pulling at the sleeve of her uniform. Trudy watched Rebecca touch her little girl's face, and Luzie giggled. Then she heard the maid singing to her daughter softly in Yiddish again, and it dawned on her that Rebecca cared for Luzie, and strangely enough, Luzie seemed to care for the Jewish maid, too.

CHAPTER 74

To complete the task of packing, Trudy decided that Rebecca was expected to work for an extra two hours after she served dinner and finished cleaning up. When Trudy sent Rebecca to the basement to sleep, Rebecca could hardly move. She was exhausted, and her body was aching. But once she heard the basement door lock and knew she was alone, her mind traveled away from this house and these Nazis. She closed her eyes, thought of her sister, and wondered where she might be. *Is she still alive? Are you still alive, Marta?* Rebecca thought. Then her mind drifted back to how she had ended up here at the home of these Nazis in the first place.

It was mid-September. A week after the high holidays. Was it four, or was it five years ago? She couldn't recall exactly. Rebecca and her sister Marta sat in the temple on a Friday night. After the service, the Rabbi, a man she had known her entire life, said, "I received a letter from Mrs. Rosenstein. You might remember her. She was the older lady who was recently widowed and moved to Berlin because her sister left her a large home. Well, anyway, she wrote to me to ask me if I knew any nice young girls who would like to go to Berlin to work for her. She said she would pay well.

Mrs. Rosenstein is currently in need of a cook and a housekeeper. If any of you girls here this evening would be interested in one of these positions, please come by my study to speak to me." Marta's eyes lit up. She turned to look at her sister. "Berlin," she said in a whisper. "We could get out of Poland and go to Germany. I'll bet we could find wealthy husbands there."

"Shhh, don't talk like that here in *shul*," Rebecca said.

"Why not? What's wrong with it? I want a rich husband. What's so bad about that?"

"Let's talk on our walk home," Rebecca said.

"No, we can't. We have to go and see the Rabbi right now before someone else takes these jobs. Then we'll be stuck here in Poland forever."

"What about Mama and Papa?"

"We'll send them money. They'll be happy if we send them money." Marta coaxed Rebecca. "You know how they always need money."

Rebecca nodded. Of course, she knew. Her parents were poor. They could hardly afford to put food on the table. If Marta told them that she and Rebecca would be earning enough money to send them some, they would be all for it.

"We'll have to quit school," Rebecca said.

"So, what were we going to do with school, anyway? You and I both know that soon Papa would make a match for us, and we would be forced to marry whoever he chose. No matter who the man was. And believe me, we don't have a dowery, so you can just imagine who we'll get stuck with."

Rebecca considered what her sister said. It was true, after all, and she knew it. Both would be married before they turned seventeen. That is, if their father could find someone willing to marry girls as poor as they were. "All right. Let's go and talk to the Rabbi," Rebecca said.

The Rabbi explained that Mrs. Rosenstein was old and feeble. She had a hard time walking and needed help with everything in her home. Both girls said they understood, and before they knew it, they were hired. As Marta expected, their parents were pleased with the situation. And in less than a month, the girls were packed and on the train to Berlin.

Mrs. Rosenstein was demanding because she was needy. But she was also very kind and quite generous. Marta cleaned the house while Rebecca did all the cooking and the weekly wash. It wasn't a bad job. They were off work on Friday nights when they would attend synagogue and all day on Saturday to observe the Sabbath. Marta, who was the prettier sister, was lively and vivacious. She attracted the attention of a boy in the *yeshiva* almost immediately. Rebecca caught them casting shy glances at each other every so often. But he was betrothed to someone else, and so Marta was disappointed. Even so, living in the Jewish sector of Berlin was fun and exciting, and both girls came to love it, except for the growing hatred of Jews that always seemed to surround them. It wasn't as if there had been no hatred of Jewish people in Poland. There was plenty of it. But here in Germany, with its mean-spirited chancellor, the hatred of Jews seemed more concentrated, more accepted, you might even say systematic and well planned. But the girls were young, and they were too happy to live in a big modern city to pay attention to the rising evil surrounding them.

Then, on a chilling night in November 1938, the old lady visited her friend who lived a few houses away. On her way home, she was attacked by a group of angry, violent youths. They beat her until there was nothing left of her but a bloody mass. Marta and Rebecca heard the riots in the street outside the house. They saw the synagogue go up in flames and then explode. They heard the voices of young men singing a terrible song about killing Jews with their knives. When Mrs. Rosenstein did not return home, they knew something was wrong. But they were too afraid to go out to search for the old woman. Two terrible nights passed, and the mobs continued wreaking havoc on the streets. They broke the windows of shops and beat anyone they could find who was Jewish and had the misfortune of being outside.

After two days passed, the violence stopped, and the mobs disappeared. The old lady never returned. And it wasn't until almost a week later that one of the neighbors came to the house and told

Rebecca that Mrs. Rosenstein's beaten body had been found. Rebecca told Marta. "If we tell our parents, they'll demand that we return home," Marta said. "Do you want to go back there?"

"No, not really, but we won't have any money to send our parents. They will know that something has happened."

"No, they won't. I know where the old lady kept her money. We can take what we need and send it home to our parents. They'll never know that anything is wrong. And if word reaches them about what happened here, we'll just say it wasn't as bad as they heard. We'll lie."

"Marta. We can't. It was terrible. It was the most terrifying thing I've ever experienced."

"But I don't want to go home. Please, Rebecca. Please, it happened. It's over. It was just a gang of thugs. It won't happen again."

Rebecca loved Marta. She would do anything for her. Even risk further danger. So, she reluctantly agreed.

Then came a period of silence. During that time, laws were put into place that denied Jews their rights. The hatred and violence towards the Jewish people grew even stronger.

CHAPTER 75

On a hot night in the summer of 1939, Marta was arrested. She had stayed out too late drinking with a young man she'd met. On her way home, she was confronted by a Nazi in uniform. "Where have you been?" he asked.

"That's none of your business," she said. The alcohol made her bold.

"Oh, you say that it's none of my business. Is that right?" he asked sarcastically. Then he ripped her blouse open and grabbed her breast.

She screamed. But he didn't stop. He pushed her up against the wall and forced himself upon her. Then, when he was finished, he took her to the police station and put her under arrest.

Rebecca awakened in the middle of the night to find that Marta was not at home. She panicked and ran outside. She searched everywhere outside the house, but there was no trace of her sister. In the morning, she went to the home of every neighbor in the area, asking if they'd seen Marta. But no one had seen her. Finally, out of pure desperation, Rebecca made a judgment call. It wasn't a good call, but she didn't know what else to do. So, she went to the police station. The Nazis knew she was Jewish, and they toyed with her until one finally told her that Marta was in custody. "Your little sister is going to a lovely place called Ravensbrück." He smiled. "I think it would be fitting that you join her."

Rebecca knew that she had no choice in the matter. She was being arrested for no reason other than that she had gone to the police station to try to find Marta.

Rebecca was put into a cell full of women, including Marta.

At first, she was furious with Marta for behaving so irresponsibly. But when Rebecca saw how red Marta's eyes were from crying, she forgave her.

They received almost no food over the next three days. Then they and all the other women in their cell were loaded onto an open-air truck guarded by two young Nazis with rifles.

Their destination wasn't far from town, only about ninety miles. But once they arrived at Ravensbrück, it was like they had left the earth and descended into hell. Two more trucks arrived within the next fifteen minutes.

———

ALMOST LIKE CATTLE, the women were herded into a line. From there, they were ushered into a shower and told they were being deloused. After the shower, their long, thick hair was shaved until they were completely bald. Marta grabbed Rebecca's hand and began crying again. "My hair," she said. "Look what they've done to us?"

Rebecca didn't answer. She just shook her head.

"This is a woman's camp," a large-boned woman in a skirt and jacket said. "Here, you trashy Jews will learn to behave like ladies."

The block where they slept was overcrowded and dirty, with overflowing buckets to be used for toilets. The bed was nothing more than straw on a concrete floor, and they were told by the older inmates that the straw was full of lice and the lice carried disease.

And so Rebecca and Marta's lives as concentration camp prisoners began.

When it came time to eat, all they received was a bowl of hot water with some potato peels. Sometimes, if they were lucky, they had a bit of potato, which was slightly sweet. Rebecca knew from the sickeningly sweet taste that the potato was spoiled. Insects often fell into the soup, and because they were starving, the inmates ate it anyway. At first, Marta refused to eat the soup, but hunger finally got the better of her, and she ate. The only treat they received all day was a small heel of bread given to them at the evening meal. Often, it was moldy, and it was always hard, but at least it was bread. And, because Marta was so hungry all the time, Rebecca shared her bread with her sister.

The women who ran the camp were cruel, perhaps even more vicious than men. They promised that the women would work hard, and they delivered. The work at the camp was daunting and often dangerous, and so was the slave labor, where the Nazis sent prisoners to work at companies outside of the camp. None of the jobs were easy.

A week after they arrived, Marta was sent to work in a pharmaceutical company on the outskirts of the compound, and Rebecca was sent to work in the camp kitchen. It was there in the kitchen that she first saw *Obersturmführer* Rudolf Schulze. She overheard him telling the female kitchen boss he was visiting from Berlin. He had been sent to check on the camp. And now he was searching for a maid because his wife had just had a baby and needed help with the child and the housework. When Rudy saw Rebecca standing nearby and listening to him, he pointed at her. "I'll take that one," he said. It was as if Rebecca was a coat or a pet. Certainly not a human being.

No one asked her if she wanted to go with the *Obersturmführer*. And because Rudy wanted to leave right away, she did not have the opportunity to say goodbye to Marta. Rebecca had no choice in the matter. She was forced to go with the *Obersturmführer* a few hours later when he was ready to leave the camp. It just so happened that Rudy was ready to leave an hour before Marta was to return to the camp from her job. So, with tears in her eyes, Rebecca begged the other girls on her block to tell her sister that she was gone and what had happened.

Rebecca was heartbroken at first. She missed her sister terribly and didn't know if she would ever see Marta again. In fact, Rebecca was so distraught that she considered suicide when she arrived at Rudy's home in Berlin. But then, she met little Luzie. And Luzie filled the emptiness in her heart. She was tiny and helpless, and Rebecca would not blame her for the sins of her parents. Luzie was not a Nazi, at least not yet. Right now, she was just an innocent child. And, because Rebecca was so lonely and needed someone to pour her love into, Rebecca gave all of her love to Luzie. Luzie's parents were too busy to appreciate the little girl who was so precious to Rebecca. And Rebecca was glad that they were.

Because Rebecca was raising Luzie as if she were her own child. It was Rebecca who saw Luzie's first smile. She was there when Luzie crawled for the first time. And she held each of Luzie's hands and helped the little girl to take her first step. Rebecca fed Luzie her first spoonful of table food. She laughed with the child when they played together. *Obersturmführer* Schulze was too busy for his daughter. He was always distracted by his work. And it seemed to Rebecca that Rudy's wife, Trudy, didn't care about her daughter. She was a difficult woman. She was a demanding tyrant who was always going somewhere with her friends. When the other wives of Nazis were around, she was the picture of a socialite. But when she was at home alone with Rebecca and Luzie, Trudy was never in a good mood. She always seemed to be angry about something. Rebecca didn't like her very much. But she stayed out of Trudy's way. She was happy to have Luzie to care for. The little girl was the only light in her life. Luzie kept Rebecca from falling into deep despair.

CHAPTER 76

Rebecca hoped she would move to Munich with the family when they left Berlin or be sent back to Ravensbrück, where she could be with her sister. But she dared not ask any questions, and no one told her what was to be her fate. So, all she could do was to be happy about the time she had left with the little girl she adored.

Trudy was always difficult, but since she had learned of the move, she had become even harder to please. She was now even more demanding of Rebecca. And Rebecca did her best to meet those demands. Trudy did nothing in the house. She hardly looked at her daughter or picked her up to play with her. Rebecca often wondered how Trudy could have a child and not feel the desire to mother her. But she didn't. Most of the time, Trudy was either out with her friends, at some Nazi woman's group meeting, or locked up in her room. Rebecca was responsible for the housework, the laundry, the food preparation, the baby, and now, for packing the house up for the move. Still, she knew she was lucky to have this job. When she had been at the camp, she'd seen plenty of women die at the hands of the Nazis. At least for now, Trudy needed her, and so she was granted another day of life. She prayed that her sister was still alive, too.

One afternoon, while Luzie was napping, Trudy struggled to carry a large box of glassware into the living room. She set it down and called for Rebecca, who came running into the living room immediately.

"Yes, Frau Schulze," Rebecca said.

"You see this? It's all crystal. All of it. It's worth a fortune. I want you to pack it carefully, and don't you dare break a single piece. Do you understand me?"

"Yes, ma'am."

"You need to have all of this wrapped and packed and prepare dinner before Luzie gets up from her nap. I am going to lie down and get some rest right now. My husband and I were out late last night, and I'm exhausted. I don't want to be awakened by Luzie's crying. Do you understand? Make sure I am not awakened," she threatened. "And I'm expecting important company for dinner tonight. The food must be ready when they arrive. I don't like to look disorganized. So, I don't want you puttering around here wasting time like the lazy Jew swine that you are. Make sure you get all of this done."

"Yes, ma'am," Rebecca repeated. She hated Trudy.

Trudy went into her bedroom, and Rebecca quickly ran up the stairs to check on Luzie before she started. Lately, Luzie had been climbing out of her crib. She would hoist herself over the side, and most of the time, she would fall to the ground, not landing on her feet. So, she would lay on the floor crying until Rebecca came and picked her up. But Luzie had not awakened from her nap. She was fast asleep. So, after breathing a sigh of relief, Rebecca ran downstairs and carefully packed each piece of the hand-etched crystal.

Rebecca couldn't help but admire the workmanship and the detail of each piece as she packed. Each glass had a forest design with a male and female deer. This same design was elaborated on the pitcher, the vase, and the candleholders. It was amazing how perfect each piece was. But Rebecca hardly had time to admire each piece. She was in a hurry, and when she finally finished packing the crystal, she ran into the kitchen to begin chopping vegetables for the dinner party. The house was silent, and so she sang softly to herself. She was humming a tune she and her sister had sung as children when she heard a loud thud. Something had fallen. Rebecca trembled. She was afraid Luzie had tumbled out of her crib again. She didn't wait to hear Luzie's cries. She had to get to Luzie before she woke Trudy. Her heart pounded in her throat, and sweat beaded on her brow as she ran into the living room. When she saw the small body lying quietly at the bottom of the stairs, she refused to believe what she was seeing. Falling to her knees beside the child, she whispered her name, "Luzie? Luzie honey?"

But the baby didn't cry. She didn't look up. Her eyes stared blankly. Rebecca lifted the child and held her close to her chest. "Sweet one, please wake up. It's time to wake up," she said, knowing that little Luzie would never wake up again. She touched the child's chest and felt for a heartbeat. There was none. She put her ear to the child's open mouth. There was no breath intake. Rebecca let out a cry so loud that it brought Trudy out of bed, but Rebecca didn't care. Trudy shuddered as she stood at the top of the stairs, watching the scene below. Rebecca looked up and saw Trudy, whose eyes were wide with shock. And for the first time since she realized that she loved this little girl, Rebecca thought of herself.

I don't know what's the matter with me. I should not have screamed. I should have run. Even though everyone in this neighborhood knows I am a Jewish servant. They are all Nazis. If any one of them saw me, they would call the police. Still, I should have tried to get away. But it doesn't really matter because Luzie is dead, and I don't know how to get back to my sister. So, what does it matter what happens to me? Luzie, poor little girl. My sweet little Luzie. Rebecca buried her head in Luzie's body and wept.

Trudy ran to the telephone and called her husband. His secretary said he was in a meeting. "Please tell him there's been an emergency. He must come home at once."

"I'll tell him as soon as I see him," the secretary said.

Trudy hung up the phone. Then she walked over to where her

daughter lay motionless in the maid's arms. "What happened?" she asked. "You were responsible for her. What did you do?"

"I don't know what happened. I think she got out of the crib the way she does and crawled to the stairs. I was preparing dinner, so I didn't hear her." Rebecca was still weeping.

"Give her to me," Trudy said, taking the child into her arms. Then she said, more to herself than to Rebecca. "I never realized how much I loved Luzie. Not until now. She's gone. She's really gone."

Time passed. No one knew how much time. Trudy walked back and forth carrying Luzie in her arms while Rebecca sat on the floor weeping.

When Rudy walked into the house, Trudy was as pale as the stark white fabric on her new living room sofa. His face was red with anger. "Why did you call me at work? What was the emergency that couldn't wait until I got home?" he asked.

"Our daughter is dead," Trudy said. "I was taking a nap, and this stupid maid you brought home, this dirty Jew, let our child fall down the stairs."

Rudy looked at the child and then at Rebecca. His face was hard, and he showed no pain at losing his daughter. The only emotion on his face was pure anger. Rudy didn't say a word. He pulled his pistol out and shot Rebecca. Her face exploded all over the child, the bottom stairs, and the wall. It had all happened so quickly that Rebecca never felt a thing.

All she knew was that now she was walking side by side with her parents and holding little Luzie's hand as Luzie giggled. In the distance, Rebecca saw Marta, who came running towards her, smiling when she saw her sister. And so, they reunited in heaven, where hatred and prejudice did not exist.

CHAPTER 77

A wicked cold wind carried sheets of rain over the streets and walkways. It pounded against the window of Margot's apartment. She was washing clothes today, so she was on her knees scrubbing the bed sheets when she sank back onto her haunches and stared out the window for a few moments. Margot was still devastated over the tragedy of losing Luzie. She thought about the little girl every day, and she remembered her smile and how clever she was. She recalled the things Luzie did that made her laugh. The funny things that she said. It was difficult for Margot to live in a world without Luzie, but she knew that she must.

Since Luzie's death, Margot had only seen Trudy a few times. But the last time she visited Trudy, she asked about the maid, and Trudy told her that Rudy was so distraught upon seeing his daughter dead that he killed Rebecca. The very thought of that made Margot sick. After all, this was an accident. Even Trudy knew it was an accident. Yet Trudy did not seem to feel bad at all about what Rudy had done. In fact, it seemed as if she thought he was quite justified. Max was there that night. He heard Trudy tell Margot what Rudy had done to the maid. Max had been furious, out of control. He walked over to Rudy and punched him in the jaw. A fistfight ensued. But Max was stronger, and he punched Rudy until Rudy's nose was bleeding, and he ordered Max to leave his house. That night, when Max and Margot returned home, Max told Margot that he was glad that Rudy and her sister were moving away because he could no longer even stand the sight of them. Margot sighed out loud. Rudy was a terrible man. And the Nazis were terrible people. She agreed with Max that it was good that they were leaving. But she wished Max had thought of Erik before he started fighting with Rudy. She was indebted to Rudy, and until Erik was cured, she was afraid she might still need her brother-in-law's influence to keep Erik in the program.

A knock at the door jolted Margot out of her thoughts. Quickly, she stood up and wiped her hands on her apron. Then she opened the door. It was a teenage boy. He was soaked from the rain. "I have a letter for Frau and Herr Kraus."

"I'm Frau Kraus," Margot replied.

The boy handed Margot an envelope. She felt sorry for him. He was wet, and she knew he was cold. "Would you like a cup of tea before you leave?" she asked.

"Yes, but I can't. I am afraid I have too many deliveries I must make before I can go home, and my mother is expecting me to be home early today."

Margot nodded. Then she took a coin from her purse and handed it to the boy.

"Thank you," he said. Then he turned around and left.

Margot closed the door behind him and sat down on the sofa. She did not get mail very often, and she was hoping this letter was from Erik's nurse. She opened the envelope, unfolded the paper, and read the letter. At first, her mind could not comprehend the words written in black ink on the white paper in front of her. But as the message sank into her brain, it felt like her heart stopped beating.

Erik was dead. The letter said that he died of pneumonia at the hospital. It was unfortunate, the staff at the Hadamar Institute declared, and they professed that they were terribly sorry because

Erik was such a nice boy. He had been doing so well with the cure. Somehow, they explained, he'd caught the disease, and his body was too weak to fight it. Margot felt dizzy. The room was spinning. Her eyes could not focus. All around her, everything seemed to be turning black. She was afraid she might pass out. So she pulled a chair over to the telephone, picked up the receiver, and dialed Max.

Max's secretary answered. "I'm sorry, Frau Kraus, your husband just left to go for lunch. But he never goes for very long. I would assume he will be back in less than an hour. Shall I have him call you back?"

"No, he needn't call," Margot said in a strained voice. "Please tell him that he shouldn't waste time with the phone. Tell him I need him to come home right away. There's been a terrible emergency with his son. Can you do that for me?"

"Of course, Frau Kraus. I know he is at the café just across the road. Would you like me to go there and let him know what you said?"

"Would you please?"

"Yes, of course."

The apartment walls seemed to be closing in on Margot. She couldn't bear this news alone. So, she tried to call her mother. *I need my mother right now.* Her hands were shaking so badly that she could hardly hold the receiver. The operator finally answered and put her call through to Adelaide and Leo's apartment. She gripped the receiver tighter with each ring until her knuckles were white. After ten rings, the operator returned and announced that there was no answer. "Please try again later," the operator said, and then she hung up. She listened for a minute to the dead line. *Could this be a mistake? Is it possible that they sent this to the wrong people?* Her heart was pounding so hard that it was like a drum in her temples. *I'll call Rudy and ask him for the phone number of the Hadamar Institute, then I will call to be sure. Maybe, just maybe, there is some mistake.* And then the phone rang. *It must be Max.* Margot practically dropped the receiver as she picked it up with a trembling hand.

"Max?" Margot said.

"No, it's Trudy."

"Oh. Trudy, is your husband at home?"

"No, he's not. He's at work. But I heard."

"You heard what?"

"About Erik. Rudy told me. He got the news yesterday."

"Rudy knew yesterday. Why didn't you call me? I just received a letter from Hadamar today. I was praying that it was a mistake."

"It's no mistake. I'm sorry to say. Poor child. But you know that Erik is better off. Let's face it: he was never quite right. One arm was a little too long. One leg, too. And that terrible epilepsy. Erik was a sick boy. And we can't have children like that in the New Germany. Rudy explained it to me. He said that it was what they call a good death."

"A good death? What the hell is good about it? My little boy died of pneumonia."

"Oh, is that what they told you?" Trudy asked in a catty voice.

"Yes. It was pneumonia."

"You poor dear," Trudy said, thinking about how Margot had Max wrapped around her finger. "It wasn't pneumonia. That's only what they told you. But the truth is, it was euthanasia. Your little son was put to sleep. Erik was given a mercy death. And a death that is not only good for a sickly child but is also essential for the growth of our Reich. We can't have damaged people like that running around in our country. We can't allow them to live and reproduce more damaged people. What the fatherland needs in its future is healthy, young Aryan men and women who are fit to rule the world."

"You're crazy," Margot said, but she couldn't hang up.

"I'm not. I'm not crazy at all, Margot. This program that Erik was a part of was very important. It is top secret, of course, so if you ever mentioned it to anyone, I would deny having told you anything about it. But I do believe because you are his mother, you have every right to know."

"What kind of program is this? A program where they kill children? You're insane. This is all just not true. I don't know why you are saying these things, Trudy, but you have always been cruel."

"What I am telling you is true. You must believe me. The program that Erik was a part of is called the T-4. And it's good for everyone involved. It takes the responsibility of caring for a damaged child from the parents as well as taking the responsibility of feeding a worthless eater off the government. If Erik had lived, he would have grown up to be nothing more than a burden on society. And he is not the only one. This is a mess that must be cleaned up. You need to understand."

Margot heard her sister take a puff from a cigarette. Margot was reeling in pain and anger.

Then Trudy went on, "You see, I knew about this for a long time. In fact, I knew right after Erik went off to Hadamar."

"You knew they were planning to kill my baby boy, and you did nothing? Rudy knew?"

"Of course, he knew. It was Rudy who told me. We both agreed that it was for the best."

Margot slammed the phone down. Then she took a pen from one of the kitchen drawers and scribbled a note to Max.

Erik was murdered by the government. His death was intentional. Trudy and her husband both knew about it, but they didn't tell us. If they had told us, we might have been able to stop it, but they let it happen. They thought it was all right because Erik was sick. I am furious. I have never been so furious. I am leaving right now for Trudy's house. I want to see her in person. I want to look into her eyes and tell her what I think of her. How did she stand by and allow this terrible government to murder an innocent child?

Then she went to Max's nightstand and took his pistol out of the drawer where he kept it in case of emergencies. The metal of the gun felt cold and merciless in her hand. But she felt merciless, too. So, she put the gun in her handbag and slipped on her coat. Then she wept as she ran all the way to the bus stop.

CHAPTER 78

T he rain drenched Margot's coat and hair. She felt like a drowned rat as she waited on the bench at the bus stop.

Due to the rain, the traffic of people taking the bus to get home from work seemed heavier than normal. And because of this, Margot was forced to wait for a second bus. She didn't care how long she sat outside in the rain. It was cold outside, but even so, her wet clothes and hair didn't affect her. The rainwater trickled down her cheeks and mingled with her tears as she sat on the bench waiting. *My sister knew they were going to murder my child, and she did nothing to stop it. If she had told me earlier, I would have gone to that hospital and gotten Erik out while he was still alive. But now it's too late. My child is gone forever. I hate these damn Nazis, but even more than them, I despise my own sister. She is my blood. How could she do such a terrible thing to Max and me? I always knew she was vain and selfish, but what kind of person has a heart like this? She's not human. She's a monster. A vicious monster. She deserves to die.*

Thunder crashed, and bolts of lightning flashed in the gray sky. People huddled under umbrellas. They looked at Margot suspiciously as she sat alone on the bench, water dripping off her.

Then the bus arrived, and Margot stood up and got in line. An old man with a cane felt sorry for her and allowed her to board before he did. She thanked him and sat beside a young woman looking at herself in a compact mirror.

It was late and still raining when Margot got off the bus. She began walking towards Trudy's house. She'd never paid much attention before, but today, she noticed that the neighborhood where Trudy and her husband lived had once been a Jewish area. Now it was populated by German families, almost all of whom had patriarchs that were members of the Nazi party. *They took these houses from the Jews. And what did they do with the Jews who lived here before? If they can kill a child, I can only imagine what they did to these people. Poor Ben. He was always a good-hearted soul. I pray he is still alive. I would never have agreed to Max joining the Nazi party had it not been for us needing medical care for Erik. And just look at how that turned out.*

Margot arrived at Trudy's house and rang the bell. Trudy seemed to be waiting for her sister. She opened the large wooden door.

"You're absolutely soaked," she said, shaking her head. "Why would you come all the way here without using an umbrella? I'm going to have to wash my floor. And you can't sit on my sofa all wet like that. It's a very expensive piece. You realize that, don't you?"

Margot didn't answer. She walked inside.

"Wait here," Trudy said, frustrated. "I'll get you a towel."

"Don't bother. I'm not staying long. I just came to ask you in person how you could let this happen?"

"Margot, I explained it all to you on the phone." Trudy seemed to be enjoying Margot's pain.

"You let them kill my son. He was just a little boy. He never hurt anyone, and you let them kill him. You allowed the Nazis to murder a child. Who are you, Trudy? The devil? I used to think you were just an overly self-centered girl. But now, I think you might be Satan himself."

"That's absurd. You're upset, and you're talking crazy. Once you settle down and think things through, you'll know that it had to be done. You'll understand." Trudy lit a cigarette.

Margot shook her head. She reached into her handbag and pulled out the pistol. She pointed the gun at her sister. Outside, there was a roar of thunder, and then the room lit up when a huge bolt of lightning struck a tree across the street.

The door flew open, and Rudy came rushing in, followed by Max. "What's going on here?" Rudy said as he surveyed the scene.

"She's gone mad," Trudy said. "She's blaming me for what happened to her son."

"You knew. You knew, Trudy, and you could have stopped it. But you didn't. You let them kill my child, and now I am going to kill you."

Rudy was fast. He grabbed Margot, twisted her arm, and took the gun away. Then he pointed it directly at her. But in the chaos, Max was faster. He pulled his pistol and did not wait to see what Rudy would do next. He fired it at Rudy immediately. Rudy fell, but he was still alive. He rolled on his side and tried to shoot Max. But Max shot him again. This time, he shot Rudy through the heart, and now Rudy lay silent and still.

"I think he's dead," Trudy said. She was shaking. Then she turned to Max and said, "I must call the police."

"If you call the police, Trudy, they will take me away," Max said, appealing to the feelings he knew Trudy had for him.

"I have something to tell you, Max. It's something you should know."

He looked at her with disgust as he pointed the gun directly at her. "What, Trudy? What else could you possibly have to say to me now? I already know what happened to Erik."

"It's not about Erik. It's about your wife. Margot is not my real sister. Your wife was adopted by my parents when she was a baby. Go ahead, call my mother. She'll tell you that this is the truth. I overheard her and my father talking when we were young. Margot is not my sister. She's the daughter of my insane uncle and a Jewish whore. Margot is a Jew. She's a Jew, Max." Trudy was screaming. "I know that you can't possibly want to be married to a Jew. I have kept this secret. I haven't said a word about it to anyone until now because I wanted to protect you from Rudy. But right now, you and I can use this information in our favor. Margot is a Jew. A subhuman. So, her fate doesn't really matter, anyway. But I can't let the police take you, so I must help you so that no one ever finds out you killed Rudy. I will call the police and tell them I saw Margot shoot Rudy. They will take her away for murder, and you and I will be safe. We will be together. No one will ever know you killed a death's head officer."

"Never," Max said, walking closer to Trudy. Then he held the gun right up to Trudy's face. "I could kill you for this. I could turn that face of yours into a mass of bone and blood. After what you did, I could easily end your life. But I won't. Not yet." Then, turning to Margot, who stood shaking, Max said, "Run, run, and keep running. Don't stop. Get as far away from here as you can."

MARGOT'S SECRET

COMING SOON!

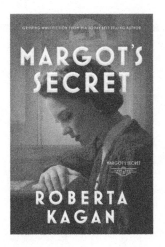

Amid the chaos of Hitler's conquest of Europe, a family teeters on the edge of utter destruction.

Trudy is still obsessed with her sister's husband, Max. But Max is torn between his loyalty to his wife, Margot, and giving in to Trudy, who might turn him in for the murder of her husband, the SS officer Rudolph.

Margot is on the run, hiding from both the Nazis and her own sister, who is threatening to expose her as a Jew. After the violent confrontation with Rudolph, she loses the child she was carrying and seeks refuge with Ben, the Jewish man she has always loved.

As the war reaches its climax, the fate of these four characters will be decided by love, betrayal, and sacrifice. Will they find happiness amid chaos, or will they pay the ultimate price for their choices?

Margot's Secret **is a whirlwind of emotion and suspense, weaving the intricate tale of how far people will go for love and survival.**

―――――

AUTHORS NOTE

I always enjoy hearing from my readers, and your thoughts about my work are very important to me. If you enjoyed my novel, please consider telling your friends and posting a short review on Amazon. Word of mouth is an author's best friend.

Also, it would be my honor to have you join my mailing list. As my gift to you for joining, you will receive 3 **free** short stories and my USA Today award-winning novella complimentary in your email! To sign up, just go to my website at www.RobertaKagan.com

I send blessings to each and every one of you,

Roberta

Email: roberta@robertakagan.com

p.s. Book 3 in the series, *Margot's Secret*, will be released on January 10th 2024!

ABOUT THE AUTHOR

I wanted to take a moment to introduce myself. My name is Roberta, and I am an author of Historical Fiction, mainly based on World War 2 and the Holocaust. While I never discount the horrors of the Holocaust and the Nazis, my novels are constantly inspired by love, kindness, and the small special moments that make life worth living.

I always knew I wanted to reach people through art when I was younger. I just always thought I would be an actress. That dream died in my late 20's, after many attempts and failures. For the next several years, I tried so many different professions. I worked as a hairstylist and a wedding coordinator, amongst many other jobs. But I was never satisfied. Finally, in my 50's, I worked for a hospital on the PBX board. Every day I would drive to work, I would dread clocking in. I would count the hours until I clocked out. And, the next day, I would do it all over again. I couldn't see a way out, but I prayed, and I prayed, and then I prayed some more. Until one morning at 4 am, I woke up with a voice in my head, and you might know that voice as Detrick. He told me to write his story, and together we sat at the computer; we wrote the novel that is now known as All My Love, Detrick. I now have over 30 books published, and I have had the honor of being a USA Today Best-Selling Author. I have met such incredible people in this industry, and I am so blessed to be meeting you.

I tell this story a lot. And a lot of people think I am crazy, but it is true. I always found solace in books growing up but didn't start writing until I was in my late 50s. I try to tell this story to as many people as possible to inspire them. No matter where you are in your life, remember there is always a flicker of light no matter how dark it seems.

I send you many blessings, and I hope you enjoy my novels. They are all written with love.

Roberta

MORE BOOKS BY ROBERTA KAGAN

AVAILABLE ON AMAZON

Margot's Secret Series

The Secret They Hid

An Innocent Child

Margot's Secret

The Blood Sisters Series

The Pact

My Sister's Betrayal

When Forever Ends

The Auschwitz Twins Series

The Children's Dream

Mengele's Apprentice

The Auschwitz Twins

Jews, The Third Reich, and a Web of Secrets

My Son's Secret

The Stolen Child

A Web of Secrets

A Jewish Family Saga

Not In America

They Never Saw It Coming

When The Dust Settled

The Syndrome That Saved Us

A Holocaust Story Series

The Smallest Crack

The Darkest Canyon

Millions Of Pebbles

Sarah and Solomon

All My Love, Detrick Series

All My Love, Detrick

You Are My Sunshine

The Promised Land

To Be An Israeli

Forever My Homeland

Michal's Destiny Series

Michal's Destiny

A Family Shattered

Watch Over My Child

Another Breath, Another Sunrise

Eidel's Story Series

And . . . Who Is The Real Mother?

Secrets Revealed

New Life, New Land

Another Generation

The Wrath of Eden Series

The Wrath Of Eden

The Angels Song

Stand Alone Novels

One Last Hope

A Flicker Of Light

The Heart Of A Gypsy